A VALLEY TO DIE FOR

THE FIRST SOMETHING TO DIE FOR MYSTERY

RADINE TREES NEHRING

ST KITTS PRESS   WICHITA, KANSAS

PUBLISHED BY ST KITTS PRESS
A division of S-K Publications
PO Box 8173 • Wichita, KS 67208
316-685-3201 • FAX 316-685-6650
stkitts@skpub.com • www.StKittsPress.com

The name St Kitts and its logo are registered trademarks.

Edited by Elizabeth Whiteker
Cover design by Diana Tillison
Cover art by Cat Rahmeier

First Edition 2002

Library of Congress Cataloging-in-Publication Data

Nehring, Radine Trees, [DATE]
  A valley to die for / Radine Trees Nehring.-- 1st ed.
    p. cm. -- (The first something to die for mystery)
  ISBN 0-9661879-9-7 (pbk. : alk. paper)
  1. Quarries and quarrying--Fiction. 2. Ex-police officers--Fiction.
3. Ozark Mountains--Fiction. 4. Widows--Fiction. I. Title.
  PS3614.E44 V35 2002
  813'.6--dc21
                                        2002002322

ADVANCE PRAISE

"*A Valley to Die For*, Radine Trees Nehring's charming debut mystery, is a story of good people fighting for their beautiful Ozark valley. Readers will delight in Carrie McCrite, a spunky heroine who faces danger and finds love. A pleasure awaits mystery lovers." —**CAROLYN HART**, author of the *Death on Demand* and *Henrie O* mysteries

"Author Radine Trees Nehring creates a fine heroine and a fascinating mystery that gets better and better as the pages roll. My wife and I love this novel about mature people finding rewarding activity and adventure in later years—including doing successful detective work!"
—**MIKE FLYNN**, producer and host of the *Folk Sampler*, heard weekly on public radio

"It's great to read fiction about the Ozarks that rings true, a book that is moral without being moralizing, and interesting without the obvious gratuitous happenings that mar so much fiction. *A Valley to Die For* has the clash of 'progress' with the inherent serenity of the hills and valleys of the Ozarks as its background theme. Its feisty and philosophical 'come here' heroine confronts in fiction some of the very problems this unique area of the nation is facing in reality."
—**DR. FRED PFISTER**, editor of *The Ozarks Mountaineer*

ACKNOWLEDGMENTS

Many menaces, procedures, and circumstances revealed in this novel were beyond my knowledge or experience when I began writing. I depended on information from a number of people around the United States, all experts in their fields, and I hereby acknowledge their willingness to help, and their patience with my questions. Any mistakes in details herein are my fault, not theirs.

Lt. Col. Dick Clohecy, US Army (Retired), and thirteen-year veteran of the Benton County Sheriff's Office, is a resource any mystery novelist would be glad to have. Dick is a specialist in small arms, a competitive pistol shooter, and a firearms instructor. He explained hand guns, insisted I hold several types, and taught me about bullets and the damage they do. Dick helped create the "beer can bombs" used in this story.

Special thanks also to Ruby Nell and Bill Gladish, and Judy and Robbie Roberson, who taught me about caves and stone quarries. Ruby Nell, an expert caver, took me deep into "Carrie's Cave."

Expert archeological and geological information came from Don Dickson, an archeologist working for Historic Preservation Associates in Fayetteville, Arkansas, as well as from the staff of the Departments of Anthropology and Geology at the University of Arkansas, and Dr. Michael Hoffman, now retired, former curator at the University Museum, U. of A., Fayetteville.

Native American historical details and legal information came from former law clerk Marlon Sherman at the National Indian Law Library of the Native American Rights Fund; and from Walter Echohawk, a lawyer with NARF, headquartered in Boulder, Colorado.

At Cherokee Nation Headquarters in Tahlequah, Oklahoma, Chad Smith, then Tribal Prosecutor, now Principal Chief of the Nation; and Richard L. Allen, Ed.D, Research and Policy Analyst, were wonderful sources of historical and legal information.

Mary Jane Lenz, Curator in the National Museum of the American Indian at the Smithsonian, was another friendly and knowledgeable contact. Ms. Lenz helped me work out the Smithsonian's small but important place in this novel.

My sincere thanks to Ozarks story tellers, Richard and Judy Dockery Young, who know all the tall tales re-told by Roger Booth.

Thanks, also, to the men and women of the Benton County Sheriff's Office and the Gravette Police Department. I have worked and spoken with many of them for several years, and I'm sorry there isn't space to name everyone. Special thanks are due, however, to former Detective J. R. Gibbs of the Gravette Police Department and Lieutenant Kenny Farmer and Sergeant Danny Varner of the Bella Vista Division, Benton County Sheriff's Office. They were the ones who most often answered my questions when I was stuck on a detail.

Media Relations Officer Russ S. Dykstra of the Kansas City, Missouri, Police Department was a perceptive tour guide, and he helped me understand what Henry's job as a police officer in Kansas City had been like.

Thanks also to Dodie Evans, Editor of the Gravette News Herald. He's a terrific local research assistant!

Cover artist, Cat Rahmeier, honors me and this book with her creative talent. Thanks, Sis.

And a big hug and thank you to my husband, John Nehring, who stands by to help with computer fix-its and so often does "the other things" while I write.

All of you—named and un-named—those close by as well as those I will never meet in person, are invaluable parts of this story. I find memories of each of you within its pages.

Radine Trees Nehring

DEDICATION

To Barbara Brett

INTRODUCTION

August, four years ago

The man still looked like he was trying to swallow a sour pickle whole.

Carrie watched in silence as he jumped in the moving van, jerked it into gear, and began the winding climb toward the county road.

He hadn't even smiled when she handed him the cashier's check. About all he had done through the long afternoon was carry and sweat and frown. And swear. Actually, swearing was what she'd heard most from the three people in the moving crew—including the woman, who looked like she could lift a refrigerator by herself. The movers swore at the trees, the rocky, uneven ground, the heat, and probably at her too, when she was out of earshot.

She hadn't gathered enough courage to complain about

the swearing. They were, after all, carrying her possessions.

Now, at last, they were gone. Carrie stood on the concrete pad in front of her garage and watched the cloud of dust on the road thin and settle. Then the grinding thunder of the truck engine faded and, except for insects, birds, and other forest creatures, she was alone.

She leaned her head back to look into treetops that arched above her new home, a six-room log cabin full of wood smell and, now, full of boxes and partially arranged furniture.

Carrie put thoughts of house straightening aside for the moment. Rob would be here in the morning to help unpack and put up hooks and pictures and curtains. Other than finding something to eat and making her bed, settling in could wait.

She began to turn slowly, still looking up into the treetops. She was, she decided, performing a symbolic ritual—turning away from asphalt, traffic, lined-up buildings, and rushing people. She was also turning away from Mrs. Amos Anderson McCrite, city wife. She was now Carrie Culpeper McCrite, independent woman, and Ozarks forest dweller.

She stood in a green well with walls unbroken by anything but the narrow window of her lane to the road.

Actually, she couldn't blame the moving people for swearing. The hole in the forest was cut for one small woman and one small house and car, not a moving van. She hadn't thought of moving vans or lumber delivery trucks when she directed the worker who helped her make this clearing. She was only thinking of getting away from the city and living her own life—living in peaceful harmony with the creatures of the forest.

The forest creatures were fitting enough company for her. Forest creatures didn't have money, and now she didn't either, though Amos had promised that they would eventually retire here in style.

Well, she was in the Ozarks all right, but she was also alone in the remnants of a world that had shattered when a bullet ended every plan Amos had made for both of them.

"Cut down in his prime," they'd said, over and over. How stupid—*stupid*—that sounded, especially when the words dripped with sympathy. Amos had been sixty-five. When was prime? If she, too, was prime, why had everyone but Rob treated her as if when Amos ceased to exist she did too?

After the awful stuff to do with his death was sorted out, moving to this Ozarks land, the dreaming place she and Amos had bought and held for their future, was all she could afford if she wanted to be independent. And she would do just fine here, no matter what everyone said.

Everyone but Rob. Her son, at least, felt she was capable of rational action.

So. It was time to move on, forget... She shook her head violently, but now the picture was back again...Amos, lying just over there on the hillside...and the blood...

Stop, *stop* it! That was past, gone! She had prayed, asked for guidance, and she had listened. Well, tried to listen, and this felt right—a fresh start, a new life.

Next week she'd begin looking for a job in one of the nearby towns. Maybe McDonald's. They hired senior citizens. Social Security and the surprisingly small amount Amos had left her weren't going to stretch very far.

No matter how he insisted otherwise, Rob didn't have room in his life for her, and he certainly didn't have room in his apartment near the university.

A teaching assistant. Soon to be a Ph.D. She said it aloud, "Dr. Robert Amos McCrite." But his life was foreign to her now, even more foreign than living alone in a forest.

Besides, she was independent, her own person. Except, except...she really wasn't sure who that person might be.

Her family and friends said she should be considering a retirement village or apartment. Women of her age, they said, glancing at each other when they thought she couldn't see them, simply did not go off and live alone in a forest.

Only Rob had supported her. She wasn't sure he understood, but he'd helped her stand firm against dire forecasts about what might happen to her, off in "that wild, lonely place."

Rob, at least, knew how un-lonely a forest could be.

"And," he'd said to Velda and Dusty and Pat and the others, "she's only seven miles from the town of Guilford, and there are neighbors less than a mile away. It isn't a wilderness, after all."

Now the sun was heading toward treetops in the west. Carrie stood very still as bird calls and cicada droning filled the air with throbbing twirps and hums. Her new world was noisier than the city had been, and she certainly wasn't alone. There was life all around her. So, why did she feel—for the first time since she'd made the decision to move here—so small and frightened? Why did she feel so very much alone?

She blinked, then said, "Carrie McCrite, you will not cry!"

Hearing the words startled her even more than it did the pair of wrens hopping nearby, intent on catching a grasshopper.

The grunt of an engine being downshifted for a turn into her lane wiped out every other concern as she realized strangers were coming to this place, where all people would now be strangers.

She wasn't ready. She needed more time! Carrie began a quick jog toward her front door, then halted.

No.

It was inevitable that strangers would come. She had to face that, so she might as well do it this very minute.

She lifted her chin and looked up the hill, standing firm as a battered grey truck bounced into view. The truck didn't stop at the bottom of the lane, but turned boldly onto the parking pad. Carrie backed up, stumbled when her heel hit the front step, and sat down with a thump as the truck's right front tire rolled to a halt beside her feet.

The driver's door opened.

The first thing Carrie saw was shoe-polish black hair that frizzed every way but straight up. Then dark eyes in a dried apple doll face peered down at her over the truck's hood, and a waxed-paper-wrapped sandwich sailed through the air, landing in her lap.

She's very tall, thought Carrie, who felt frozen in place, incapable of getting up to greet her guest. It was as if she was standing aside, watching herself, and trying to figure out whether or not to be frightened.

The woman's words rushed out. "You alone? Thought so, house didn't look like it was being made ready for two, heard the movers leave, hope you like turkey, 'n if you don't, we'll call it funny ham. We can sit here on the step and eat, y'don't have to ask me in yet."

The stranger was dressed in a faded chambray shirt and jeans tucked into stove-pipe boots. She came around the truck, stepped over Carrie's feet as if they were obstacles she faced every day, and opened the passenger door to take out two bottles of lemonade and a package of cookies.

The tumble of words began again while she was folding her long legs to sit beside Carrie on the step. "JoAnne Harrington, your nearest neighbor." A finger pointed. "Live that way along the ridge. Got high boots you can put on? After we eat, I'm headed to check on the Jerusalem artichokes by the old fence, thought you might want to come along. We can harvest them together this fall. I'll share, they're on your land anyway."

The woman's laugh was surprisingly girlish.

Carrie hadn't the slightest idea what to say, but in a moment she began laughing too.

CHAPTER I

"If nothing else works, we'll sit on the dynamite."

That's what JoAnne had said last Saturday, looking around at the seven of them, her eyes challenging any reluctance...or fear.

Impossible!

Carrie had looked around too, checking the expression on each face in Roger and Shirley's living room. She was sure not a single one of them was willing to do such a stupid, dangerous thing, no matter how much they yearned to save the valley.

They'd all lived long lives, but that didn't mean they were now willing to throw life away, to "put it on the line for a cause," as JoAnne was urging them to do.

As far as Carrie was concerned, life became more precious with every passing year. It was not older people but the young ones who too often didn't appreciate its value.

JoAnne hadn't seemed to notice the silence that greeted

her pronouncement, but then JoAnne was like that—single-minded, fearless, always a willing fighter for a cause she believed in—and bullheaded as a goat. Uh, no, that must be thickheaded as a goat. (One had to be completely honest, even about one's best friend.)

Now, sitting safely in her own kitchen a week later, Carrie wondered what set dynamite off. She hadn't asked, mostly because JoAnne seemed to know, and JoAnne would be scornful if Carrie admitted she didn't. Probably you lit a fuse.

But was that all? What happened if you dropped it or wiggled it or...sat on it?

There had to be information somewhere. Maybe an encyclopedia...

Rob probably knew, or could find out on the Internet, but then he'd have to know why his mother was asking such a question, and when he found out, why, of course, he'd have a fit.

One fit from her son would be an excuse to get out of the whole mess. But wouldn't that make her a traitor to the cause—a cause she really did believe in?

Carrie pushed aside the coffee mug that said, "MOM for President," and stared out into the awakening forest. She pictured the valley caves with their exotic formations and the layered bluffs, clear creek, wildflowers, and berries, all about to be blasted to oblivion just to make road fill, for goodness sake.

On the other hand, maybe dynamite wasn't what they used today. Everyone knew now that explosions could be done with some sort of fertilizer.

If the blasting came, what they used sure wouldn't matter much. The results would be the same. Beauty and peace in their valley would become a monstrous joke.

Did the quarry people think raw rock piles were beautiful?

Probably. Smashed rock meant money to them, and, for many people, money equaled beauty. They'd see the valley's limestone bluffs as a pile of money, nothing more.

She shut her eyes and thought about walking along the quiet valley road in early summer, pausing, as she always did, where wild hydrangea bushes tumbled down the southern bluff to the very edge of the berm left by road graders. She gathered bouquets in her mind, filling her arms with clusters of tiny florets surrounded by popcorn puffs of white blossoms—so beautiful against the dark green leaves.

Now, in November, the bushes displayed empty seed heads ringed with papery brown blossoms, a left-over beauty she could take freely. She never picked the summer blooms lest she rob quail of food, or humans of viewing pleasure.

She had put a bouquet of dried wild hydrangea on the coffee table last weekend, a subdued arrangement that suited the fall landscape outside her windows.

Unlike JoAnne, Carrie had rarely been a protestor. After more than sixty years on earth, she was wise enough to realize that most people who knew her didn't have any idea what protests she might be hiding. Life had always been easier that way; and now, it seemed safer too.

She thought about courage and wondered if she had it.

Maybe, just maybe...standing up for what one believed in...?

But it would still be no more than a gesture—only putting off the inevitable—unless they found a legal way to stop the quarry.

And, maybe they had found something, or, at least, maybe JoAnne had. She'd sounded different over the phone last night, excited even, and had been about to tell Carrie why when her cat dumped a jar over on the kitchen counter. She'd stopped talking then, said she had to go clean up the cat's mess, and Carrie would have to wait until today and hear about it with all the others. Then JoAnne had giggled. Drat! JoAnne wouldn't care if wondering about what the news was kept her friend awake all night—which it hadn't, since Carrie knew it must be good news from her Thursday meeting with the State Environmental Commission in Little Rock.

A twinge of pain crossed Carrie's forehead, and an involuntary frown deepened the lines there. JoAnne accomplished so much, she was so very capable! Carrie wished she, too, had good news to report. She didn't. No one at the meeting would look at her with hope and admiration showing in their eyes.

Down in the hollow, fog was drifting through dark tree trunks, but when the sun lifted above the ridge, the fog would fade, and they'd have a good day for the meeting. She looked up at her blue and white wall clock, then shut her eyes again, thinking she should pray for the valley. Even before words could form, ringing music from Handel's *Messiah* boomed into her head:

"Every valley shall be exalted."

Exalted, yes, but how could they keep it *safe*?

Her lower lip pushed out. It wasn't a pout—far from it. She'd begun using the gesture as her own small act of defiance years ago, when her parents insisted that their only child *must* eat liver. In protest against what she saw then (and, even now) as incomprehensible adult behavior, she'd stuck out her lower lip.

It did no good. Her parents ignored the gesture. By the time she was in first grade, she'd given up on even that protest and it was eventually forgotten. Now, seated in her blue and white kitchen, Carrie remembered, pushed out the defiant lip, and felt much better.

When you came right down to it, blowing up the valley was yet another adult action that Carrie Culpeper McCrite found incomprehensible.

"Can't stop progress," the County Judge had told her only yesterday. "Road department needs stone, needs a quarry nearby. Save tax money. You folks that pay taxes oughta be glad, not doin' complainin' about one valley bein' messed up a bit. That's progress.

"Now, there, Mrs. um, MacWhite, you go on back home and enjoy your bird watchin'. I'll run the county in a proper manner, do what's best for all you folks."

He had squeaked forward in his chair and smiled up at her. "Can't stop progress, now, can we?"

Progress! Well, it depended on how you defined the word. At that moment, Carrie McCrite almost forgot herself. She'd wanted to reach across the desk and shake the man. If only she'd had the courage. Remembering, she smiled at the thought of it and wondered what that big man would have done if a pudgy, five-foot-two, grey-haired female grabbed his fleshy shoulders and shook him 'til his head bobbed.

He'd see. He was young. He didn't understand anything about tough women. He didn't know JoAnne Harrington or...or...the rest of them.

That County Judge had something to learn.

Carrie shoved her chair back with a bang, went to spoon more instant coffee into her mug, poured hot water, then returned to her place at the kitchen table. She leaned forward and stared out the window again, trying to re-capture the feeling of peace and well-being that early morning in Blackberry Hollow brought to her.

Day came late to the hollow, especially when there was fog. Sun was just now edging down through the trees, but her bird feeders had been busy for some time. Cardinals, indigo buntings, woodpeckers, chickadees—a colorful bunch. The "tink tink" of the cardinals always cheered her.

Even if the stone quarry came, she'd still have her own twenty-five acres of protected forest. But every time she drove down to the Booths' farm, she'd see not a valley but rock piles, dust, blasting, heavy machinery, and an army of growling trucks.

Thinking about it, Carrie, who never swore, murmured, "Just like Hell," into her coffee mug.

A sharp crack from over the hill punctuated the words, and she winced.

Deer rifle! Close. Too close.

It was like this every November.

Crack.

Sounds were funny in the woods. Maybe it wasn't that close after all.

Carrie knew hunting thinned out a deer population that could be too plentiful, but during hunting season her woods were a new and dangerous world. Posting didn't always stop those who came into the area with guns; some hunters ignored the markings.

When she walked through the forest during hunting season, she wore her old orange ski jacket and a hunter's hat and sometimes even sang aloud or carried her portable radio tuned to a music station. But why should she have to be afraid on her own land any time of year?

Because she knew all too well how far a shot from a deer rifle could carry. One had carried far enough to kill Amos.

She'd found the bloody remains of a butchered deer in

the woods last November and, for a time, that brought back the nightmares.

Now they were out there again, hidden among the trees, shooting.

Until that awful November five years ago, the woods had always been a sanctuary for her—a cozy, welcoming place.

Amos, on the other hand, had loved these rocky, tree-covered hills because they made him feel masculine and strong. He'd never said anything to her, but she'd understood. She'd known exactly why he was planning to move here when he retired from his law practice in Tulsa, and why he agreed so quickly when she urged him to buy this land early so they could visit it on weekends. She'd won him over completely when she mentioned, very casually, that he could cut their firewood here, and, in November, he could hunt.

If only she hadn't mentioned hunting.

Amos had almost swaggered that morning as he and his friend, Evan Walters, headed out to harvest deer. The two men had talked about the opening weekend of hunting season for months. They'd built the deer stand in late summer and begun putting out dried corn in the fall.

Since the weather that weekend was warm for November, Carrie offered to come along and serve a picnic. She didn't mind waiting, sitting in a lawn chair reading or poking about in the woods near the road.

But, only minutes after they left her, there had been a shot, a cry from Evan. She could still hear that cry.

Then he had crashed back wildly, faced her, and...

It all felt like a bad dream now. It was as if, over the last five years, she had become disconnected from the real event, the horrible thing that was "only an accident."

Now, for her, the horror usually stayed in its own dim shadow, hidden away, and the friendliness of the woods had returned. But Evan couldn't seem to forget that day, even after five years—even after he'd been cleared of any homicidal intent by the courts. Thank goodness she no longer needed to see the man.

You couldn't change the past, so why didn't he just get on with his life? After all, she had! She'd been on her own for a long time when, at age twenty-nine, she married Amos McCrite. Their marriage had never been more than a friendship, so now, well, being alone was just fine, and she was proving she could cope, no matter what her age. No matter what, period!

It took her a moment to come back to the present and realize the phone was ringing. She looked at the clock again. Still early. It would be JoAnne.

Carrie had never decided if JoAnne didn't understand how she valued her early morning quiet time or understood completely and didn't care. One thing for sure, JoAnne herself didn't spend much time being quiet. JoAnne was a lot like Amos.

But it wasn't JoAnne, not at all. Henry's rumbling voice apologized for disturbing her.

"Is JoAnne there?" he asked. "She wanted help organizing the notes from her meeting with the Environmental Commission and asked me to come by this morning, but when I got there, she didn't answer the door. The cat came to the window and yowled at me, that's all. Did she forget?"

Carrie wasn't surprised. JoAnne was always going off on spur-of-the-moment quests. She had simply found something she considered more interesting or important than a meeting with her neighbor, Henry King. Still, it was odd that, given her opinion of all men, she'd invited Henry's help in the first place, instead of asking Carrie to come.

Not only was Henry male, he'd been a cop. To JoAnne—who had pushed against lines of uniformed men during the war in Vietnam, had marched for civil rights, the ERA, and even chained herself to a log skidder in the Ozark National Forest—being in any kind of law enforcement was about as low as a man could go. Nothing Carrie could say softened JoAnne's opinion about that.

She wondered if JoAnne had ever faced off against a woman law officer. She must remember to ask.

Once more Carrie checked the clock. Wherever she was now, JoAnne would be back for the Walden Valley Committee meeting in an hour and a half. After all, having the meeting was her idea in the first place.

A rumble coming from the phone broke into her thoughts. "Carrie, hello, are you there?"

"Oh, sorry, Henry, I was thinking about JoAnne. No, she's not here, and I haven't heard from her this morning. I have no idea where she might be. She's usually up and busy quite early. She may have gotten into some new project hours ago and just plain forgot you were coming, or she could be out wandering the valley again, or maybe she's just gone to town for cat food or milk or something."

She knew she was babbling, but couldn't think what else to say. Evidently it didn't matter, because when Henry spoke again, he changed the subject.

"Cara, maybe we could go for a walk in the valley after the meeting, just the two of us, then drive into town for lunch?"

His use of the nickname, as well as his invitation, made her feel strangely warm, and she wondered—as she had more than once before—if Henry wanted a closer friendship. Some types of friendship could intrude on her independence if she let them. She was aware of that, even without JoAnne's constant reminders.

But Henry was such a comfortable person to be with, and he'd never said or done anything that wasn't suitable. It wasn't a male-female thing at all.

She said, "Sorry, but I can't. I'm baking caramel rolls, sort of a brunch. Everyone is invited to stay for rolls and coffee after the meeting, and then I need to work on the new brochures for our racks at the tourist center. I've got boxes of them to go over before Monday. Don't worry about JoAnne. I'm sure she'll be back in time. She'll just have to make do without your organizing help."

His voice was suddenly sharp. "She'd better get back, it's her meeting."

He paused, then said, more gently, "Will you be through with your work by supper time?"

She almost laughed at this follow-up, but stopped the laugh and was quiet for a moment. There could be nothing wrong in going to supper together. She would enjoy it, and he always treated her like an intelligent fellow human. How else should she expect him to act, at their age?

In this case, JoAnne just didn't know what she was talking about. There was no harm in going out with Henry. He wasn't going to make holes in her independence. He probably wanted to discuss plans for the valley protest, that was all.

So she said, "If that's an invitation, may I call you about 3:30? I'll know by then how my work's going. I would enjoy eating out." She bit off saying "thank you," hearing JoAnne's voice warning her that thanking a man for something you wouldn't thank a woman for was subservient.

Instead, she finished, "See you at the meeting," put
the phone down, and went to sit in her chair again. Henry
didn't know JoAnne well enough to understand her odd
ways, but Carrie sure understood why he was interested in
what the State Environmental Commission in Little Rock
had to say on Thursday.

She frowned as her thoughts went back to the quarry.
Though everyone on the committee but Roger and Shirley
Booth lived in the hills around Walden Valley, they had all
come to feel the entire area—hills, bluffs, the Booths' pastures and carefully tended dairy herd, even Walden Creek
itself—belonged to each of them. It had been quiet coun-
tryside for so long.

Too bad none of them had paid attention to the abandoned farm next to Roger and Shirley. Even that was pic-
turesque, with its collapsing barn and the pink brick chimney that stood tall, years after the home it had once warmed
burned to the ground. No one had wondered what might
happen to that old farm. Now they knew too well. Quarry
operators had bought it.

Well, all right. Her lip went out again. They would
win this fight! Surely there were other places less valuable
that a quarry could go if, indeed, the county really needed
another quarry.

The blue and white clock reminded her it was time to
get ready for the meeting, and she went to set out plates
and cups. One of these days she'd better buy some kind of
coffee maker. Guests probably thought instant coffee was
pretty tacky. Well, they probably thought any ready-prepared food was tacky. Who cared? Hospitality was about
feelings, not food.

She opened the refrigerator, took out three pop-open
packages of breakfast rolls, got her cookie sheets, then

turned on the oven. Maybe she'd heat some of those cute little frozen sausages too. It was chilly, folks would be hungry.

As she worked, Carrie began humming a song she'd invented for Rob's bath time when he was a toddler. He'd reminded her of it last summer, saying he still couldn't keep from chanting it to himself in the shower, though its original purpose had been to make a game out of cleaning his ears—as well as under arms and between toes, where he was ticklish.

"Down in the valleys, under arms and toes.
Make the valleys clean where the washcloth goes.
Valleys are (whish and sw-o-o-p) CLEAN!"

Another rifle shot cracked. It sounded very close, and she flinched, imagining a bullet whistling by her house.

She wondered if JoAnne had heard the shots, wherever she was. JoAnne didn't like hunters on her land. JoAnne didn't like hunters, period.

Well, nothing she could do about it now.

Carrie looked around her kitchen, then nodded to herself. It would be all right. This was her sanctuary, her home. No one would intrude on that.

She was singing Rob's valley song loudly enough to drown out any whistling bullets when she left the kitchen and went to finish getting dressed for the meeting.

CHAPTER II

Roger and Shirley arrived first. When Carrie opened the door, Roger pointed to his truck, which he'd squeezed in a space between two trees that was only inches wider than the truck's fenders. "Okay to leave 'er there?"

"Sure." Carrie looked around the clearing, suddenly seeing it through Roger's pale, grey-blue eyes and supposing he wondered why on earth she didn't make more space.

"I know I should cut some trees," she said, thinking he could never understand how she felt about the trees. "I'm sorry for drivers of delivery trucks, but I can't decide what to cut, so I just don't, and the trees keep growing."

"Well, trees're better fer your health than trucks," said Roger, punctuating his words with eye twinkles and adding a grin when he noticed Carrie's surprise.

Both Roger and Shirley Booth were lean Ozarks natives who towered over her. She had once been sure no Ozarks native was concerned about protecting the envi-

ronment, especially if doing so involved some kind of regu-
lation. Roger and Shirley, however, were proving her wrong.

In fact, Roger had been the first one to warn people
along Walden Road about the quarry. He'd begun contact-
ing his neighbors after he heard a few rumors and decided
to go over to the county seat to "see 'bout an abandoned
farm I just might think of makin' an offer fer," as he said
he'd told the nice clerk at the court house in Bonny.

"Happens," he explained to Carrie when he called her,
"that some fella from over the border has spoke fer that
land. I asked my cousin who lives that-a-way to check up
the name fer me. He says the fella runs an old used-up
quarry near Martinville. Hank also says the place is a mess.
Some heifers got sick when they drank the crick water last
year."

Carrie had translated to herself while Roger talked. The
quarry in question must be in Missouri, and it must have
somehow polluted the creek near Martinville. Roger was
concerned about his own herd of Holsteins. Those cows
were so carefully babied Carrie was sure Roger and Shirley
would buy bottled water for the stock tank if they had to,
but none the less, there it was—a call to action by the most
laid-back hillbilly on Walden Road.

And as far as the Martinville cousin was concerned,
Carrie was enough of an Ozarker now to know that "cousin"
could mean any degree of relationship at all, but also might
really be a cousin. She was beyond surprise when learning
about intertwined family relationships throughout these
hills and hollows. In fact, Roger had once told her, "Only
reason we're glad Yankees come here is 'cause now we don't
always have to marry our cousins!"

Roger and Shirley accepted cups of instant coffee without commenting about the method of making them and

eased down on the big couch in the cabin's main room. They had never been inside her home before, and their eyes roamed over the walls covered with bookshelves. "Just like a library," Shirley said finally. "You like to read!"

"Many of the books are about Arkansas and the Ozarks," Carrie replied as she enjoyed the warmth of the smile on Shirley's thin face. She returned the smile with real pleasure and a sudden feeling of companionship and shared...what? She had thought she had little in common with this woman, though they must be about the same age. "I do quite a bit of research in my work for the Department of Parks and Tourism. But, yes, I like to read."

Shirley set her coffee cup aside carefully and got up to inspect the books, touching a few with her fingertips as she walked along the shelves. "I didn't learn to read much 'til after the kids went to school," she said. "Just hadn't been interested. Figured I didn't need to read books to them when they were little—I could think up plenty of stories in my head, and I knew Bible stories by heart. Then the oldest started school, and I was 'shamed when she brought stuff home and saw I didn't know what it said. So I studied with the literacy folks in town. Now I'm pretty good at reading." She looked over her shoulder at Carrie, and the wrinkles around her eyes deepened in another smile. "I read my own Bible now, and other books too."

Carrie started to reply, thinking that there must be books on her shelves that Shirley would enjoy borrowing. Just as she was puzzling about what to offer, the knocker interrupted, and she went to open the door for Jason Stack and Mag Bruner.

Jason's Buick was parked in front of Carrie's garage, but Mag had walked from her house at the head of the road. She liked being outdoors as much as Carrie did and never minded walking a few miles if the weather wasn't too bad and the roads were passable.

"Road's in good shape," she said as she handed over her jacket. "No dust, no mud, can't get better than that."

Carrie knew all too well that road mud could stick to boots until they weighed twice as much as they ought to, and if it was dry, dust raised by passing vehicles choked walkers.

Today Mag's feet were clean, though she wiped them carefully on the entry mat. In the country that gesture was automatic.

Jason, who was keeping records for the committee, carried a notebook with papers sticking out at odd angles. Everything about his appearance—from grey hair frizzing at the edges of his tweed cap to rumpled slacks—proclaimed a disorganized person, but Jason Stack didn't fit that mold. He was very businesslike, something his appearance denied now and had probably denied when he was head of a large manufacturing plant back in Ohio.

"I'll bet he's caught a lot of people off guard," Carrie had once said to JoAnne, "because he's about the most organized person I know."

The fact that Jason's wife Eleanor was back in Ohio with a daughter who had just produced her second child wouldn't have disrupted his always orderly thinking.

Jason drank de-caf black when Eleanor was present, but today he accepted regular coffee with sugar and milk, then asked if JoAnne had learned much at her meeting with the Environmental Commission.

"I talked with her last night, and she seemed quite excited and pleased about something," Carrie said, "but the cat knocked over a jar on the kitchen counter just as she started to tell me about it, so she said she'd save the news for the meeting today and hung up."

Mag's thin mouth twisted in disgust. "I went to lunch at JoAnne's once and that cat was sitting on the table. Could barely manage my meal after that. FatCat is a stupid name for such a skinny thing anyway. She told me some crazy story about the cat coming from a rich family—whatever that's got to do with it. You'd think she'd have a dog, living alone and all."

Carrie said nothing. Mag seemed to have forgotten that she, like JoAnne, had no dog and that the Booths had several cats. Carrie hadn't the foggiest idea where the Booths' cats ate.

Mag started to say something more, and Carrie was afraid she was going to continue making a fuss about FatCat, but Shirley spoke up first. "Our cats wouldn't get away with jumping on the table. Roger'd swat them."

Roger's lop-sided grin told Carrie he probably wouldn't swat them at all. Funny, Roger didn't need anything or any action to help him feel masculine, and he was really one of the gentlest people she'd ever met. She doubted that he and Amos would have gotten along, but then, Roger could probably good-old-boy anyone into friendship, even Amos, who hadn't had many close friends besides Evan Walters.

"Time to start the meeting," Jason said. "I'm not surprised JoAnne's late, but where's Henry?" He turned his round face toward Carrie and winked. "I thought surely he'd be here before anyone else."

Carrie, who'd never blushed in her life, supposed Jason expected her to do so now. Instead, she stared at him, trying to show no emotion—then swivelled to stare at the front door instead as Henry opened it and walked in.

She hadn't locked the door after the early arrivals but was still surprised when Henry came in without knocking.

It wasn't like him, and his assured action startled her. This was her private home—her own space. She didn't get up to greet him, held in her chair by a tongue-tied confusion she didn't know how to settle. He acted like he owned the house. What he'd done reinforced Jason's typically masculine insinuation, which she realized would get sparks out of JoAnne if she heard about it.

Of course, it was possible she and Henry had been seen by someone from here the few times they'd gone to dinner together, even though they always chose restaurants in Bonny or Rough Creek. In her experience, if one person in the area knew anything, then everyone did.

Well, who cared if they'd been seen? She was a mature adult. She did hope no one mentioned it to JoAnne, though. JoAnne would be quick to tell her what to do, and Carrie was far from eager to have any more discussions about Henry with her.

Henry glanced around the room, then looked at Carrie. "JoAnne?" he asked and continued without listening for the obvious answer. "I went by her house, and there was no sign she'd come back. Do you think someone should check? You have a key to her house, don't you, Carrie?"

"Is she off wandering again?" Jason asked, sparing Carrie from the need to reply. "Let's just get started. She'll probably be here soon. Roger, you first. How did you and your cousin get along?"

Roger leaned forward on the couch, rested his arms on his knees, and looked slowly around at all of them with his familiar grin.

He's enjoying this, Carrie realized with surprise, glad to turn away from worrying thoughts about Henry. Roger Booth, bless his heart, had an audience of move-ins. He knew quite well they were going to be entertained by how he told his story, and, far from being embarrassed, he was enjoying it!

"Well, Herb and me," Roger began in an exaggerated drawl, "we decided he needed a load of stone fer somethin' 'er other, so we took his old truck and went to the Martinville quarry. They've about blasted away all the bluffs along Spider Crick. It had rained the night before and, let me tell you, that crick was milky with rock dust.

"Fella there wasn't the owner. Said the boss wasn't around much. That was better fer us since this fella, he enjoyed talkin'. He'n Herb had seen one another at the café in town so they was like old friends, and we got along fine.

"I asked if they might be lookin' fer help, said I had a boy needed a job, and the fella said he was going to need a job soon hisself 'cause they was fixin' to shut that quarry down. Said they'd about come to the end of that property and couldn't buy more around there, which was no surprise, seein' the mess they made of what they had.

"So I said, was there any plans fer more quarryin' someplace else? Maybe my boy could travel. He said he'd heard they planned a new quarry over th'line in Arkansas, but he didn't want to travel that far from home if he could get work closer by.

"Then Herb acted real interested in how they did the quarryin' and asked the fella to show us how it all worked, said it seemed pretty dangerous to him what with the blastin' and heavy rock. Since the fella was there by hisself and it was an off day fer customers, with them runnin' out of stone and all, he was real proud to show us the works.

"We're right about the blastin'. There's lotsa that, and lotsa dust. Mountains of busted rock, and machines big enough to move mountains. They got a couple of ponds supposed to hold rain water until the dust settles out, but they looked pretty full of muck themselves, and, if they work, why was that crick milky?"

Roger's smile had disappeared. "Let me tell you now, Herb says that valley was a beauty before the quarry came. Clear water where folks fished and went swimmin', and high bluffs with different layers of rock. Once he went to a church picnic on the farm there, and kids picked bunches of wildflowers. Some kid even climbed part way up a bluff and got some kinda flower there."

He looked at Shirley, and she said, "Wild columbine."

"Yeah, those. They had it all, huckleberries, blackberries, walnuts; birds and other creatures everywhere, just like we got in our valley now.

"Well, maybe since that quarry has been there more than fifteen year, they could do things rougher than they kin now, what do you think? Maybe there's new rules?" He looked around at the group again, still not smiling.

Jason spoke up. "Let's not forget our objective—that is, what we want to do—is stop the thing altogether. Get everyone told how destructive it'll be and get it stopped."

Carrie winced, wondering if Roger had noticed Jason's pompous assumption that he wouldn't understand the term "objective," but Roger simply shrugged.

"May not work that way, Jason. The quarry owner may have friends we can't fight, and that land didn't come cheap, even if it had been abandoned fer years. It's good farm land fer around here, so the quarry folks got real money tied up. It may be all we kin do is figure out a way to keep 'em from lettin' that dust fly everywhere or run into the crick. Most of the regular folk, those of us been here, think if the county government is behind it and the place holds a few jobs out like a carrot in front of a mule, ain't no way any of us is gonna stop it. County's gonna think more about money than care fer one more little ol' valley bein' smashed up."

Everyone was quiet, and Carrie felt her own hopes sag. Were they losing the will to fight? Maybe JoAnne's report—whatever it was—would make the difference.

Jason turned to her. "You're next," he said. "What did all the officials say?"

Carrie's assignment had been to talk with people on the town council in Guilford, seven miles downstream on Walden Creek, as well as the state congressman, members of the Quorum Court, and the County Judge.

She reported first on what the judge, who was the chief executive officer of the county, had said about needing rock for road work, then added, "The others *acted* sympathetic, but no one knew of any state or county laws that could stop a quarry as long as owners got approval of their plans for maintaining air and water quality. Roger's right, there are new laws about that. The best anyone could suggest is that national environmental regulations be looked into. Also, they said we might contact the State Game and Fish Commission and ask about endangered species in the area, maybe in the caves. Perhaps there would be something there. I wonder if the Environmental Commission told JoAnne the same thing?

"Anyway," Carrie finished, "though a few of them seemed to understand how we felt, and the people in town are concerned about the creek, not one of them was ready to oppose the quarry. I think it's all going to be up to us."

Silence held the room until Henry said, agitation evident in his voice, "Well, the next step seems to be what JoAnne found out in Little Rock, so where is she? Why isn't she here?"

Carrie got up. "I'll call her house and then bring back

something to eat. Everyone want sausages with their rolls and coffee?"

Shirley followed Carrie into the kitchen, bringing the tray of used coffee cups with her. Without asking for instructions, she turned on the kettle and began spooning instant coffee into cups. Carrie punched in JoAnne's number and pictured FatCat pacing around the offending noise on the desk in the kitchen.

After fifteen rings Carrie gave up and went to get the plates.

CHAPTER III

The committee ate Carrie's brunch as eagerly as if she'd spent all morning in the kitchen preparing it.

There, she thought, that proves it. It doesn't take a zillion-ingredient recipe and stacks of dirty pans. All it takes is friends getting together—then no one cares whether your kitchen helper was Julia Child or the Pillsbury Doughboy!

Carrie's helper was much more likely to be the Pillsbury Doughboy. By the time she married Amos, she had established a casual approach toward culinary efforts in her nearly-spinster life. Frozen dinners and simple, one-dish meals suited her just fine, though sometimes she did enjoy creating specialty edibles from unique and often bizarre combinations of basic ingredients. She had frequently surprised guests with dishes whose origins were long lost in "Carrie's kitchen fiddling," as Amos called it. Since he preferred to work late and eat alone at the Tulsa Legal Club, it hadn't mattered to him whether she cooked fancy or didn't cook at all.

And, as far as their son Rob was concerned...well, he'd been used to ready-prepared food from the time she opened the first Gerber jar. When she'd tried to apologize to him recently for what she had begun to suspect was a warm-fuzzy-home-cooked-meal-deprived childhood (was it something she'd read in a magazine?), Rob only laughed and asked how she thought he'd manage alone today if he hadn't learned her cooking methods early on.

Perhaps it was no surprise that, over the years, Carrie's friends had given her cookbooks. She always thanked each giver with the same burst of enthusiasm that inspired her special kitchen creations, and every one of them went away feeling that all Carrie McCrite had lacked was the right cookbook. She shelved each book in a special maple bookcase Amos brought home from his office, dusted them all twice a year, and sold them all—in mint condition—right before her move to the Ozarks. She kept only a small file box with a few favorite recipes and a hand-written notebook that preserved the details of her more successful kitchen experiments.

Now she felt a warm satisfaction as she watched Jason, whose wife was a dedicated cook-from-scratch woman, pick a last scrap of caramel topping off his plate, lift it to his mouth, then lick his fingers carefully. After a short pause for appreciation, he looked around at the group and said, "We can't wait any longer for JoAnne, so we might as well adjourn the meeting. It's important to find out what she learned from the Environmental Commission before we plan our next move."

Roger and Shirley looked just as placid as they had when the meeting opened, but it was easy to tell that everyone else was annoyed by JoAnne's absence.

Mag said sourly, "It's just like her to plan a meeting
and then run off after some will-o'-the-wisp at the last
minute, not caring a bit if it bothers any of us."

The group agreed on the necessity for taking some kind
of action as soon as possible, so Jason suggested they meet
again the following Saturday, making sure JoAnne would
be there. Mag invited them to get together at her house.

"Jack'll be busy around the farm," she said, "so we'll
have the place to ourselves."

Carrie had met Jack Bruner on one of her rare visits to
Mag, and she saw him in Guilford occasionally, but that
was all. Mag was certainly opinionated and outspoken, but
at least she was friendly enough. Friendly was the last word
Carrie would have chosen to describe Mag's husband. He
was dark and moody, taciturn to the point of hostility.
Carrie thought of him as one of those people you'd never
want to be alone with in a dark alley—or anywhere else.

Whenever Mag's sharp tongue tried Carrie's patience,
she'd remember Jack and pray for the Lord to help her be
kind and loving toward his wife, and to love Jack too, al-
though that seemed impossible.

Carrie couldn't help suspecting that Jack was an abu-
sive husband. Without meaning to pry or be a busybody,
she'd find herself looking for bruises or other signs of in-
jury every time she was with Mag. So far, she'd seen no
outward signs of abuse, and Mag had never said anything
to suggest such a terrible thing, but Carrie often wondered
if Mag's sharp, thoughtless tongue wasn't the result of an
unhappy life.

Everyone on the committee had been surprised when
Mag asked to join them in the effort to stop the quarry.
Carrie herself was quite sure the Bruners didn't care about
the valley one way or another. She had decided Mag just

wanted a chance to get away from the farm and Jack—though now she had invited them to her home. Maybe what she wanted was friendship with her neighbors.

After Jason closed the meeting and everyone left, Carrie finished cleaning up in the kitchen, thinking all the while that she should walk down to JoAnne's house.

No one in the group seemed worried about JoAnne, simply because she was so well-known for leaving home to pursue any quest that interested her at the moment. But what about the cat? JoAnne usually called when she was going to be gone more than a few hours and asked Carrie if she'd look in on FatCat—a request that was always irritating, since Carrie worked full time and felt she had better things to do than go stroke a spoiled cat while JoAnne went off on a lark.

JoAnne could leave food and water out to cover most absences but said she didn't want her cat to feel lonely, so would Carrie mind stopping by for a moment to make sure the cat was all right, and maybe give her a love pat or two?

Carrie'd finally had enough nerve just the other day to tell JoAnne how she felt about tending the ego of a cat. She thought JoAnne had ignored her protest, but maybe she'd listened after all. Maybe that was why she hadn't called about FatCat before she left.

JoAnne was like Amos. She was certain of her opinions, self-assured, smart, easy to be jealous of, easy to admire and love. Carrie had understood from the beginning why she was drawn to JoAnne, and she sometimes felt overwhelmed because two such people had come into her life, taking, in their turn, the position her father once held.

But right now, checking on the cat did give her a good excuse to check JoAnne's house, and she didn't feel like settling down to her work until she'd done that.

The two women had worn a path through the forest between their homes, and as she walked the familiar, leaf-padded trail, Carrie wondered if notes from JoAnne's meeting with the environmental people might be on her desk in the kitchen. She would have taken good notes.

Why on earth, though, had she asked Henry to go over the notes with her? Did he have some special training or knowledge about such things? He had been a real estate agent after he left the police force. Maybe he knew something important about property law that would help them? It would have to be very important, or JoAnne would never have asked his help.

It was cold, getting colder, and the sky was clear. That meant there could be frost flowers in the woods tomorrow morning and since they only appeared a few times each winter, she didn't want to miss a chance to see them. She'd go for a walk before church, carrying her portable radio so any trespassing hunters would know she was in the area.

When Carrie came out of the woods into the sunny clearing around her friend's house, everything looked normal, and very quiet. The place where JoAnne parked her grey truck was empty. Carrie knocked on the door, listened to the silence, then, feeling an increasing skin-prickling nervousness, picked up the third flower pot by the front steps, got the key, and opened the door. She called JoAnne's name, timidly at first, then more loudly. There was no answer. Of course not.

The house felt cold. Was there no heat going?

FatCat appeared from the direction of the kitchen and rubbed against her boots, making little noises that sounded like soft yips.

Carrie took off her glove and bent to stroke the silky

back. Peculiar cat. It had traits from so many ancestors that nothing could be decided about its background, according to JoAnne at least. The cat looked and sounded something like a Siamese but had faint stripes in her coat, and her blue eyes were set in a large head.

Well, whatever else FatCat might be, she was not fat, which accentuated the largeness of her head, and now she was definitely hungry. Carrie went to the kitchen, and both she and the cat stared into two empty bowls. She put water in one and found the box of dry cat food. It was almost empty, but there was enough for today's meal. Possibly JoAnne really had gone for cat food and got side-tracked somewhere.

While the cat ate, Carrie surveyed the desktop, pushing papers around carefully with one finger. She wouldn't have to tell JoAnne she'd looked for the report. All she needed was a quick peek to see if something hopeful had been offered. Then she could go home in peace and wait until JoAnne came back.

The top of the desk was neater than usual except for scattered mail. There were a couple of bills, ads, a catalogue. No notes.

Carrie walked into the living room, rocking her feet carefully from heel to toe at each step to keep her shoes from making any noise on the wood floor between the braided rugs. She looked at table tops. Nothing.

Next, the bedroom. In the silent house, Carrie heard her breath swishing in and out as she turned down the hall. Could JoAnne be sick? That possibility hadn't occurred to her before. The house was so cold, it just felt empty.

Except for a cat, she amended, as FatCat brushed past her leg and disappeared through the partially closed bedroom door. She didn't follow the cat immediately, but stood outside the door, shaking with a sudden chill. Maybe she had no business searching her friend's house, but now she had to check the bedroom, in case...

She used a finger to push the door open and realized she'd been holding her breath. She gulped in air when she saw the bed, empty except for a cat who had rolled into a circle on the pillow and was just now squeezing her eyes shut.

The bathroom was empty too, and JoAnne's pajamas were hanging neatly on the back of the door.

Carrie found the thermostat outside the bedroom door, set at 55—okay if the woodstove was in use. She returned to the living room and put her hand close to the stove, then touched the surface of the black iron box. Cold. JoAnne hadn't started a fire this morning. Strange. Had she planned to come back, feed the cat, and get the stove going before the meeting at Carrie's began?

Carrie walked into the kitchen again, thinking she should check the back porch. She started to turn the dead bolt knob and realized the door—always kept locked— was not locked.

She stood in the open doorway for a moment, glancing around the clearing toward the dense forest. There was a noise that might be a squirrel rustling in leaves. She shut the door quickly, turning the dead bolt.

The small click did nothing to settle her unease. Now all she wanted was to be out and away from this cold, silent house.

She hurried back into the kitchen and hesitated, staring at the desk. Six drawers.

JoAnne had sounded so excited Friday night, and her notes must be here somewhere. Curiosity began to burn again, dulling Carrie's fear. Okay, she would look, but first...

She went to the hall closet and opened the door slowly. Her thumping heart seemed to be shaking her whole body. She peeked around the door, imagining someone bursting out and knocking her down, but, at the same time, acknowledging this was undoubtedly fantasy, like the mystery novels she read. JoAnne had simply forgotten to turn the back door dead bolt. There was a first time for everything, wasn't there?

And now the closet door was wide open. Nothing. The interior looked ordinary...normal. But JoAnne's hiking boots were missing. Her faded jeans, red jacket, and knit cap weren't there either, so she was dressed in rough outdoor clothing and not for the meeting when she left.

FatCat had lost interest in a nap and was following Carrie closely again. Remembering Mag's admonition that women living alone should have a dog, Carrie was grateful for even this small presence.

She checked the bedroom closet next. Everything looked normal there too. The door clicked loudly as it shut. Then she bent to look under the bed. Nothing but dust fuzzies.

She really was alone in the house.

Feeling calmer, Carrie returned to the desk. Six drawers. In the center drawer a tray of pencils, pens, paper clips, and other desk equipment faced her. The bottom left drawer held files labeled for household bills, insurance records, and personal information; the drawer above it had phone books and JoAnne's familiar red address book. Drawers on the right had writing paper, envelopes, a greeting card assortment.

There was a sealed pink envelope on top of the cards. Carrie, whose birthday was later in the month, turned it over. It had her name on it. She turned the envelope face down again and shut the drawer.

The final drawer had nothing in it but old correspondence. No report.

Carrie went back to the living room and sat down to think what to do. FatCat came along, jumped on the arm of the chair, and shoved her head under Carrie's hand, moving it aside before stepping gently into her lap, where she curled into a ball and began purring.

FatCat's attention bothered her almost as much as the unlocked door had. The cat always allowed Carrie to pet her, but she'd never before been willing to sit in her lap, no matter how much JoAnne or Carrie coaxed!

After a moment, Carrie began stroking the cat, accepting her friendship while wondering what had caused it. And what now? Take the cat home? Go get more food? Actually, FatCat ate only one bowl of food a day, so she was okay as long as she had plenty of water. There was no need to worry about her again until tomorrow, and surely JoAnne would be back by then.

Surely.

Carrie looked down at the framed photo of a young couple with a baby that was the only ornament on the table beside her. JoAnne's niece and her family. Susan Burke-Williams lived in Kansas City with her husband and son and, according to JoAnne, was her only living relative. The girl's mother and dad had been killed in an auto accident a few years ago. JoAnne loved the girl as much as Carrie loved her own son Rob. She had lived near her sister and brother-in-law in Kansas City so she could watch Susan grow up.

Maybe she should call the niece. No, the girl knew the ways of her aunt better than anyone. She'd probably think Carrie was a meddling busybody.

So then there was nothing more she could do here,

other than put out plenty of water for the cat. And, even if she was being a busybody, she should think about calling Susan if JoAnne didn't return soon. How long was too long before it would be right to call?

As usual, indecision made her feel awful. The sensible thing to do, she told herself, would be to simply go home and forget the whole thing. Except for the cat, of course.

Carrie shut her eyes, willed her bouncing thoughts to calm down, then said aloud, "Dear Lord, what shall I do now?"

She often prayed for guidance, but wasn't usually sure about getting an answer.

Silence. Well, she hadn't exactly expected to hear a voice anyway. So, go on thinking...

Susan worked at the home office of a national brokerage firm in Kansas City. Henry could probably tell her the company name if she needed to call Susan at work. He was from Kansas City too and might even have a phone book.

She'd never asked if he'd known JoAnne or her family when he lived in Kansas City. Neither he nor JoAnne had mentioned any connection, and they barely spoke when they were together. Besides, JoAnne closed her advertising agency and moved to the Ozarks a dozen years ago, and Henry had only been in the area a little over a year.

Carrie was sitting very still.

Oh! She wouldn't have to ask Henry or anyone else how to reach Susan. There was JoAnne's address book—the number would be there. Why hadn't she thought of that?

Yes, why not? Carrie lifted FatCat gently and put her in the chair seat. Then she went to the desk and took out the dark red book, putting her thumb on the place for "B" names.

The "B" section was blank.

Well, maybe it was under Williams.

No, JoAnne had the address book before Susan was married, and...

"W" was blank.

She flipped the pages quickly. There were no entries in the book at all. Every page was blank.

But she'd *seen* JoAnne use this book many times. Her own number was in it. She'd watched JoAnne write it down four years ago! She had seen this book with writing in it!

Carrie closed the book. It looked right, even a bit rubbed and scratched. Was there another book like it?

FatCat was with her once more, winding slowly around her ankles.

Carrie piled the drawer's contents on the desktop, looking for another red book, then pushed everything back inside the drawer and checked the rest of the desk again.

Nothing.

The address book that JoAnne had often used while Carrie watched, the mate to the blank one, was missing.

Just like JoAnne.

CHAPTER IV

Carrie locked the front door, put the key under the flower pot, then stood on the porch for a moment, imagining she heard "muwouuu" from behind the door. FatCat had wanted to come with her, no doubt about that. Later...if JoAnne was gone much longer...

But now, it was time to get on with her work. She turned away from the house and started down the path toward home, kicking loose rocks out of the way as she went.

Funny how rocks popped out of the ground. New rocks certainly showed up in her garden each year, no matter how many she cleared away or how much compost she added. Rob and JoAnne both said it was the freeze-thaw cycles that pushed them to the surface.

She preferred Roger's explanation. He said every Ozarks child knew (because their parents told them) that the sandman planted stone seeds at night, and they grew up into Ozarks rocks. "'N I'm sure that's true," he'd added, grinning at Carrie, "because if the sandman's smart enough to figure out how to get kids to sleep, then he's sure smart enough to know the Ozarks is a good place to grow rocks."

"I'll share your theory with Rob," she'd said, keeping her face straight—and then was sorry she hadn't just laughed. As soon as the words were out of her mouth, they sounded pompous, or even like she was making fun of Roger's humor. He might not understand how much she enjoyed hearing his tall tales, as did her son, a very logical-minded geoscientist at the University of Oklahoma.

But, uncertain how to explain all this to Roger without making things worse, she said no more.

Roger, dear man, hadn't seemed to take offense.

And, she did tell Rob the story.

"Oh, I'd believe it," he said, "but I seem to recall you're the one who once read to me about a flying elephant, and Roger told me his absolutely true stories about whoofenpoofs and booger bears last summer. So...should I question this? What's *your* advice, Mom?"

Her foot slipped on a rock hidden in the leaves, bouncing her thoughts back to the present. She continued along the path more slowly, kicking some rocks, and picking others up to check for fossils before she tossed them aside.

Rob did believe the stories fossils told.

JoAnne, however, was the one who had taught Carrie to enjoy rubbing her fingers over the waxy chert and to recognize fossils—Crinoidea, Brachiopoda, and Bryozoa— in limestone rocks. JoAnne even made sure she got the names of the fossils right, saying there was no point knowing something if you didn't know it correctly.

When she'd first come to the Ozarks, Carrie had read about the warm oceans that once covered the area and about the marine life that developed in those oceans during the

Paleozoic Era, such a very long time before her own arrival. It all seemed far away and abstract until JoAnne showed her fossils remaining from that earlier life.

Carrie kicked a rock too hard, then stared at the new scar the rock had made on her heavy walking boot.

Drat! Where *was* JoAnne anyway? It was selfish of her to go off and miss the meeting. What had come up that could possibly be more important?

At least there was no need to worry about her being out in the woods after a fall or other trouble. Her truck would still be at the house if she'd gone hiking. And if she was sick or had been in an accident, someone would have called, because they'd put each other's names on those billfold cards that asked whom to notify in case of emergency.

Well, it was very possible something new and exciting had happened. Everyone's guess that JoAnne was simply involved in an interesting new project was the most likely explanation.

Ahhh, Carrie thought, forgetting about kicking rocks for the moment. She's met a tall, handsome stranger...silver hair...tweed cap. He's a professor, studying...studying something, and JoAnne meets him, and...he says what he's studying can save the valley, and, well, what a joke on JoAnne, he's a man!

"Oh, stop it, stop it," she said aloud, startling herself when her voice mingled with bird calls and the rattle of rocks and twigs under her feet.

Now she really was being ridiculous, though, she thought, kicking another rock hard enough to startle a rabbit out of a brush pile near the path, JoAnne could still have called me.

She quit walking and pushed back her coat sleeve to look at her watch. One o'clock. No more muddling over

JoAnne. It was time to get to work on the brochures. She wanted to finish that job and take them to the tourist center before dark. She also planned to go to the big grocery store in Bonny for a few things that the store in Guilford didn't carry. She'd add cat food to her list, just in case.

Carrie normally didn't go to the Bonny Tourist Information Center on weekends this time of year. There was always a waiting list of retirees living in the area who were eager to take over. Like all center employees, they enjoyed talking with the tourists and could, with a part-time custodian, manage weekend traffic quite well after the fall color season ended. But there was snow in the forecast for Monday, and Carrie didn't want to carry boxes from the employee parking area in bad weather. Since she needed to go to the grocery store, she'd planned to leave her brochure boxes off too.

She always had her contact at the Arkansas Department of Parks and Tourism send new brochures to her at home. She liked to read each offering before putting it out in the racks at the center. As she looked at the material, she made a list of things to put on the events calendar and wrote short descriptions of the activities for her tourist consultants. That kind of work was hard to do at the center because it had no private office. The area originally intended for an office had been sacrificed to expand restroom facilities and add baby changing stations.

That was one reason the department didn't mind if center managers like Carrie did some of their office work at home, as long as tourists were cared for and the centers ran smoothly. That was also one reason Carrie liked her job. She could spend some of her work time sitting in an office that looked out into Ozarks forest, rather than standing at a counter facing trucks and cars.

When she'd first dreamed of moving to the Ozarks, she hadn't known she'd need to get a job, but after it became clear how little Amos had left her, there was no choice. This job with the state opened up at the right time, and she was so grateful for it that she was more than willing to put in extra hours at home if necessary.

The answering machine light was flashing when Carrie walked in the house, and, thinking JoAnne might have called, she punched the message button before she took off her coat.

"Carrie," said Evan's soft voice, "will you be coming to Tulsa soon? I'd like to see you. We can have lunch someplace nice, my treat of course. I'm home all day. Please call me."

Carrie hooked her coat over a chair at the dining table, made a cup of coffee, and sat down to stare out the window. She didn't want to talk with Evan. All their conversations since Amos died had been awkward, and now they were pointless. She wanted to be through with Evan Walters and his memories of her husband's death, but he kept calling, and even her coolness hadn't stopped him.

Sure, she had private thoughts about Amos, but she hated talking about him, especially with Evan. She hated having to keep on soothing Evan when surely, if anything, it should be the other way around! Too bad the man had never married and didn't have a wife to talk with. Amos had been his only close friend so far as she knew, and Evan hadn't mentioned any new friends, since...

I wonder what Evan would do, Carrie thought, if I cried or—just once—made a scene about how difficult things are? What would that be like?

She didn't know. Would everyone around her be shocked? Evan probably would, and Amos sure would have.

She frowned out the window, disgusted at herself.

"Carry on, Carrie," her father had often said. Well, she was carrying on, and doing a good job of it. Even when Amos was here, there had been no one to lean on. The only time she'd really wanted to break down was when he laughed and said to someone, "Carrie's a real stoic."

Stoic. She'd looked the word up to be sure, and the definition still screamed in her heart.

A stoic was a person who should be apathetic, without passion, above joy or grief, and accept unavoidable things with no complaint.

Or, she thought, at least a person who acts that way.

So she'd never shouted, never said in defense, "Well, that's what people want of me, especially you!" She'd learned how to live inside herself, even while she was living with Amos. That way, things people did couldn't hurt her.

Come to think of it, her whole life with Amos had been preparation for being alone.

And alone was what she was. She wanted nothing to do with people entanglements now. She had her carefully constructed life, and being an independent woman suited her just fine. That's why her friendship with JoAnne was so important. JoAnne reinforced independence.

But that didn't mean she couldn't enjoy Henry's company. He made no demands on her, and they had good, light-hearted times together. No deep emotions.

Of course, she and JoAnne enjoyed being together too, but even an independent woman knew that talking with a man was different. "Not better, just different," was how she explained it to JoAnne, who always seemed jealous when Carrie mentioned Henry.

Not better—just different. A tiny ripple of pleasure moved inside her as she thought about Henry, and she wiggled her shoulders in response to the feeling, even as she wondered what caused it and warned herself not to give in to that type of pleasure. Anyway, it was silly. They didn't know each other that well. Their talk was always light and very carefully neutral.

So, later this afternoon, she'd call him, and they could go to town together. He wouldn't mind stopping at the grocery and the tourist center. Maybe he'd like to go to the new catfish restaurant that had opened about a mile from the center. She'd been wanting to try it out. In fact, she and JoAnne had talked about going there this weekend.

The memory chilled her, and she sat still, coffee cup held stiffly, half-way to her mouth. Last night JoAnne had suggested they eat there together...tonight.

And JoAnne never missed a chance to eat out.

Well, what more could she do than keep calling JoAnne? If there was no answer by 3:30, she'd ask Henry if he had a Kansas City phone book and could help her find Susan's number. Carrie didn't remember Susan's husband's real name. She'd never heard him called anything but "Putt." Surely there'd be only one Burke-Williams anyway.

In the meantime, she'd have to deal with Evan.

She was sure he didn't want to talk business. Over his strong protests, she'd transferred her few investments from his office to a broker in Bonny when she moved. She wanted everything close to her new home and, she admitted now, to be finished with Evan.

He answered the phone immediately. "Oh, Carrie, hi, thanks for calling. Um, I was hoping you might be planning a trip to Tulsa soon. I've, uh, wanted to see you..."

Carrie knew better than to ask him to make the two-hour drive to visit her, even if she'd wanted him to come. He hadn't been near Blackberry Hollow since Amos died.

"I really hadn't intended to come any time soon, Evan. It's getting into the time of year when there might be ice or snow. I've told you about the stone quarry they're planning to put in our valley, and we're busy organizing the fight against it. It may be a while..."

"Oh, Carrie, you can't be that busy. How about next Saturday? We'll, uh, meet, talk over good times here in the city, even go to a show at the Performing Arts Center, or whatever you want. You must miss being able to attend city events."

When she said nothing, he changed the subject. "Um...in the meantime, tell me what's new from Rob. Has he been over?"

Now she could talk with honest enthusiasm. "Not recently. He's busy with his new job at the university. He likes his department head and class assignments. Says there are good research opportunities too. He'll be here for Thanksgiving."

"Any daughter-in-law in sight? Is he seeing anyone special?"

She laughed. "I don't know. He has a very good friend in the art department at the university. He seems to spend a lot of time with her, but I haven't met her yet."

"Carrie, I feel I have a part in this. Um...do you remember that I first met you and Amos when you came to see me about opening an investment account for Rob's college back when he was six?"

Good heavens, how could Evan think she'd forgotten that? She kept her voice light. "Well, he put his college money to good use, didn't he? We'll be calling him Dr. Robert Amos McCrite by next spring. We both have a lot to be proud of, Evan."

"Amos should be here to see it."

"Well, yes, but he's not, and Rob's fine, and I'm doing fine." She heard her words tumbling out and stopped, changing the subject. "Evan, as you can tell, I really avoid coming to the city. It has nothing to do with you. I've turned into a real country girl."

"Uh...so you're doing all right then? Are your investments doing well? Satisfied with our office there?"

"Yes, Evan, and you know I have a good job, so I'm fine."

"At your age you shouldn't have to work. You should be enjoying playing bridge, and trips, and whatever you want. You should have a man...um...take care of you. Huh-hunh."

His laugh sounded really strange, and now she was losing patience. "Evan, we're not that old. I like my job, and you know I don't play bridge! Some day I might travel, maybe take one of those senior citizen bus trips, but not now. I'm too busy helping other travelers find their way around Arkansas."

"Yes, yes, the bus trip would be a good idea. I'm glad you're thinking of that. Perhaps we'll plan to go together."

She was too shocked to answer and, after an awkward silence, he said, "Well, tell me more about what's going on with that quarry."

She talked a few more minutes, filling the time, then stopped, anxious to get off the phone.

When Evan realized she wasn't going to say more, he finally told her goodbye, finishing with, "You'll call me soon?" Then, at last, he hung up.

Good heavens, why did Evan have to be so interested in her? And the man had taken her seriously when she mentioned the bus trip. Senior citizen bus trip indeed—the last thing she wanted to do was go on any kind of bus trip, let alone with Evan!

Still, the folks who came to the center in tour buses always seemed to be having a good time, like they were members of some special club.

But, she reminded herself, she had never wanted to join any club, either. Too many people, too close together.

Carrie put her coffee cup in the sink, then made a cheese sandwich, piled carrot sticks beside it on a plate, and poured a glass of orange juice. She took the food to her office, setting the glass in the copper coaster Rob made for her when he was in eighth grade metal working class.

The coaster was ugly. Rob had never been any cleverer at making or repairing things than Amos. Being a teacher suited him.

She began sorting brochures, stopping every few minutes to punch re-dial and listen to the phone ring at JoAnne's house. She wished she'd left JoAnne a note asking her to call when she returned. She hadn't done it because she hated to admit she'd been in the house, but then, JoAnne knew she might be expected to check on the cat under the circumstances.

An hour and a half later, the brochures were all sorted, she had made the notes she needed, and also finished all the food, including the carrot sticks. She couldn't think of anything more she wanted to do in her office. It was nearly 3:30.

After one more call to JoAnne's still-empty house, she punched in Henry's phone number.

His familiar rumble sounded a bit breathless. "Oh, hi, Carrie. I was getting more firewood in, supposed to be very cold tonight. Heard anything from JoAnne yet?"

"No, but Henry, I thought I might call her niece if she's not back soon. Do you have a Kansas City phone book? I'd like to have Susan's phone number. The name is spelled B-u-r-k-e. Burke-hyphen-Williams."

Carrie suddenly felt very awkward. She didn't want to tell Henry about searching JoAnne's house and finding an unlocked door and a blank address book.

"Hey, she'll surely be back this evening. I wouldn't worry, you know how she is. Do we have a date for supper?"

His quick dismissal of JoAnne's absence made Carrie feel once more that she was overreacting. After all, under some circumstances, she might not even know JoAnne was gone, and there could be a perfectly logical explanation for both the unlocked door and the missing address book.

"Yes, that's great, Henry, at least if you don't mind if we stop by the center to leave my brochure boxes, and also take time to go to the grocery. I need some things I can't get in Guilford. I should drive this time. My turn."

"Nope, I'll drive, and I need to get milk myself. Guess you're bringing your cool chest? Where do you want to eat?"

"Have you tried the new catfish place? It's just a mile south of the center. How about that?"

"Sounds good. I'll pick you and your boxes up in an hour. Don't forget your cool chest. Mine still smells like fish from last summer."

Carrie didn't realize until after Henry hung up that he hadn't answered her question about whether or not he could help her locate Susan's phone number. Well, of course, he wouldn't think it was that important anyway.

CHAPTER V

Henry's old Volkswagen Rabbit came bouncing down the drive at exactly 4:30 by Carrie's clock. One might never worry if JoAnne was late, but it was time to worry if Henry was late for anything.

Carrie was prepared. She'd had the brochure boxes, cool chest, and her coat ready at the door by 4:15, and her teal blue knitted cap was already on her head.

She always wore sensible hats when it was cold. This one didn't exactly go with her outfit, but it was fuzzy and warm, and she liked the color.

As a matter of fact, just two weeks ago Henry happened to mention—quite casually, of course—that the cap matched her eyes. Most people called her eyes hazel, and Amos always said they were green. The color had been more noticeable when it was accompanied by the red hair she'd once had. "An Orphan Annie mop" was what her mother called it. Now the red ringlets had been replaced by coarser grey curls, and her eyes, too, were a quieter color. But it was nice Henry noticed the color and had perhaps seen something of youth there.

Carrie was out on the porch with the first box in her arms by the time Henry circled around in the drive and got out to open the hatchback. He didn't rush to take the box from her or act like she wasn't capable of carrying it, but simply went to get the next one from the stack.

When they were both securely belted in, he reached over to squeeze her hand and smile before he put the car in gear. She stiffened and then, embarrassed, looked out her window as the little car joggled its way up the hill.

When Henry's full attention had turned to maneuvering the rutted county road, she faced forward, then, turning her head as little as possible, glanced at him. He was such a big man, with a strong square face and black hair going grey. He made quite a contrast to her own short, round body and wide oval face. Like Hercules and—she almost laughed aloud when she thought of how she might look to others—an ancient cherub in clothes!

Oh, well. She felt, what was it, giddy? No, not that exactly, but she did feel surprisingly light-hearted. Did a smile and a hand squeeze from a man do all that?

She relaxed, settling into the contours of the seat. Without willing it, she found her thoughts lifting above the problems of the day. She was really looking forward to the evening with Henry. This was fun, almost like going on a date when she was sixteen. She hadn't forgotten!

They didn't talk until they were on the paved highway since the rocky road made for noisy travel in almost any car.

Hoping to keep conversation away from the quarry for a while, Carrie asked Henry how well he knew Jack Bruner.

"Oh, not well, but we always seem to end up in the barber shop at the same time. We talk some." He looked over at her. "I think men talk to each other in the barber shop even more than women do in a beauty shop. Too bad the old barber shops are disappearing. They don't have those dryers making noise to interrupt conversation."

She grinned. "Gossip!"

"Well..."

"What *do* you talk about?"

"Oh, most of what Jack says is about his farm—chickens and cattle—and also taking care of his land. He seems pretty big on following guidelines for spreading chicken litter on pastures, avoiding run-off into the creek, things like that. I guess he's a good farmer. Maybe it's all PR, but he seems sincere."

"Surprising. I wouldn't have expected that from him. I smell their chicken houses sometimes when the wind is from the south, don't you?"

"Yep, live in the country, smell the country."

"Maybe, but I'd just as soon live a million miles from any confinement hog or chicken houses, denuded forests, human pollution, or too-close neighbors."

"Carrie, you don't mean all that. Besides, you put manure on your garden. As for neighbors, don't forget your house is less than a mile from mine if you walk through the woods. And...there's JoAnne, close enough."

She was silent for a moment. "I guess I like my privacy too much, hm?"

"I like privacy too, but, well, people need people sometimes."

The tone of his voice had changed. She glanced over to see such sadness in his face that she turned away involuntarily, then bowed her head when he spoke again.

"Carrie, you've probably never needed someone like I did once. You've probably never had someone turn on you when you needed them most."

After a silence, she said softly, still not looking at him, "I do know, Henry. Even if Amos was still here, he wouldn't be the kind of person who could offer understanding, or comfort, or support. I've had to stand on my own pretty much all my life. I don't know how it was with you, so maybe it isn't the same, but..."

"Amos never turned against you, never lied, never tried to make you suffer!" His words were full of pain.

Now she turned toward him again. "No, no, he didn't. I'm sorry. You mean it was Irena? Irena did that?"

Carrie knew very little about Henry's marriage except that his wife had left him five years ago, about the same time Amos died. That was one reason the two of them were drawn together in the beginning. They had each been alone for about the same length of time, and in most ways both of them were comfortable with their single lives. That added to companionable understanding in a relationship without commitments. But other than saying he had been married, his wife had left, and there were no children, Henry had offered nothing, and Carrie hadn't wanted to ask.

JoAnne, who seemed to know a lot about Irena's family—probably from reading the society pages of the Kansas City papers—had reported to Carrie that the family had lots of "old" money. JoAnne said that when Irena's last relative died, she inherited all the remaining wealth. At least Henry didn't need to worry about supporting his missing wife. Maybe Irena was supposed to be sending him alimony! Surely that wasn't what he meant.

"This is a depressing conversation, isn't it, Carrie? Let's change the subject."

But she couldn't help asking. "Did you get a divorce?"

Henry's smile returned, though he didn't look at her. "Yup, no attachments!"

Now why did I have to ask that, Carrie thought. She'd opened her mouth before thinking!

The grocery wasn't busy, and she walked beside Henry as he pushed her cart through the almost empty aisles.

"Ah, Kitty-Kat Krunchies," he said, enunciating each "k" and "t" sharply and rolling the "r." She started to laugh as she put the box of food for FatCat in the cart, and, with that encouragement, he began reading more product names aloud. Even though most of the brands were known to her, somehow Henry's sonorous voice rolling out, "toe-MAH-toe bits," and, "Be-a-nie-We-e-enie" made the names sound ridiculous—and hilarious.

No one could mistake us for an old married couple, she thought. We're acting too silly.

After the sacks of groceries were safely stowed in the back seat of the car and the milk and meat put in the cool chest, they headed toward the highway. "Shall we eat or go to the center first?" he asked.

She looked at her watch. "Eat," she said. "The center will be closed now anyway, and I'm starving."

"Ah, and you're a fine woman, Carrie McCrite," said Henry.

He became pompously chivalrous when they arrived at the restaurant, and they were laughing again by the time he bowed over her hand and helped her onto one of the rough-hewn wooden benches. Staring at them, the young hostess in cap and apron laid brown paper menus on the trestle table.

When she was out of earshot, Carrie said, "She can't wait to get back to the kitchen and tell everyone about the strange old folks with odd manners."

"Should have stayed," Henry said, "might have learned something."

The overall-clad waiter who came to take their order couldn't be a day over sixteen, Carrie decided, as she began by asking for separate checks. She and Henry always went dutch.

Henry looked up at the boy and winked. "I can't stand independent women, can you? No, suh, this lady goes on my ticket."

Carrie, thinking she should be angry about his reference to her independence as well as more mindful of JoAnne's admonitions, responded by holding the menu over the lower part of her face and batting her eyes at the confused boy. Then she looked at Henry and said, "Why, thank you, Colonel. You are most kind."

Oh, goodness gracious, what was wrong with her?

"Was that supposed to be Scarlett O'Hara?" Henry asked when the boy left.

After that beginning, thought Carrie while they ate, I probably could have eaten the box of Kitty-Kat Krunchies and not known it.

The meal, however, was delicious. Henry obviously enjoyed it too, and even ordered extra hushpuppies as soon as he and Carrie finished a lengthy discussion about who was going to eat the last one on the platter.

"You just ordered more," Carrie told him as they got up to leave, "because I ate the last one! But," she said firmly, "I counted. They brought us eight, and we each had four.

Fair is fair, and I no longer care a twit about a girlish figure."

"Hm," Henry said, keeping his eyes on her face as he
held her coat, "I like a bit of roundness here and there
myself."

Oh, my, Carrie thought, oh, my.

When they went outside, the cold air was sharp against
their faces though the wind had died. Stars sparkled, even
in the city-lit sky. "Sure is cold," Henry said unnecessarily
as they got in the car.

"Sure is. Probably there'll be frost flowers in the morning. We haven't had them yet this year...hasn't been cold
enough. I plan to go for a walk tomorrow morning and see
if I can find some."

"Is that the curvy ice that comes out of the ground? Is
that what you call them? I haven't seen very many, but then
I guess I'm not in the woods as often as you are. What
makes them?" He glanced away from the traffic for a moment, and his brown eyes twinkled at her. "I'm willing to
bet you know."

"Fairy ice, frost flowers, they have lots of names. They
happen when plants retain moisture in their roots after the
tops die in the fall. When the air temperature is cold
enough, the remaining moisture freezes and expands. Ice
is pushed out through rows of tiny splits in the stems. That's
what makes the fantastic swirls. The ice swirls stop appear-
ing as soon as all moisture inside the plant is gone. JoAnne
told me those facts. I prefer to think it's magic.

"Of course, they only occur in places where the weedy
wildflowers are left alone, and most of society moves too
fast to notice them when they do appear. Conditions have
to be just right, and they don't last long. They're usually
gone by ten o'clock, a transient beauty."

"Yes, and I'd like to see more of them. Would it be all right if I went with you tomorrow? Besides, you probably shouldn't go by yourself. Hunting season, you know. I saw trucks with gun racks along the road today."

"You can come if you want to see the frost flowers, but I'll be perfectly safe alone. I wear hunters' orange, and to-morrow I plan to carry my radio and play loud music.

"We usually find the best display on the hill beyond the creek, which is about half-way between your house and mine, I guess. I want to go out early so I'll have time to get home and dress for church. I'll call you around eight, and we can meet on the hill if you like."

"Whatever you say," he agreed and was silent.

Maybe I should have asked him to go to church with me, Carrie thought. So far as she knew, Henry didn't at-tend any local church, but he was always the first one to bow his head for a quiet table blessing when they ate out together.

Still, she was silent too and wondered if she wanted Henry to go to church for his good...or hers.

The Tourist Information Center parking lot was bright with mercury vapor light, and Carrie had no trouble finding her key to open the door while Henry followed with the first box. She didn't turn on any inside lights. They could see quite well by light that came in through the windows. She showed him where to put the box and went back to get another. She was just putting it in the corner when he came in behind her with the last box, stacked it on top of the other two, then turned at the edge of the counter, block-ing her exit. He leaned against the counter for a moment, studying her in silence.

She began to feel like she was floating in another time, clear back to her first year of high school. She was standing on the shadowy porch at her parents' home with Christopher Kneeland, the first boy who had ever kissed her. But the big, powerful-looking man standing over her was not Christopher.

Nor was his kiss like Christopher's.

Henry's arms tightened around her, and without a thought of caution or regret, she welcomed the warm, strong body against hers. Carrie was almost beyond surprise when she recognized the stirring of feelings she barely remembered from long ago...long, lonely years before Amos died.

After several minutes she turned to put her cheek against Henry's rough jacket, trying to calm her thoughts.

Then she looked up at him. "Oh, my," was all she could say.

"Carrie," he said, very softly, then shook his head. "Should I apologize? I don't want to."

"No," she answered. "No, you don't need to apologize."

He picked the teal blue hat off the floor, handed it to her, then waited in silence while she locked the office door. She couldn't think of anything to say except a rather formal thank you as he held the car door for her.

Henry turned the heater up as he headed the car down the highway, and Carrie, who was shivering now, welcomed the warmth. Had he expected this? Had he thought about it ahead of time? She certainly hadn't.

And now she was scared. She didn't know what she should think or say. She didn't even know how she should feel. Passion was a word she never used, but was that it? Was remembering the warmth of Henry's closeness wrong—the wrong feeling, the wrong time?

For the shortest moment, back there in the darkness, she had thought of the marriage ceremony, and two being one.

And she had felt so quiet, so safe, and so...unlonely.

True, it had been one heck of a day, but still, was she seeking escape from mental muddles over Evan and JoAnne and the quarry by responding to—no, welcoming, even encouraging—hilarity, and then...then... She'd certainly never acted like that in her whole life. She was going to have to think about Carrie as well as Henry. What was wrong with her? Or, what was wrong with this person in her body that really couldn't be...had never been...her.

After they'd driven several miles, she backed away from her tumbling thoughts and struggled to make casual conversation, commenting on an early Christmas tree in a window they passed and wondering aloud how many times snow and ice would knock out their electric power this winter. Henry followed her lead, talking quietly, his earlier roles of comedian suitor and tender lover held back by what she supposed was either propriety or perhaps something akin to the shock she felt.

He helped carry her groceries into the kitchen, took his milk, and headed back toward the hall. He didn't offer to stay, nor did she want to ask him. At the door he looked at her seriously for a moment, then smiled, brushed his gloved finger gently across her cheek, and bent to touch her mouth with his in the slightest whisper of a kiss.

She said thank you—meaning the dinner—then, after the door closed, realized he might not know just what she had thanked him for. Maybe she should have been more specific.

Awash in confusion, Carrie stood by her front door listening as the little car chugged up the lane toward the road, carrying Henry away into the night.

She put two logs in the wood stove before going to get ready for bed. She wrapped herself in the fuzzy robe Rob had given her last Christmas and sat in her chair by the stove for a long time, deciding she was almost as confused by Henry's actions as she was her own. He had always been friendly, but that was it. He'd never touched her, unless it was to take her arm as they entered a restaurant or make some other polite gesture. His touch and kiss tonight had been rather more than polite.

Was this all wrong? Or could it be, somehow, all right? Why didn't she, a sensible, independent, mature woman, know the answer to that? And how was she going to face tomorrow, and the next days, when she would see Henry, and other people would be there, and when she would look at him and know...know about tonight. What was she going to do?

Do? She didn't even know what to think!

Well, one thing she must not do is be alone with Henry again. At least not for a while.

She'd come to no other conclusions when she closed down the damper on the stove and went to bed.

CHAPTER VI

Carrie awakened from the dream slowly. The images wavered, faded, and she let them go reluctantly.

Oh, my, just like the romantic movies of her childhood, and just as unreal. Silly.

She lay quietly under her down comforter, totally involved, for a brief dream-time, in memories.

Then, suddenly alert, she pushed memory away and sat up so quickly it made her dizzy. It was just a dream, but the man in the dream had been Henry, not Amos!

I'm carrying on as if I were a teenager instead of a mature woman, she thought. I must get this out of my head.

Carrie willed her thoughts into daylight and turned to look out the window. First light. The sun would come soon. Time to go see about JoAnne, and it would be a beautiful morning to share a woods walk with Henry.

No...oh, no, not now. That she could not do now, no matter what she'd promised last night. Besides, he undoubtedly regretted his actions, maybe was as embarrassed as she was and didn't want to be alone with her either. That's what he must be thinking. He would be wondering what had gotten into the both of them.

Several times before last night, they had talked about independence and agreed it was so important.

She turned from thoughts about Henry and began a prayer for JoAnne, then side-tracked, thinking that God must understand she hadn't wanted Henry as anything but a good friend...someone who understood and was kind.

That person didn't have to be a man, though Henry had seemed both understanding and kind. A real gentleman—if she overlooked his coming into her house without knocking yesterday. She hadn't had the courage to ask about that.

Well, JoAnne was a good friend. She was intelligent, quick, loyal, and witty. But she was not gentle or kind.

The prayer, which strayed between Carrie's own need for comfort and her concern for JoAnne, ended with, "Please let her be home, and thank you for taking care of all of us. Guide us...me...in doing Your will."

Of course, JoAnne could be quite safe away from home. It might not have occurred to her that Carrie would worry.

She shook her head in frustration. Why hadn't JoAnne confided in her? They were supposed to be good friends!

Well, she'd just left it in God's hands. She should live up to her prayer.

Now it was time to check and see if JoAnne was home, then go look for frost flowers. Henry, remembering last night, would understand why she hadn't called.

She pushed her comforter back, slid out of bed, put on her robe and furry slippers, and hurried into the living room to start a fire in the woodstove. As she got closer to the iron box, she could feel the tiny bit of friendly warmth that remained from last night's fire and, when she swung the heavy latch and opened the iron door, saw there were healthy coals glowing beneath the ashes. She selected kindling and two split logs from her wood box, put them on the coals over sheets of crumpled newsprint, and watched to be sure the fire had a good start before she went to make her coffee.

While the water was heating, she punched in JoAnne's number, thinking, "Please answer, please answer," as if this incantation would somehow help.

There was no answer.

So. She'd have to go feed the cat before she went walking.

Suddenly Carrie felt anger replace her worry. JoAnne simply *assumed* she'd take care of FatCat! She hadn't phoned because "Carry-on Carrie" would always take over. Well, if JoAnne wasn't back when she got home from church, she'd bring FatCat and all the cat paraphernalia here. If it snowed, she wanted the cat at this end of the forest path until JoAnne came to claim her. Let JoAnne worry if the cat was missing when she returned!

Still, Susan should be notified. It was time someone else worried about JoAnne's behavior.

Carrie decided she'd dress and eat first, then it wouldn't be quite so early and seem so much like an emergency. Surely Kansas City Information could find the number. The name Burke-Williams wasn't exactly common. She wasn't going to bother Henry about the number again; he hadn't acted like he wanted to talk about Kansas City. Probably something to do with the bad experience he'd hinted at last night.

She ate a bowl of cereal, then put on her jeans, a turtleneck, and a heavy sweat shirt.

Information in Kansas City did have a listing, and Carrie dialed the number. Susan answered and greeted her warmly. The baby was crying in the background, and Carrie remembered how Rob had sounded years ago.

She got right to the point. "Susan, have you talked with your aunt JoAnne recently? She left home yesterday morning and hasn't returned or been in touch. I thought I'd better tell you."

"We talked Thursday night. We were making plans for getting together there at Thanksgiving. She was fine then. Do you think something's wrong?"

In the background the crying stopped. Probably Susan's husband was tending to the baby. Nice. Amos wouldn't have.

"Well, no," Carrie said, "not exactly. You know how she is, but I am a bit worried. There's the cat. She didn't call to ask me to take care of FatCat."

Silence. Carrie heard a man's voice, then Susan's, explaining. The man said something else.

"Carrie, Putt and I both think someone should be notified. I know Aunt JoAnne's in good health and all, but, if it's been a whole day and no word about taking care of FatCat... Who can you call there? Would there be a police department or missing persons?"

"No, out here it's the county sheriff. I'll call him. I'm really sorry to bother you, and I don't want to make a big deal about this, but still..."

"Yes, we both know Aunt JoAnne, but, as you say, there's the cat. After you've talked to the sheriff, will you call me back?" Susan's voice betrayed her worry.

"Right away. I'll hang up and call now."

Carrie wasn't sure if she should call 911 or the regular

number for the sheriff's department. She didn't want to
make this sound like it was life-threatening or anything.
She dialed the regular number.

The pleasant, low-key female voice that answered asked
a few questions about JoAnne and her truck, then told
Carrie that nothing sounding as though it might involve
JoAnne had been reported. She took Carrie's phone number, saying she'd re-check all the reports from deputies and
from the hospitals and put out a description of JoAnne as
well as the grey truck. Checking would take a little while.
Would Ms. McCrite be at this number?

Thinking quickly, Carrie decided she'd better feed the
cat now, and she really did want to go walking. She explained she had an answering machine, thanked the dis-
patcher, and hung up.

After calling Susan to report that the sheriff's office
had no reports of any problems involving JoAnne, Carrie
put on her orange jacket and hat and, taking her portable
radio and a plastic bag with cat food in it, went out into
the bright morning.

She hurried along the path and let herself into the
house. She emptied the bag of food into FatCat's food bowl,
re-filled the water bowl, then hesitated. Perhaps she'd better do another walk-through.

In the door of JoAnne's bedroom, she stopped. Had
she left the closet door open after she looked inside yesterday afternoon? Surely not. But she must have. It was open
now. JoAnne wouldn't be happy if she found out. FatCat
had once shown a lively interest in the sweaters on shelves
at one side of the closet.

Carrie took a quick look. The sweaters seemed undis-
turbed. She shut the closet door, hearing the latch click.
Odd, she remembered that sound from yesterday.

She re-checked the rest of the house. All was quiet, very normal, and empty of any movement except for a friendly cat.

Instead of heading back along the path to her house, Carrie decided to climb down the hill behind JoAnne's, cross the creek, and make her way at an angle up the opposite hill to their favorite frost flower spot. There were several places where it was easy to step over the spring-fed creek that ran through the hollow, and the creek disappeared completely before it got to the end of JoAnne's property, leaving the rocky bed dry except when there had been a heavy rain.

She and JoAnne often puzzled about where their water went after it sank out of sight through the rocks. They had imagined it must be busy underground, creating a beautiful cavern full of all kinds of exotic mineral deposits. There were small caves with such formations in the bluffs overlooking the valley and, of course, magnificent ones, large and small, in many other places throughout the Ozarks.

The two of them had talked about pouring a bottle of red food coloring into their creek, then walking along the big creek in the valley to see if any pink water showed up. Later this winter, they'd do just that.

She started up the hill and turned on her radio, tuning it to a program of gospel music. If any hunters were in the area, they'd sure know she was coming.

As she climbed, she began scanning the forest floor for the magical ice formations. Nothing, yet conditions were right. JoAnne had mentioned that it was about time just a couple of days ago.

Then, suddenly, sunlight in the clearing ahead of her sparkled bits of diamond fire from the forest floor. She'd expected to find a few, but here were dozens of the fantastic twists of ribbony ice rising from the ground, creating the now familiar flower-like swirls, loops, and sugary folds. No matter that she understood how fairy ice was formed, she'd always think of these ice formations as magic. She stood still, savoring the beauty, and feeling sorry, for a moment, that she hadn't called Henry. Maybe it was wrong to rob him of this pleasure.

Well, he was certainly capable of going on a walk by himself, and she had told him the best display was usually on this hillside.

The first fall after she'd moved here, JoAnne took her into these woods, promising a spectacle she'd never forget. As usual, JoAnne had been right.

Carrie turned the radio off, listened, and looked around to see if Henry had come out by himself. A person could see long distances in a winter forest, but now she saw nothing and heard only birds and squirrels.

Hunters might be here, but they were always quiet.

She turned the radio on again, then took off a glove and bent to touch one of the delicate ice formations, feeling it give under the light pressure of her finger.

The radio announcer said it was 9:15. She should head back toward her house and the phone.

It really was too bad Henry had missed this show.

She started downhill on her regular walking path, planning to cross the creek on the old earth dam at the pond and climb the gentle slope below her house.

This was the best time of year to be in the forest. Undergrowth had dried, and she could see so far. She paused and tilted her head up to look at tree branches making crisscross lacework against the sky. She was near home, almost to the old fallen tree and the creek. It would be safe to turn off the radio and listen for birds. Safe...

What was that by the old tree? Something, a trick of shadow—just the shadow of memory from when Amos had died there—a memory returning to her for the first time in many months.

She was very calm. Trick of shadow. That was all.

She shut her eyes for a moment, then opened them to walk again. The crunch of her steps in dry leaves sounded too loud.

Sunlight and shadow. The tree did have something.

Carrie felt cold, as cold as frost flowers.

Amos! "Oh, no. Ohhh, dear God!"

No! No, no, not Amos...impossible. She shook her head back and forth, hoping the image would clear away, but it didn't.

It was very real. And it was JoAnne.

JoAnne, with her head and shoulders propped against the giant tree trunk. So cold...where was her red coat?

Now Carrie moved fast and sank to her knees beside her friend, unaware that she was kneeling on rocks. For a few moments everything was still, she was still. All she could hear was the scream of a crow, echoing around her, and the sound of someone breathing.

The side of JoAnne's head wasn't bright red like Amos's had been, but it was the same unreal, unhuman mess. This was a familiar death, one Carrie had lived through before.

Blood. Where was the blood? She knew there should be a lot of blood.

She dropped the radio, took off her glove, and reached for her friend's bare hand. When she touched it, her own fingers felt ice, and she realized JoAnne's hand, as cold and hard as ice itself, was lying on a crushed frost flower.

Carrie shut her eyes in bewilderment. Why was it happening again, and where was the blood?

Words from the 23rd Psalm raced through her head: "Yea, though I walk through the valley of the shadow of death...I will fear no evil...thou art with me...thou art with me...thou art...shadow of death...comfort me...comfort me...thou art with me..."

She didn't cry.

Time passed, but how much, no one would ever know or care. Eventually Carrie was aware that she was shaking with a cold, hard rage. Hunters! But when? Not recently. Nothing here was warm. No life had wisped away on this hillside this morning.

And she had heard no shots. Not this morning. Yesterday! The opening day of hunting season.

She got to her feet and began to move as quickly as she could over the forest floor, trying to control her shaking with quick movement. It was impossible to run, there were too many rocks and fallen branches. Slow down, no need to run. Falling could be disastrous, and for JoAnne it now would make no difference how fast she did something. Or even, Carrie realized, whether or not she did anything at all!

She stopped walking. So why do anything? Her thoughts rushed crazily. It would be fair. She'd already coped with one death on this hillside. Go home. Dress. Go to church. Let someone else find this and deal with it.

No! The hunter would pay, and if no one else found him—or her—Carrie would. Yesterday morning! Oh, dear God, it must have been the shots she heard yesterday morning. She would ask, would find out who had been in the woods, and that person would pay. Her rage carried her home in a rush, and this time she did dial 911.

After she'd explained—very slowly—exactly what she had found, Carrie gave directions to her mail box and from there to her house. The person on the phone asked her to stay at the house, though Carrie protested she should go back to JoAnne, who had now become "the body." It had occurred to Carrie that the hunter who shot JoAnne might return to remove evidence, though actually she hadn't any idea what that could be, especially after a day had passed. A shell? Maybe he dropped something, something that would say who he was. She hadn't looked around at all.

And she should be with JoAnne, make sure nothing and no one came to harm her. Then it occurred to her that, now, JoAnne was beyond harm.

The man on the phone said a deputy would be there within thirty minutes. Did she have someone to come be with her?

Who would that be, Carrie wondered. JoAnne was the only close friend she had. There was Rob, of course, but he was three hundred miles away. She and JoAnne had once talked about the fact that they had Rob and Susan and, after that, only each other.

Oh, no, Susan! She was going to have to find a way to tell this to Susan.

Perhaps Henry could. Maybe he'd come over to be with her. He was—after all—a kind friend.

But, she discovered, Henry wasn't home to answer his phone.

For a minute she thought of Roger and Shirley. But they'd be busy with milking.

So, she'd have to carry on alone. She picked up the phone and prepared to give the terrible news to the little family in Kansas City.

The door knocker sounded just as Carrie finished her conversation with Susan's husband who, thank goodness, had been the one to answer the phone. The sheriff's man, it seemed, had made good time.

She opened the door, and Henry, looking much older than she remembered from last night, stood on the porch holding out her portable radio.

She stepped back. As he came toward her, he spoke. "You found her?"

"Yes," she said. Then, while she was standing there, looking at his crumpled face, something inside her broke loose.

The ice that had been there for so many years cracked and melted as she went to him and, as soon as she was safe in the circle of his arms, Carrie McCrite began to cry.

CHAPTER VII

Carrie's tears finally stopped, but she didn't look up. She kept her eyes closed, her head down, and listened to the thump—thump—thump in Henry's chest. The calming vibration and warmth made her think, suddenly, of the flutter of Rob's heart when he was a baby.

How many times had she rested her cheek against her son's tiny body, then brushed her lips against his tummy?

A heart was life. But JoAnne...

She couldn't think coherently. Being hugged was all that mattered.

Henry's hand moved, patting her back gently. She wiggled her body, snuggling closer, and sighed. It came out as a long, shuddering sound.

The strong arms tightened around her, and for just an instant there was no memory of death.

Then the spell was broken. Her nose was going to drip. She pulled a tissue out of her pocket and blew her nose, trying to be quiet about it and failing miserably.

Her thoughts vaulted to the future. She had to make plans. She'd have to arrange for time off work, take care of Susan and her family. She was executor of JoAnne's estate, and then there was the cat.

She'd always said no one is given challenges that God doesn't have enough strength for. So, there it was. And now she was crying again. No! She couldn't!

Henry stood quietly. He didn't seem to be alarmed by her silence, or the sigh, or the tears. He said nothing, asked nothing, just continued to hold her while she assembled her thoughts for the necessary actions ahead. But, of course, he couldn't know what she was thinking. Well, that was one plus. He was certainly patient.

At last she pulled back and glanced up.

Henry had wet eyes! She hadn't heard anything, but there were tear tracks down the creases in his cheeks. Carrie resisted an urge to feel the top of her head to see if it was wet.

Were the tears for her? He had barely known JoAnne, though, God knows, what they had both seen on that hillside was enough to cause distress.

She said, "I'll make coffee. Let's sit down."

Henry looked too big to be really comfortable on the chairs at her dining table, so she carried the coffee mugs to the oak table between the chairs by the wood stove. He remained silent, seeming to be deep in thought, and Carrie, feeling as if she was living in a world full of fog, was glad to be quiet too. She could hear JoAnne's angry voice chanting familiar words, over and over. "Crime against the land, crime against..."

But JoAnne had meant the quarry, not her own death! This crime was against JoAnne, who couldn't have known.

Finally, Carrie looked up at Henry and found him watching her. "You've never mentioned," she said. "Do you hunt?"

"No."

She swallowed, willing tears away so she could speak clearly. "We'll find the hunter—the murderer," she said. Even in her own ears, her voice sounded defiant.

"Yes," he said very slowly, staring into his mug now.

She was glad he agreed with her. "Susan and Putt are coming. I'm to call them back after...after...uh... They said a memorial service in Guilford. Susan and the baby are flying here Wednesday, and Putt will drive down Friday."

She went on, steadier now, knowing what she must do for JoAnne. "I heard shots just before you called me yesterday morning. Did you? I heard the shot that..."

"I heard the shots. Carrie, I—"

The sound of a car stopped him, and after a moment Carrie got up to go to the door. As the knocker banged, she was sorry she didn't have time to check her face. She realized with surprise that she hadn't worried about what Henry saw on her face.

The man standing there looked very businesslike and rock-solid in the conviction that he knew how to handle this and any other difficulty in the county. He carried a small bag and had on a brown jacket with the insignia of the county sheriff's department, as well as a black belt almost hidden under an assortment of attachments and pouches. He introduced himself as Deputy Sheriff Leon Faraday.

Carrie stood aside silently, wondering if the man wanted to come in. She was glad when Henry appeared beside her.

"I'm Henry King, a neighbor of Mrs. McCrite's. Do you want us to take you to where the body is?"

"Yes," said Faraday, "will you show me, or...?" He looked at Carrie.

"I'll go," she said, "but I'd appreciate it if Henr—Mr. King—came along."

"I'll wait while you get your coats on," said Faraday, stepping back onto the porch.

Henry had already gone to get their coats, but Carrie stopped him. She could not put on that orange coat and hat again. She got her blue down jacket from the closet and pulled a stocking cap over her ears.

She led the way to the creek, following the path that her own feet—and JoAnne's—had worn during many woodland walks. When they got close to the fallen tree, she hesitated, then stopped, pointing. Henry went ahead, with Faraday close behind.

The two men stood beside the body, looking down and talking, then Faraday knelt and looked more carefully at JoAnne and the ground around her, touching nothing. Henry began talking again, and Faraday nodded, then looked up, listening. Carrie couldn't hear what was being said and didn't want to watch them if they touched JoAnne, so she began to circle around the hillside, thinking maybe she'd find something that would lead her to the murderous hunter.

Henry called to her. "Carrie, don't move around. Let him look first."

Understanding at once, she stopped where she was. She, with JoAnne's help, had developed an ability to read signs on the forest floor and supposed Faraday had too. Now that the sun was higher, she could see a trail of disturbed leaves leading up the hill toward the old fire road. Some-one had come straight down or gone up the hill. Shuf-fling? Maybe the hunter had a limp or had barely lifted his feet as he walked. The trail wasn't made by an animal. Their paths didn't disrupt leaves in a long straight line and, anyway, if something like a coyote had come, well, JoAnne probably wouldn't look like she did now. Carrie thought of the buzzards and the eagles that returned to the area every winter. There really were a lot of creatures in the woods, large and small, that ate, uh. Oh! Dear God.

She blinked tears, shuddered, and suddenly felt very tired. She wanted to go back home.

She started toward the men. Faraday was talking into a cellular phone. She waited until he finished, then pointed uphill. "Did you see the path in the leaves? I didn't make it. I came down the hill over there. You can still see where my boots ruffled the leaves. I imagine Mr. King came that way." She pointed to the opposite angle, up the hillside. "His house is that way, but," she wrinkled her brow and looked at Henry, who simply returned her gaze and said nothing, "I don't see signs."

"Yes," said Faraday, "someone must have dragged her in from straight uphill. The body shows evidence of being pulled over rough ground. Most men could have carried her, but the body had stiffened so, well, dragging might have been easier."

"Why would the hunter drag her here? What would be the point? Was he trying to hide her?"

Henry began to walk toward her. "Carrie, we, that is, the deputy, doesn't think JoAnne was killed by a hunter."

"But, did you tell him we heard the shots?"

"Yes, and I think the shots we heard came from somewhere in the woods between your house and mine. You're right, they sounded like a hunter's rifle. But it looks like JoAnne was killed with a handgun."

Carrie stared at him. "But, why would someone come

here with a handgun? What would they be shooting at? Target practice? Squirrels? Well, *what?*"

"There'll be more people joining Deputy Faraday here soon, and questions like that are what they're trained to answer. They'll probably want to talk with you eventually, and Faraday has a few questions now. Then, wouldn't you like to go home?"

"Yes," said Carrie, "I would."

Faraday's questions were all about how she had found the body and whether she had touched anything. She wasn't paying much attention to what she said but supposed she was giving answers that satisfied him, because his voice went on smoothly as if from a great distance, asking a new question after she'd answered the last one.

"When I touched her hand," she said, interrupting him, "there was ice under it, a frost flower."

That stopped the questions, and Faraday stared at her. Finally Henry said, "Frost flowers—ice formations that come out of the ground in the early morning this time of year."

"Yes," said Carrie. "And they wouldn't have been here until early this morning. She wasn't *here* until this morning."

After a long silence, Faraday nodded his head as Henry took her arm. "I'll walk you back now. I said I'd meet the other people who are coming and bring them back here."

As Henry went with her up the hill on her side of the creek, Carrie remembered the red coat. "Why didn't JoAnne have her red coat on?" she said aloud, then decided she'd better tell Henry about being in the house. She stopped to catch her breath and turned to face him. "I looked through her house a bit yesterday afternoon. I went to check on the cat. I, well, I guess it wasn't the right thing to do, but I also looked around. Mostly I was thinking about the report, which I didn't find, by the way, and I was worried. So I even looked inside closets and...places like that. JoAnne's red coat and hat were gone."

Henry spoke gently as they started up the hill again. "I think that's one thing you'd better tell the people who come to ask you about JoAnne."

When they got to the house, it was Henry who offered to make more coffee, and he headed toward the kitchen. Carrie, saying she didn't want any, went to her chair by the wood stove, sank into it, and closed her eyes.

She heard the teakettle shrill, the clink of spoon on pottery, and then Henry's heavy steps as he came to the chair beside her and put his coffee cup on the table. In the silence a log popped loudly in the woodstove, and though it was a familiar sound, Carrie jumped.

"There's something you should know about me before the people from the sheriff's department come," he said at last. "Something I've tried to leave behind, but it won't stay in the past now."

He was speaking very slowly, as if he had to think before saying any sentence aloud.

"I never told you much about my police work in Kansas City. I retired as a major in the homicide unit. Things like...this...were what I worked on. I retired as soon as I could. There were getting to be too many dead kids. I couldn't...well, I'd had enough.

"Then I began selling real estate, and Irena left. I thought I was through with murder." He paused, sighed, and went on. "Now, here it is again. Faraday already knows I used to be a homicide detective. I never wanted you to see Henry King, the cop, and I darn sure don't want to be him, but I know too much about what's going to be happening here, and you'll realize that very soon. I do know, all too well."

He was silent for so long this time that Carrie thought he was finished, but then he began again, sounding like he was talking to himself.

"Some people in Kansas City think I left police work because I was becoming a coward, too soft-hearted. Maybe I was. Irena thought so. Not all women hate being married to a police detective, you know. She didn't. She gloried in the danger of my life. It gave her some kind of thrill, being married to a man who 'put his life on the line,' as she said. And she loved the sympathy that being a common policeman's wife got from her society friends and her family. It was like I was Irena's personal charity case. After I quit being a policeman, well, I guess her only reason for staying married to me quit too."

Carrie was taking all this in with more interest than Henry could have imagined.

"I guess what I'm trying to explain is pretty hard for an outsider to understand."

She lifted her head and looked at him. "No, I don't think so. It seems to me your work was...well, about justice, wasn't it? And that's good. The two of us can help find justice for JoAnne. Oh, I know the sheriff's department investigates these things. But they don't care like we do and don't know this area like we do. We have something to offer. It's good you know how to go about it."

"Carrie, we can't interfere with the sheriff's investigation. I wouldn't have welcomed such help, and I'm sure they won't. They would see it as interference, you know, and I wouldn't blame them. Besides, it could be dangerous for us—or for them."

"We'll work in the background and not bother the sheriff. We knew JoAnne, or I did at least. They don't."

A sudden shock of power and excitement surged through her as she said, "I don't think we can help being involved anyway. We were her friends, all of us on Walden Road."

He hadn't answered when the knocker sounded.

Three men stood at the door this time, two dressed all in black, one in jeans and a sheepskin jacket. Black looks nice on the tall blond one, thought Carrie, swallowing an urge to giggle. The man looked so stiff and haughty!

He stepped forward and said, "I'm Harrison Storm, County Sheriff, and this is Detective Sergeant Don Taylor." He didn't introduce the third man and was beginning to talk again when the man interrupted him.

"Mrs. McCrite," he said, "I'm Julian Baker, the County Coroner. I know how awful this must be for you..."

"Yes," said Storm, barely glancing at Baker. "May we please go to the scene of the crime at once."

He was making a statement, not asking a question.

Carrie hesitated and turned to look at Henry, who had followed her to the door.

"Mrs. McCrite has had a terrible shock," he said quietly, "and I can assure you she's not going to leave the area. Can't she remain here while I show you?"

"I'd prefer she go with us," replied Storm, narrowing his grey eyes at Henry as he spoke.

Henry helped Carrie into her coat and held her arm as the five of them retraced the path back to the hillside.

Yellow tape was now tied from tree to tree in a large area around the place where JoAnne lay. Faraday could be seen walking up the hill away from them, following the path of scuffled leaves that Carrie had pointed out. He was bent toward the ground, moving very slowly. When he heard the group approaching, he turned and came back to meet them, circling away from the trail.

JoAnne's never been still for so long, thought Carrie, covering up what began as a choked sob with a loud cough.

Henry and the coroner looked at her with concern. The other men glanced away.

"Wait over there, please," said Harrison Storm, pointing. "We'll be with you in a few minutes."

Henry led her to a large rock, and Carrie sat there while he stood beside her. She couldn't hear what the men were saying but winced and shut her eyes when one of them touched JoAnne's body, though that didn't shut out the picture of JoAnne lying there.

Then she heard footsteps and opened her eyes to see Sergeant Taylor crouching beside her, notebook in hand.

"Now, Mrs. McCrite, would you describe how you found the body, and tell me what you were doing on the hillside."

She told him, explaining that JoAnne had been missing since Saturday morning and trying to make him understand that this was really not unusual, not for JoAnne. She said she'd fed the cat, then come up the hill to look for frost flowers.

It was quite obvious he had no idea what she was talking about. Probably Faraday hadn't told him about the crushed ice under JoAnne's hand.

"Well, they're gone now," she said stiffly. "It's too late in the day." She wasn't going to waste time explaining such lovely, fragile things to this cop.

Oh, dear, she'd forgotten. Henry was a cop.

And, without being conscious of doing so at first, she left out all mention of Henry while she talked and didn't say anything about their plans to find the frost flowers together. Let Henry tell them that himself if he wants to, she was thinking, as she continued her story of every move she could recall until the time when she found JoAnne.

"And," she finished, "her red coat and hat are missing. You'd better find those."

"How do you know they're missing?" Taylor asked.

"Because, of course, I saw they were gone from her closet yesterday afternoon."

He was quiet for a moment, writing, then looked at her steadily as if he expected her to say more.

I can do this as long as you can, Carrie thought, lifting her chin to stare back.

"So you've been in her house more than once since she disappeared," he said, making it sound like an accusation.

"Of course. I'm, I was...I am, her friend, and I told you I needed to feed her cat."

"We'll go to her house in a few minutes," he said, shutting his notebook and turning back to the group of men.

She looked up at Henry, then stood so she could speak to him without raising her voice. "Were you out looking for frost flowers this morning? I didn't see you."

He lifted his eyebrows, but before he could say anything, Taylor was headed toward them again. He began by asking almost the same question Carrie had.

"Mr. King, how did you spend your morning?"

"Reading the paper," said Henry. "Then I decided to go for a walk since I'd heard there would probably be frost flowers on the hillside this morning. That's when I found Ms. Harrington, and since Mrs. McCrite's radio was on the ground beside her, I thought she had probably been out walking and found the body. I went on to her house to make sure she was all right."

"Radio?" said Taylor.

"Yes," said Carrie firmly. "To keep hunters away."

This time she ignored Taylor's stare.

During what seemed like an eternity, several more men in black arrived on the hillside. Pictures were taken, and every inch of forest floor around JoAnne was studied. Finally, her body was lifted and put in a long black bag. Carrie stared into the woods while her friend was carried away from the hillside where she had walked so many times.

At last, Taylor and Storm were ready to accompany Carrie and Henry back to her house so she could take them to JoAnne's. Carrie wondered if Henry was as hungry as she was. She decided she'd better not ask if she could take time for lunch.

She did ask for a moment alone inside her own home to "freshen up" before she went with the men. Once inside, she ate some crackers, then dawdled, hoping Henry would come in too. She wanted desperately to confer with him before she spent more time with these inquisitive men. She understood why they had to ask questions, but she wondered what Henry expected her to tell them. Should she say anything about the fact that he'd gone to JoAnne's house and found her not at home yesterday morning? Or should she just say that they'd known JoAnne was missing when she didn't come to the meeting? Should she mention Henry at all?

In their time together after finding JoAnne, he hadn't said she shouldn't tell everything. But then, maybe neither of them had been thinking clearly. Of course, it made no difference what Henry had done, everything would have a simple explanation. And none of it had anything to do with JoAnne's death. None of it.

When it was obvious that Henry wasn't going to come in the house to get her, she returned to the porch and saw him wiping his hands. Sergeant Taylor was taking fingerprints!

She glanced at Henry's face. He looked as tired as she felt, and quite worried. Did his worry have anything to do with the fingerprinting? Something had furrowed his forehead, and when he spoke, offering to accompany Carrie to JoAnne's house, his tones were higher than the usual low rumble.

The Sheriff told Henry they'd rather he returned home. "We'll talk to you later, Mr. King," Storm said, trying to smile. Don Taylor wrote down Henry's address and phone number and a description of how to get to his house. After shaking hands with the two men and smiling—a real smile—at Carrie, Henry walked off through the woods.

Well, never mind, she thought, as Sergeant Taylor rolled her inky fingers on his card. I'll figure out what to say by myself. Maybe they won't ask more questions.

After she'd wiped her hands, Taylor helped her into the back seat of the car marked "Sheriff," got in the driver's seat next to Harrison Storm, and followed her directions to JoAnne's house. When they arrived, she started to get out, but after asking her where the key was, Taylor indicated she was to wait in the car. She sat back and watched the men carry two large bags into the house.

They're going to look for fingerprints, she thought, so they had to have ours to eliminate them. She began speculating about whose fingerprints they might find. Hers, of course, and Susan's and Putt's. Well, if fingerprints lasted a long time and JoAnne hadn't done too much cleaning, Mag's would be there, and a repairman or two. Since the quarry committee had never met in the house, and Henry had never been inside, that would probably be all.

Time passed. The car was warm enough with the sun shining on it, but eventually Carrie began to fidget and think about how hungry she was. She wondered how FatCat was reacting to the strangers. They'd probably shut her in the laundry room. She hoped they'd moved her water and the litter box there too.

It was very quiet. She didn't even hear bird calls in the nearby woods.

Then, suddenly, there was the sound of JoAnne's voice again: "Crime against the land, crime against the land."

All right! They wouldn't let this crime interfere with their fight to stop the quarry, and now they had to win that fight for JoAnne as well.

Finally Sergeant Taylor came out, opened the car door, and perched backwards on the front seat, looking at her.

"Let's see," he began, "as I recall, you said you were in the house yesterday afternoon and this morning, looking around. Tell me everything you saw that was unusual."

That's not really a question, thought Carrie. He acts like he knows I searched the whole house pretty thoroughly.

"Well," she said, "the back door was unlocked, and JoAnne's address book—it was gone."

"And?" he said.

"The red hat and coat too," she replied. "I told you."

"Mrs. McCrite, I think you'd better come in the house with me, but for now, please don't touch anything."

Puzzled, Carrie went with him to the front door. He moved aside, and she stared down the hall at the heap of things spilling out of the closet door. He indicated with a hand gesture that she should go in, so, stepping carefully over the jumble on the hall floor, she turned into the kitchen. The contents of the desk had been dumped everywhere.

Since Carrie's visit at 8:15 that morning, someone who didn't care what kind of mess they made had searched the house. And, she thought, I'll just bet these men think I did it.

CHAPTER VIII

No one ever mentioned lunch.

After Carrie looked at the mess—hoping her unfeigned shock would help convince the two men she had nothing to do with making it—she answered questions through what seemed like three meal times.

First, Detective Taylor had her stand in the door of each room and look around carefully, telling him if she noticed anything odd or missing.

Other than chaotic heaps of JoAnne's belongings, Carrie saw nothing to talk about. She did not say what seemed obvious to her, if what the searcher was looking for had been hidden in the first place, how was she supposed to know it was gone?

One thing was clear—the person hadn't been looking for money or valuables. JoAnne shopped with checks and credit cards, so she kept no money, except in her purse, which she presumably took with her when she left. The few good pieces of jewelry she owned were dumped on the floor with everything else. The television and VCR were untouched.

Carrie did notice two things missing, but didn't say anything about them, because they seemed so trivial. She didn't see the pink envelope with her name on it or the picture of Susan and her family. When she'd told Sergeant Taylor about the missing address book, he hadn't seemed very interested, and she supposed he'd think the missing card and photograph were even more trivial. Perhaps they were concealed in the mess somewhere and would turn up later.

After she looked through the door of each room, Taylor asked her where she usually sat when she visited JoAnne. He had her sit there, and the questions continued.

Storm and Taylor alternated, and she soon realized they were actually asking the same things over and over, putting questions in different words but repeating themselves anyway. And, she thought, they might as well be asking the cat.

"Why would someone search this house? What did JoAnne Harrington do or know that could put her in danger? What did she talk about? Describe her life here. What did she do in Kansas City? Tell us all you know about her past. Tell us all you know about her family and friends. What did she do Friday? What did you do Friday? Saturday?" And, "Mrs. McCrite, couldn't you have forgotten to lock the back door when you came to feed the cat?"

Carrie talked, and answered, but everything came out sounding very simple, normal, and unimportant.

The men didn't ask her any questions about Henry. They wouldn't think there was any reason to, she decided. After all, he was a fellow cop.

Both men kept their voices low and were obviously trying to appear reasonable and kind. Sergeant Taylor managed it quite well, but Sheriff Storm didn't. By late afternoon, Carrie was imagining herself screaming at him: "She grew bigger tomatoes than I did"—a statement JoAnne would have appreciated, since Carrie had never admitted it before—"so I killed her and searched the house for her secret fertilizer recipe." Then Harrison Storm could breathe a sigh of relief and get on with whatever he usually did on Sunday afternoons.

Well, she thought, as her stomach rumbled loudly enough for everyone to hear, this is hardly my idea of an ideal Sunday afternoon either.

Finally she protested, with a choked sob that was as much frustration and anger as grief, "Look, JoAnne was my best friend, and if I knew anything about her that seemed dangerous, or sinister, or unusual, I'd tell you. I don't. We're all boringly normal here. Now I'm tired, I'm hungry, I'm upset, and this has gone on long enough!"

Conceding—probably, she thought, because she was now telling them the same things over and over—they ended the questions. Taylor drove her, FatCat, and all of FatCat's necessities home, saying he'd be back later that evening.

Leaving the cat to explore on her own, Carrie called Susan to report and make plans. Then she punched in Henry's number, wondering if he really was at home, since Storm had almost ordered him to go there. For whatever reason, he did answer his phone quickly, and the low, quiet "hello" warmed and comforted her the minute she heard it.

After telling him what had happened at JoAnne's, she asked if he knew what they might expect next. "I had thought Susan and her family could stay at JoAnne's house," she said, "but I guess they can't now."

Henry was quiet for a long moment before he answered. "It's probable Storm won't allow you or Susan in for a while, especially if the house was torn up by someone doing what sounds like a pretty thorough search. What the sheriff does depends on when his department thinks they've learned all they can there. We'll have to expect that it will be off limits. Could Susan stay at a motel in Bonny?"

"No, not with the baby. I couldn't let her do that. They can stay with me."

"You've got lots of extra things to do right now," said Henry, "so maybe I can help by inviting them here." There was a pause before he continued. "Shall I ask them here?"

"That's nice, Henry, but I have the extra room, and Susan really doesn't know you."

Another pause. "That's right, she doesn't."

"Well, then." She sighed and looked at her watch. "It's almost six. I'm going to take a hot shower and fix something to eat. Storm's hospitality didn't include lunch. Have you eaten?"

"Yup, TV dinner," he said.

"Thank goodness for those. I'm too tired to fix anything else. Have you called anyone? Roger and Shirley, or Jason?"

"I called them all," said Henry. "They're horrified, of course, and I don't think it seems real to anyone yet. Shirley said we're to come there for dinner tomorrow night. She didn't know when to call you and admitted she wasn't comfortable talking to answering machines. I told her we'd be there. Is that all right? It sure won't be TV dinners."

"Of course I'll come. Would you mind telling her for me? And tell her I'm glad to have the dinner to look forward to. It helps."

"Good, I'll call her now. Jason thought we should wait until after next weekend to plan anything more about the quarry. We won't meet Saturday, of course, but somehow it seems getting going on this quarry thing and beating it would be the best possible memorial to JoAnne. Maybe everyone will be willing to talk about it tomorrow evening."

"Yes, we must plan...something. It's even more important to me now too."

Carrie, dressed in flannel nightgown, robe, and slippers, had just been finishing the last of her Hungry HE-MAN Roast Beef Dinner when Storm and Taylor came by to tell her JoAnne's house was sealed, and no one was to enter. If they had learned the answers to any of their questions, they didn't say so.

Sergeant Taylor did have one piece of interesting information, which he mentioned just as the men were leaving.

It seemed that when things were important enough, even state officials got asked questions on Sunday. Don Taylor had called the head of the Environmental Commission at home in Little Rock. She reported back that JoAnne had never contacted them, nor met with any member of the commission.

Carrie was brushing her teeth some time later when it occurred to her that Henry had said JoAnne asked him to come by and help organize a meeting report that could not have existed. So, someone lied! Why?

She couldn't seem to follow any logical reasoning about that. By the time she was ready for bed, she had discovered that challenging dark memories of the day was more than enough for her mind to handle.

She sat up in bed reading her Bible for almost an hour before turning out the light. Carrie's last conscious thoughts that Sunday night were in the form of a silent prayer for JoAnne and her family.

And now, eating breakfast, getting dressed, and driving the familiar highway toward the tourist center, there was plenty of time to puzzle over more than one mystery.

She had already acknowledged that this was no hunting accident. Hunters wouldn't tear a house to pieces, then take nothing of value. And, how would strangers know where the key was? There was no sign of forced entry. Unless, she thought, JoAnne's keys were in her purse, she had it with her when she was shot, and the killer took her keys.

And where was JoAnne's truck? Was the purse in it? Of course, if you accepted the fact that JoAnne had been killed with a handgun, and not by a hunter, then someone must have meant to shoot JoAnne, and that was beyond understanding.

No matter how many times they had asked the question, the sheriff and Sergeant Taylor couldn't get her to recall any reason why someone would intentionally kill JoAnne.

That's because there is no reason, thought Carrie.

But, as she turned into the parking lot at the center, she decided the most worrying question was the lie about the meeting notes. And who had lied? Henry? Or JoAnne?

Was the "crime against the land," the quarry, part of all this somehow? She thumped the steering wheel in frustration. She, as JoAnne's best friend, really should be able to accomplish things the sheriff's men couldn't.

If she did discover something of value, deduce something important, and do it by herself, then it would prove to Henry—and everyone—that she could be clever, smart, and capable, without help from anyone, a woman to be respected and reckoned with!

"JoAnne, what would you do?" she asked aloud.

Wait. There was something. And it was something only Carrie herself knew. Some time ago, JoAnne had told her about hiding a box with contents she wanted kept secret, said she had told no one else, and explained where the box was. After asking Carrie to repeat the description of the hiding place, she made her promise not to look there or tell anyone, except in dire emergency. And now...

When Carrie had tried to question JoAnne, she'd just shaken her head and refused to discuss the matter further.

Of course, what was hidden probably wouldn't have a thing to do with her murder, but...then again...

JoAnne had harbored quite a few quirky notions, of course, and could have kept something secret that most other people would display openly—a book she was ashamed to own, for example.

Nevertheless, thinking about finding evidence of any sort, and maybe even something that would help identify JoAnne's killer, made Carrie hope she wouldn't have to stay at work very long.

News about JoAnne's death was being reported on area radio stations and had arrived at the Bonny Tourist Information Center before Carrie got there. Everyone was determined to be sympathetic, but it was also obvious they could barely control their boiling curiosity, so, as simply as possible, she told them what had happened.

Talking about finding JoAnne wasn't as painful now. It had almost become someone else's story, since she'd already repeated it so many times for the detectives. It was a bit like the stories she used to read to Rob. They'd read his favorites so often that she sometimes paid no attention to what she was saying. Rob still talked about having to remind her to turn a page when she continued with the familiar words beyond events pictured on the pages that lay open in front of them.

The employees on duty at the center were quick to understand when she said she'd just be there for the morning, then must go home to get ready for the coming week and the arrival of JoAnne's family. She was, she explained, executor of JoAnne's estate, and there was lots to do.

She really wasn't sure yet just how to go about it all. Though Amos's law practice had brought many wills and estate closings into his business life, he hadn't shared information about what was going on; and others had been there to help her when Amos died.

After calling department headquarters in Little Rock to explain why she was taking a few days' emergency leave, Carrie spoke with center employees about the new special events she'd put on the winter calendar. When she went to unpack the boxes of brochures she'd brought from home, her thoughts suddenly hurtled back to Henry and Saturday night. She stopped and stood motionless, staring into the distance while a stack of brochures slid to the floor.

Startled and embarrassed, she bent to pick them up, hoping no one had noticed; but Sarah Simmons, senior tourist consultant, came over quickly, took her by the arms, turned her toward the door, and gave her a brisk pat on the behind.

"Go," said Sarah, "take care of things for that young woman and her family. We'll manage just fine."

Carrie gave Sarah a hug, put on her hat and coat, and though she'd only been at work three hours, headed home.

First she'd check to be sure FatCat was all right, though the cat seemed to be getting on fine in her new quarters.

True, she had yowled unhappily when Carrie made it plain last night that she was not sharing the down comforter on her bed with any cat, not even a bereaved one. The complaints had stopped when Carrie found an old down pillow with most of its stuffing gone and put it on top of the mattress in the wicker cat bed. Carrie was pleased with herself. Rules were rules, and FatCat was, after all, a very intelligent cat. She was catching on quickly to the new ground rules.

When she got home, Carrie parked her station wagon by the door to save time. She needed to go into Guilford as soon as possible to get JoAnne's will out of her safe deposit box and take it to the attorney.

Both she and Susan had seen the will when JoAnne made it a year ago; it left a nice amount to the Self Start Project in Rough Creek that aided single mothers, and the rest went to Susan.

But first, she'd find what JoAnne had hidden. The will would have to wait that long.

No cat greeted Carrie at the front door, but almost at once FatCat came loping toward her from the bedroom. She rubbed against Carrie's ankles, making noises that sounded like she was trying to start a muted Vespa. It was rather nice to have someone come say hello, Carrie thought as she bent to rub the cat's back.

She headed for the bedroom to get her gardening jeans and oldest sweat shirt. The morning's cloudiness had faded, making the snow forecast a sham. Leafless trees outside the bedroom windows barely filtered the bright sunlight falling across her bed. Carrie looked at the round indentation in the middle of her comforter, then went to the bed and put her hand in the cavity. Warm. Much warmer than the rest of the sun-lit bed.

She looked down. FatCat was gazing soulfully up at her while the black-tipped end of her tail curled slowly from left to right and back.

"We aren't going to discuss this," said Carrie. She looked back at the bed and its sun-lit down pouf. How wonderful it would be to curl up in the sun, just like FatCat had obviously done, to feel the softness...to forget... She sighed. "Cat, if I'm going to adopt you, you have to learn that bed is *mine*. No cats, no sharing."

FatCat watched her from the floor while she changed clothes. As she left the bedroom, Carrie picked up the cat basket with one hand and tucked its owner against her side with the other. She dropped the cat in the hallway and shut the bedroom door firmly.

"*No*," she said, wondering if this was going to work. Since the woodstove provided most of the heat in the house, she couldn't leave the bedroom door shut very long. Well, the cat was simply going to have to learn the rules, that was all! For now, she'd leave the door shut. Maybe the message would get across. She carried the basket to a sunny spot by a window in the main room and put it down. That would have to do until she had more time to think about getting her new companion to understand house rules.

Carrie stood at the kitchen sink looking out into the woods while she ate a peanut butter and jelly sandwich and drank a glass of milk. Then she put on her old coat and gloves and, carrying her hat and full-length good coat, went to the car. She would change coats at JoAnne's and go straight into town to save time. If she had her good coat on, few would realize she had gardening clothes under it.

When she pulled into JoAnne's driveway, the house that had once seemed so friendly and welcoming stood sharply four-square and cold. For the first time, Carrie noticed that dead flowers remaining in the pots JoAnne left on the porch year-around looked dusty and broken. The bright marigolds of last summer were now represented by these shadow plants. Still, she thought, the seed heads are there. I'll bring an envelope and collect memory seeds for my garden...and Susan's.

Tape at the doorway reminded everyone that the house was off-limits and, shivering, Carrie was glad it was. She couldn't face being alone in the house right now. But, no matter how she felt, she'd have to straighten the mess inside before Susan saw it.

Would Susan sell the house right away? It was hard to think of new people, but then, such a house should share its setting in the living, natural world with living people.

Curious, she looked under the third flower pot. No key. Evidently, the sheriff had taken it. Well, never mind. She had her own extra key if she needed it, and Susan did too.

She looked around carefully and listened for a moment before heading into the woods below JoAnne's tool shed. She didn't want anyone seeing her now. Her heart was thumping, reminding her, if her head hadn't already done so, that this might be a very important venture.

She climbed down to the place below the tool shed where the hillside stopped its gentle slope and dropped into a sheer rock bluff. The bluff front couldn't be seen from the house. It was only about eight yards wide, a horizontal limestone scar along the hillside caused by some wisp of geologic action that Carrie couldn't begin to imagine.

According to JoAnne's instructions, she'd have to get to the middle of that sheer face. The idea terrified her, but there was no other way, and if JoAnne had done it, well, she could too!

Starting from the slope at the edge of the bluff, she began to slide carefully along the vertical wall, bracing her feet on rocks and tufts of grass at the bottom of the bluff face and edging toward the small ledge and opening in the rocks that JoAnne had told her about. The only hand-holds now were dead weeds growing out of the bluff. It was slow going, and her feet slipped several times, sending rock showers into the valley below her.

After what seemed like a very long time, she got to the ledge. It was at least a foot above her head, and, no matter how she stretched, she couldn't reach over it.

Carrie wanted to wail in frustration. But, of course, JoAnne had been several inches taller than she was. What on earth was she going to do now?

What she did was rest against the trunk of a tree growing close to the bluff face and consider possibilities. Henry was certainly tall enough, but JoAnne had made her promise to tell no one about this. And would Henry be the one to tell anyway? Thinking about Henry and JoAnne, she was suddenly uneasy; she wondered once more who had lied about Henry's invitation to help JoAnne with her meeting notes. And why? No, she mustn't ask Henry for help.

But she was so close. She had to find a way, even if she didn't get to town before the bank closed.

Carrie looked more carefully at the bluff face, searching for some way to climb. The rock wall was almost straight, and its surface was weathered. Small chunks of chert and limestone fell every time she moved.

Could she bring a short ladder and brace the bottom of it against the tree she was leaning on? That was it, and JoAnne had a stepladder in her tool shed! Forget the will and the lawyer for today. Carrie wanted to see what JoAnne had hidden in the crevice above her head.

She reversed her slow movements until she got to the slope and then hurried as fast as she could through the dry winter underbrush on the forest floor. She'd have to use her key to JoAnne's house because JoAnne had kept the tool shed locked, and the key to it was on a hook by the back door. She'd just reach inside around the door frame and get the key. She probably wouldn't even have to break the tape, so the sheriff would never know.

Still, the whole business was creepy, and Carrie was glad when she had the ladder out and had returned the key and re-locked the tool shed and the house. She would put the ladder in the back of her station wagon when she was finished and return it later.

It was very difficult to edge along the bluff front with the ladder over one arm, and the darn thing was surprisingly heavy. Her feet slipped several times and, when they did, the ladder banged against her side. Nevertheless, she was glad it was wood. It seemed sturdier for bracing against tree trunks than aluminum.

When the small ledge was above her head again, she laid the ladder against the bluff with its legs hooked on either side of the tree trunk, and used the steps to help her climb while she held on to the ledge. Just now a slip might send her bouncing down the hillside. After what seemed like an age, her head was over the top, and she could see the opening clearly. When she got to the top step, she freed her right hand by holding firmly to the ledge with her left and reached slowly toward the tiny cave, moving very carefully so she wouldn't go off balance and send the ladder over sideways.

When her hand was inside the opening, she couldn't feel anything but empty space. Then she saw that the cave opened wider behind the face of the bluff, and there was clear space around the edge on either side as well as straight back. Her gloved fingers groped back and forth and still felt nothing. She changed hands, holding on to the top of a fallen cedar tree on the right, and reached up and back with her left hand. A smooth object resisted, then moved, and she heard the scrape of metal against rock.

Something was there, but she had moved it farther away! Carrie wasn't too keen on sticking her hand in the dark hole without heavy gloves on, but there was no other way. She tried not to think about what might be using the cave for shelter and took off her left glove, stuffing it in her coat pocket.

She reached again and touched a cold metal surface. It was a box, and...yes, there was a drop loop handle. How else could JoAnne have pulled the box in and out? She curled her fingers under the metal loop and pulled. The box grated on rock, moving toward her. Once it was sticking out of the hole, she saw that it was no larger than a cash box.

She tested its weight, pushing it up with her fingers.

Fairly heavy. She'd have to risk pulling it over the edge with one hand and just pray the ladder wouldn't tilt off balance. She tugged slowly until the box teetered and, struggling to brace its weight with her stiffened arm, she pulled it free, holding tightly to the handle. It came over the edge and dropped, yanking her arm painfully as she resisted its pull so she could keep it from shifting her body or the ladder sideways.

After a breathless moment, she was able to begin backing slowly down the ladder, holding the box with an arm and hand that were almost numb.

CHAPTER IX

Carrie inched her way back to the slope, lifting the box and holding it against the side of the bluff ahead of her while she slid toward it. When the box was finally secure among the dry leaves and rocks on the hillside, she went back for the stepladder and had just finished moving it to the slope when she heard a car, no, two cars, pull up in front of JoAnne's house.

Oh, no! The sheriff's men, of course. They would come back now! She huddled against the hillside in a panic. Why hadn't she realized that they might come back? Well, there was nothing to do but act her way out, since her car was there, plain as day. But she could not—would not—let anyone else know the box existed. She'd have to hide it again, and quickly.

She looked back at the bluff. No, she couldn't put the box back in the little cave. There were too many fresh scrapes and scratches there. If they searched the hillside before forest creatures and weather had covered the signs of her presence, they'd surely find the box.

Well, nothing for it but get the thing as far away as she could before they came looking, and she'd have to be careful how she moved, or they'd hear her.

She felt more exhilaration than panic now. She was accomplishing something important and doing it on her own. She just wished—here, her lower lip went out—that Velda and Pat and Dusty could have seen her crawling along that bluff face. They thought she was over the hill, and instead she was practically scaling mountains.

She was Carrie McCrite, Private Detective. That certainly had a nice sound to it, though she knew her friends and family would laugh.

Well, what of it? Maybe she couldn't match Emily Pollifax, but, of course, that woman's feats were pure fiction. Carrie McCrite could be her own kind of detective, and there was no doubt she had an important mission.

She felt a twinge of guilt that this was all the result of JoAnne's murder, but one did have to carry on in the face of adversity. So, carry on she would, and she'd better get with it.

Hugging the box to her chest, she began edging her way carefully down the slope. She had to make it to her own property! Thank goodness the men were talking loudly. There was no way to be completely quiet on a hillside covered with brush and dry leaves.

She continued to move downhill, half sliding, until she got to the bottom where there wasn't so much heavy growth and she could walk more quickly. She kept to gravel bars along the edge of the creek and almost ran toward her end of the hollow. The voices stopped, and she did too, holding her breath until she heard a door slam. Probably all the men had gone inside. She fervently hoped so.

When she reached the woods below her house, she pushed the box into a hole left by a heavy tree that had toppled after several days of soaking rain last fall. She hurriedly covered the grey metal with leaves and rocks, dropped a broken branch over the place, and stood back for a quick survey. Not bad. Since squirrels, skunks, and other creatures were constantly ruffling up small places on the forest floor, it would do. She headed back downstream toward JoAnne's and was just starting up the hill below the tool shed when she saw Detective Sergeant Taylor looking at her from the top of the hill.

"Oh, hi, there," she called up to him. "Just came over to borrow JoAnne's stepladder so I could get some leaves out of my guttering and heard a pileated woodpecker calling. Thought I'd see if I could find it. So you're back to look around again?"

The man stared at her in astonishment, then, for a moment, his eyes narrowed. But after all, he was only about thirty-five. I hope his mother does *lots* of things he considers peculiar, thought Carrie.

She reached the place where she'd left the ladder and stopped to catch her breath. "I just dropped the ladder as I followed the bird and didn't realize I'd brought it so far downhill."

She lifted the ladder, trying to make the task of bringing it back uphill look easy, because she didn't want him coming down to help her, at least not until she was above the area beside the bluff.

Taylor did start down toward her, so she hurried as fast as she could, not daring to look sideways to see if the rock face was safely out of sight.

She must have been past the spot by the time they met

on the hillside, or he was too interested in what she was doing because, without so much as a glance to either side, he lifted the ladder with one hand, reached for her arm with the other, and turned toward the house. At least the fact that she was out of breath made it unnecessary to say more.

When the ladder was safely stowed in the back of her station wagon, Carrie went up JoAnne's front steps and sat in the wicker rocker on the sun-warmed porch. Though she was wild with curiosity about what was in the box, she also wanted to know if the men had any new information.

"If you don't mind, think I'll sit and listen for the wood-pecker for a few minutes," she said.

Don Taylor actually smiled at her. "What do they sound like?" he asked, dropping onto the porch swing.

"Well, it's sort of a kuck-kuck, kuck-kuck," she replied, hoping she was close to right. As she remembered, that was the sound, but for the life of her, she couldn't keep all the bird calls straightened out. She just hoped Taylor wasn't trying to fool her and that he didn't know the call of any woodpecker, let alone a pileated.

They sat in silence for a few moments, until, unwilling to play the game any longer, and full of curiosity about what was going on inside JoAnne's house, Carrie spoke up.

"JoAnne's niece and her baby are coming Wednesday. I had hoped they could stay here."

"Yes, it's tough that there aren't any motels close by," he said, "but even when we're through with the house, there may be legal hurdles to get over before heirs can use it. Did you check with a lawyer?"

"Well, I'm executor, and I was going into town this afternoon to get the will out of my safe deposit box and see JoAnne's lawyer." She looked at her watch. "The bank'll be closed before I can get there now. I guess I shouldn't have taken time to come pick up the ladder."

He changed the subject. "How well did Mr. King and Miss Harrington know each other?"

Startled, she replied, "Oh, not at all. They'd barely met, just saw each other on the quarry committee."

He was looking at her intently now. "Well, then, why would his fingerprints be in her house? Did he have a reason to call on Miss Harrington?"

"Uh, well, about the quarry maybe."

"You a special friend of Mr. King's?"

"We, that is, he... We're friends, that's all."

Taylor was still watching her closely. "It is interesting that his fingerprints are all over this house. In every single room. Yours, too, of course."

Carrie gulped. "But—" She looked at Taylor, forced her mouth to grin, crossed her fingers inside her pocket, and went on, "Well, well, never know, do you! The sinful old fox. He and JoAnne...my, my."

After that, Carrie couldn't get away fast enough, in spite of the fact that odd thumps and bumps were coming from inside the house. She rose and, as if they'd been enjoying a social afternoon, said she must be going.

Taylor, acting as relaxed as if the two of them really had been having afternoon tea on the porch, promised to call by noon tomorrow to let her know if she could clean up the house for JoAnne's family.

As she started toward her car, he said, "And Mrs. McCrite, please do not go back in the house or tool shed again until we say it's okay."

Without answering, Carrie got in her car and drove away. She couldn't have said another word to Taylor if she'd wanted to.

Henry and JoAnne? No! There was no way at all to explain such a relationship. JoAnne was—had been—wary of all men and specifically avoided Henry. What on earth could have been going on? Not...not, well, they just couldn't have! He wasn't that kind of...

His fingerprints in every room? The picture of JoAnne with Henry was too much. Carrie would not believe it. Then another possibility rose out of her tossing thoughts. Had Henry been the one to search JoAnne's house?

No, not possible either! He was too careful, too meticulous, to make a mess like that. And why would he want to anyway? Well, she'd just ask him!

As soon as she got home, she walked straight through her house, out the back door, and started down the hillside as fast as the rocky terrain would allow. She couldn't wait any longer to see what was in that box.

Then she heard voices and the sound of crunching feet coming from JoAnne's end of the hollow. She stopped, listening and thinking. They probably were searching the entire area between the house and where JoAnne was found. She tried to decide what reason she'd have for being out roaming around in the hollow if they saw her. She couldn't risk being caught with JoAnne's box.

If they'd seen signs of disturbance along the bluff face, they'd be wondering what made them, and Taylor knew she'd been down there. He'd probably tell them to search the area even more carefully, especially if they found the little cave in the bluff and scuff marks where she'd slid the box. He knew, of course, that she had been carrying nothing but a ladder when he first saw her. He might wonder, though, if she'd taken something away to hide.

She had to get that box safely inside as soon as possible. Her hiding place wouldn't withstand a thorough search. They'd find the box for sure.

She hurried back to the house and located FatCat, who was napping in her basket by the window. She got JoAnne's large pet carrier out of the garage, put the cat's down pillow and a scrap of blanket inside, and pushed the cat in after them. As she headed out of the house, she could hear FatCat grumbling about her impromptu ride.

"We're on a secret mission," Carrie told the cat softly, speaking in what she hoped was a soothing manner, "and it's going to take the two of us to manage it."

She was still hurrying but kept as quiet as she could and looked around carefully after each step, until she reached the tipped-up tree and the hidden box.

She couldn't see anyone, though the noises were closer. She hurriedly dug up the metal box, wrapped it in the blanket, and shoved it through the door of the carrier past the pillow and protesting cat.

"I'm sorry," she whispered, "but we must do this."

She had climbed about ten yards up the slope when Leon Faraday appeared on the hillside. Thank goodness it wasn't Taylor. She wasn't sure she could bluff through a second hillside escapade with him.

"JoAnne's cat," she said, puffing, genuinely out of breath. "It got out. I finally caught it. The cat isn't used to being outside but got past me when I came home and opened the door. Had quite a tussle catching it." She pointed back to the disturbed area where the box had been hidden. "It was hiding there. If I'd known you were out, I'd have asked for help. Guess you're searching for JoAnne's hat and coat?"

"Among other things," Faraday said. "Here, I'll carry that up for you. You're out of breath."

She couldn't think of any reason not to give him the

carrier. "How nice," she said, handing it to him carefully. "But don't let it tilt or sway. The poor thing gets seasick."

"Sure is a heavy cat," Faraday replied as he started back up the hill, and FatCat began to yowl. At least there could be no question in Faraday's mind that there was a cat inside.

"Yes," Carrie said, hoping the pillow would keep the box from sliding.

She opened the back door, indicated where Faraday could put the carrier on the rug, thanked him, and shut the door.

"We did it!" she told the cat as she let her out and gave her a pat. "Special treats for you when I can go to the store." Then she lifted the metal box into her arms.

When the box was sitting safely on her kitchen table, Carrie stared at it in dismay. She hadn't thought about a key. The box was obviously locked, and a lock obviously needed a key. JoAnne had never mentioned a key, and the thing was probably somewhere in her house, possibly on the key board by the back door, probably right next to where Carrie had found the key to the tool shed!

She considered. The lock didn't look too sturdy. Maybe she could break it.

One screwdriver and two minutes later she had easily popped the lock open. So much for security. But then, JoAnne had only needed protection from gnawing critters.

Carrie looked at the plastic-wrapped parcels inside the box, concentrating so intently she didn't notice that FatCat was up on the table staring into the box with her. When she started to lay out the contents, she bumped into a cat.

Her reaction was immediate. She flailed her arms, sweeping the cat off and catching the box just in time. FatCat yowled, but obviously only her dignity was hurt, and she stared at Carrie malevolently from the floor.

"Boy, I've got to break you of a lot of bad habits," Carrie told the cat, then turned back to the box, leaving FatCat to nurse her wounded pride.

She pulled open the seal on the first bag and lifted out the contents. Baby things! A pair of pink booties. A delicate gown with lace. A hospital bracelet that said, in pink letters on tiny white beads, "Harrington."

"Oh, dear God."

A second package was flatter. Papers. Legal looking. A birth certificate for Susan Elizabeth. Mother: JoAnne Elizabeth Harrington. Father: Henry Jensen King.

It was several minutes before Carrie set the birth certificate aside and picked up the next document. At first it looked almost like a will, but it only took a glance at the words to tell Carrie it was anything but.

There were the "whereas" prefixes and stiff wording—a lawyer document. As she read, Carrie's heart twisted at the implications of what was being set forth in this paper. Henry Jensen King was renouncing any right or claim to the child, Susan Elizabeth Harrington, as his issue. He, under penalty of law, was forbidden to make any contact with this person as child or adult, or to in any way reveal his identity to her.

Furthermore, Henry Jensen King would have no legal responsibility for this Susan Elizabeth Harrington, either financially or as a parent or guardian. Nor was he to have any future contact with the child's actual mother, JoAnne Elizabeth Harrington, or with parents who would adopt the child.

Would such a document hold up in court? Surely not, but to Henry, it wouldn't matter. There was obviously a lot she didn't know about Henry King, but she knew him well enough to realize he'd never break this compact. He was honorable to a fault. But, then, then... Wouldn't he hate JoAnne? She, not Irena, must have been the one he was talking about, the one who had caused him so much pain.

Forgiving the earlier indignity, FatCat jumped into Carrie's lap, leaned against her warm body, and looked up. Absently, Carrie's hand rubbed down the cat's back, over and over.

There was one more thing in the box. A small envelope.

"The contents of this box must never be revealed unless there is an absolute medical necessity. Susan Elizabeth has no right to know and, I hope, will never need to know who her birth parents are."

Carrie understood instantly. One evening last summer when she had been at JoAnne's house, they watched a special nature program on public television. After the show, a teaser for the next program had been run. It was about adopted children who were trying to locate their natural parents. Carrie was surprised when JoAnne left the program on and intently watched it all.

One of the reasons for seeking birth parents that had been covered during the program was in the instance when family medical history, or even organ donations, were needed. JoAnne hadn't commented, but it was so unlike her to care about anything on television other than the nature programs that Carrie clearly remembered the evening. And it was only a few days later when JoAnne told her about the hidden box.

As she sat staring out the window, Carrie said aloud, "Dear God, JoAnne, dear God. This is too much for me. Why did you do it? I don't want to know this! I don't want to carry this secret. Not now. Especially not now."

FatCat trod a few careful steps on the soft lap, then curled up in cinnamon-roll fashion and shut her eyes, filling the room with a loud purr. Carrie didn't notice. She folded her arms on the table and put her head down on them. Like the cat, she shut her eyes, but Carrie made no sound.

She didn't cry, but if the pain inside had formed into tears, there would have been a lot of them.

CHAPTER X

"Amos never turned against you, never lied, never wanted to make you suffer."

Carrie could still hear the anguish in Henry's voice.

She had supposed his emotion was the result of something Irena had done. Now she was sure it was not Irena, but JoAnne, who had been the cause.

Henry was alone, and Susan's adoptive parents were dead. It would be natural for him to want to be united with his daughter, but JoAnne and the document she and her family had him sign, as well as Henry's own stiff integrity, stood in the way.

Carrie tried to picture his thoughts and actions. He must have moved to the area for one of two reasons. Either he was still in love with JoAnne, which she just could not believe, or he hoped that being close to JoAnne would give him a chance to convince her Susan should now be told who her natural parents were.

The strength of JoAnne's dislike for Henry was puzzling. It had been too intense, even for someone who didn't like men in general, and cops in particular. He was, after all, father of the child she adored. And, at one time, she surely must have loved him!

Henry's attitude toward JoAnne was easier to figure out. He must have been unhappy with her because of the forced separation from Susan. Carrie thought back over the few times she had seen Henry and JoAnne together—always as part of a larger group. He had been cool, polite, stiffly proper. But, was there fire behind that ice? She squirmed, thinking about Saturday night at the tourist center. Until now, those few moments had seemed very special, a caring closeness she wanted to treasure, even if she and Henry could never be more than good friends. Irena made no difference to that friendship, nor did Amos; they were in the past. But, JoAnne and Susan—especially Susan and what her existence proved—did make a difference.

What Carrie really wanted to do was phone Henry and say, "I know all about Susan, so tell me the whole story. Just exactly what happened?"

But that was childish and would probably turn Henry against her, shutting him away, burying him deeper inside his own thoughts.

Or would it simply infuriate him? Was there a temper buried there?

She needed to think clearly, more clearly than she ever had in her life! She needed the wisdom of Solomon if she was to help Henry...help everyone.

"Please, God, I don't know what to do."

She just didn't know enough yet. Was it possible Henry didn't really care about Susan?

If he didn't care, why did he move here? Thirty years

could have given him enough time to wipe Susan out of his memories. How much did he care today?

And did he care enough to kill? What would JoAnne's murder gain for him? Carrie couldn't see any gain, unless...

Think, oh think!

Henry must have asked JoAnne to tell Susan about her past.

JoAnne would have refused. Now, JoAnne was dead.

There were the fingerprints in JoAnne's house. Henry must be involved. Was he angry, and had he...

Carrie rubbed her forehead with two fingers and tried to picture what could have happened. He'd shown no signs of an uncontrollable temper but, under the circumstances, maybe he would have, could have... No!

If she'd only known about Susan earlier. She'd have convinced JoAnne. JoAnne was a proud women, but Carrie would have convinced her to acknowledge Susan as a daughter.

But wait. JoAnne already *had* Susan. As niece and aunt, the two women were very close, especially now that JoAnne's sister was dead. So JoAnne really had nothing to gain if her secret was revealed. And keeping the secret meant she didn't have to share Susan with Henry!

So just Henry was left out. There would be no way to bring father and daughter together unless the role of the birth mother was revealed. And that, Carrie saw now, was something as unlikely as Ozarks snow in July.

JoAnne was proud of being an example of strong womanhood for Susan, she'd said that often enough. She disdained sexual attraction and believed in a strong moral code. She never would have admitted she was Susan's unwed mother.

Henry probably thought he could eventually win

JoAnne over. Without JoAnne, did he have any proof he was Susan's father? Was the only proof right here in the box?

There would be records in Kansas City...no, the birth certificate was from some maternity home in New York State.

The records could have been traced, especially if Henry had any idea where Susan was born. But why would he know? It was unlikely JoAnne or her parents had told him.

And, even if Susan knew she was adopted, there was still no guarantee she'd want anything to do with a father who, she might assume—or perhaps had been told—abandoned both child and mother. Only JoAnne could tell her the truth about that.

JoAnne wouldn't. And now, JoAnne couldn't.

JoAnne's death, as Henry must see it, had put an impassable barrier between him and his daughter. No wonder he had shed tears!

And naturally, he couldn't have killed JoAnne.

Carrie realized with a start that he must have searched JoAnne's house to look for the very papers she had in front of her. It would have been like JoAnne to taunt him by telling him she had the papers here in Arkansas, using them as her own personal form of punishment for what had happened long ago, but was, until Saturday, very fresh in the minds of at least two people. And now only one of those people was left.

Carrie's thoughts were leaping wildly.

If he'd searched the house looking for the papers, then he'd been upset enough to forget completely about leaving fingerprints, though, if she was reasoning correctly, he'd known JoAnne was dead by then. Otherwise, he surely wouldn't have chosen Sunday to search the house.

Stupid, stupid! And he'd been a law officer for thirty years, he should have known better! Everyone knew you wore gloves for committing crimes. Oh! Oh, dear.

Carrie sat up stiffly, and FatCat stirred, then settled. The purring began again.

His crime was...what? Breaking and entering? To some people, it might look like Henry had reasons to kill JoAnne, especially if he had lost his temper, if they had quarreled.

What would the sheriff think? He didn't know the events or the people who were involved.

Leave it alone, she thought. Let the sheriff and his men do their work.

No, she couldn't leave it alone. Not now.

Henry really was a good person inside. He had hugged her, comforted her. He'd understood. And he had shed tears. Even the kisses Saturday night meant nothing next to what was revealed in that hug, or those tears. He just could not be a killer. Why, he didn't even hunt! He probably didn't even own a gun.

Law enforcement officers dealt only with facts. And cold facts had nothing at all to do with the truth in this case, or with Henry's fingerprints in JoAnne's house.

But, what would the sheriff think? She wished she knew just what the sheriff was thinking right now.

And what was she going to do? Well, for one thing, she'd better re-hide the contents of the box.

After going over options inside her house, she decided to put the few important documents she kept at home in the box on top of JoAnne's papers. She could take Susan's birth certificate to her own safe deposit box later, if she hadn't figured out some way to get Henry and his daughter together in the meantime.

When she added her papers to JoAnne's, there wasn't

enough space left for the baby things. She put the box in a cabinet in her office, then roamed the house, carrying the plastic bag with its tiny reminders of a baby girl who had undoubtedly been loved, but not welcomed, by the parents who conceived and bore her.

After rejecting a number of hiding places, Carrie decided she'd put the bag inside FatCat's mattress. No one would ever look there. She removed the mattress and down pillow, tucked the plastic bag under the flap in the bottom of the mattress cover, tied it closed again, then fluffed up the down pillow and put it on top. There, that would do, and FatCat, who had been prowling the house with her, would never talk. JoAnne's cat could guard JoAnne's secret.

She looked at her watch. Time to get ready to go to the Booths', but first she'd pick out a book to take to Shirley. She was standing in front of the bookshelves when the phone rang.

"Hi. Dinner's to be at 6:30, after Roger finishes with milking. Shall I pick you up about 6:15?

Carrie made an instant decision. "Can you come a little early, Henry? We need to talk."

She was stepping out of the shower when the phone rang again. Grabbing her towel, she went to the bedroom to answer.

"Carrie, I just saw a bit in the Tulsa paper about your friend JoAnne Harrington being shot! It doesn't say much. What happened? Um, are you all right?"

"Oh, hello, Evan. There isn't much to tell, really. She was killed sometime on Saturday and put in the woods behind here, near where...well, you know the area. I found her when I was out for a walk and now all the manpower in the county sheriff's department is roaming the hills. I don't know much more than that."

"How awful for you. I guess it was a hunting accident? Didn't you tell me she liked to walk in the woods?"

"They don't think a hunter shot her. Something about the wrong kind of gun. I suppose they'll get it all figured out eventually."

"So, ah, they've talked to you about it?"

"I'll say! Lots of questions about what I was doing, and about JoAnne. Of course I didn't know anything that would help them."

"So you...they...have no ideas about how it happened?"

"Well, I sure don't, and of course they aren't telling me what they think."

"What about JoAnne's family? Are they coming there?"

"A niece and her husband and child are the only remaining relatives. Susan, the niece, is flying here Wednesday. Her parents—JoAnne's sister and her husband—were killed several years ago in an automobile accident."

"Terrible thing. Do you have to play hostess? Guess the niece can stay in her aunt's house, though."

"She'll probably stay here. It may not be legal for her to be in JoAnne's house. The sheriff has sealed it."

"Do they think your friend was killed in her house?"

"I have no idea." She was tapping her foot, impatient to be done with this conversation.

After a silence, Evan asked, "What can I do?"

Carrie was sure he was simply being polite. She responded, "Nothing at all, Evan, thank you."

But he said immediately, "I know what, you must come here until things are cleared up; um, get away from all the fuss. Surely the girl could stay someplace else."

"Goodness no, Evan. I don't think the sheriff would like it if I left, and I'm executor of JoAnne's estate. There's a lot to do for that, I'm sure. I'll go to see the lawyer first thing tomorrow."

"Fine. Just let the lawyer handle it all. They can do that. Talk to the sheriff. Surely he doesn't really need you. You can't be a suspect."

Carrie noticed excitement in Evan's voice now, and he was talking faster and faster.

"I'll come get you. I'll pick you up at your house to-morrow afternoon, and you can stay in the guest suite at the office. Ask for a leave of absence or a vacation from your job."

Carrie was stunned. This was a new Evan, and every-thing he said was aggravating her. Still, he was just trying to be kind, and offering to come here to get her must be hard for him.

"Thank you, Evan, but no, I do feel I need to be here. It isn't that bad, now that the initial shock is over. I appre-ciate your kindness. Maybe I can come later."

"Will you keep me posted then? I am concerned about you...I worry about your safety..."

"I'm fine, Evan. It's nice you're concerned, but I may not have time to talk to you for a few days. After I get back from the lawyer's tomorrow, I hope I can get into JoAnne's house and begin cleaning it up. Then I—"

"Cleaning up?"

"Yes, someone searched the place and pretty well trashed it."

"That's odd, isn't it?"

"Sure it is, but then all of this is. Look, I've got to hang up. I'm going to dinner at a neighbor's house, and I need to get ready."

"Who?"

"Who? What do you mean? Oh. The Booths. They have a dairy farm in the valley. I'm sure I've told you about them."

"Oh, yes." He paused, and she thought he was through, but then he asked, "Have you called Rob?"

"Actually, it hadn't occurred to me. Maybe I should if the story is showing up in newspapers. I can call him tonight when I get home."

"I'm just so sorry you're there alone. Do consider coming over here. I think it would be best for you."

"Thanks, Evan, but no, and I've really got to go. We'll talk later."

What an old maid, Carrie thought as she hung up. I always did think he was a bore. Now he's getting to be a pest as well. I'm sorry he saw that piece in the paper.

Then, ashamed of herself, Carrie tried to think good thoughts about Evan as she went to get dressed.

She was waiting on the porch when Henry pulled up by the steps. He leaned across, pushed the door open for her, and, after saying hello, was silent as he waited for her to fasten the seat belt.

She looked up at him. "Henry, there is no time to be delicate about this. The detectives found your fingerprints all over JoAnne's house, *all* over it. Have they talked to you about it?"

He shut his eyes for a moment, then said, "Not yet."

"Well, they mentioned it to me, trying to shock me into saying something indiscreet, I imagine, or giving away some secret I'm supposed to know. I did neither. I simply implied that you and JoAnne were lovers."

"You did *what?*"

His voice banged against her ears, and she winced. "Well, wouldn't that cover the presence of your fingerprints simply everywhere?"

Henry started to laugh, but the sound held no humor.

This was awful, and she wanted to scream at him to stop laughing. She'd reasoned it all out. Wasn't her plan the only way to explain the fingerprints safely? Maybe she was hurting him, but she couldn't help it. The very presence of those fingerprints proved he wasn't thinking clearly. It was obvious he needed her help to get him out of this mess.

"Henry, stop it. It will not be funny if they arrest you for JoAnne's murder."

"Tell me why anyone, especially you, might think I killed JoAnne?" The laughing had stopped, and he turned his head away from her now. His voice was so low she could barely hear him.

"Well, it's ridiculous, of course, but how do they know that? Unless you were her lover, how would you explain the fingerprints to them—tell them you searched the place? Won't they ask why? I didn't know you'd been in the house, so, of course, I was honest when they first asked me if you and JoAnne knew each other, and by the time I learned about the fingerprints, it was too late. I had already told them you were barely acquainted. We do have to explain the fingerprints in a logical way. You and JoAnne were lovers. That ought to do it."

The silence wasn't much better than the laughing. Finally, he said—his words still quiet and full of an emotion she couldn't identify—"Why are you doing this...lying!"

"Lying?" Her voice shook, faltered, but she pushed the words out. "It could be true. I thought you'd be grateful!"

She wondered if her tone revealed what she was thinking, that he *should* be grateful to her for trying to help him. "And, how do I know that you and JoAnne were not lovers?"

"If you don't know that..."

Now he sounded furious. This was going all wrong! She said, "Well, it makes a logical story, doesn't it?"

"Did it ever occur to you that I was as curious about those meeting notes as you were? Didn't you search the house for them? Why wouldn't I do the same thing?"

"If you barely knew her, why on earth would you expect the sheriff to believe that, casual-like, you just walked in and searched the whole place for the dumb meeting notes? For heaven's sake, Henry, the place is a mess. Why did you make such a mess, and why on earth didn't you wear gloves?"

She was almost shouting, but was too upset to care.

"I did not make a mess, and I didn't wear gloves because I couldn't know anyone would ever care whose fingerprints were in JoAnne's house, now could I!"

He twisted to look straight at her, and she dropped her head. She didn't want him to see her face. The light was dim, but what if he could tell she knew he was lying? She wanted to open the car door and run and run. She wondered if he'd follow her if she did.

He went on. "Yes, I searched JoAnne's house, but I did it early Sunday morning. I went there again, hoping she'd be back. I wanted to ask about her meeting with the Environmental Commission, and I thought I'd have time before I went with you to look for the frost flowers. Of course, she wasn't home, so I decided to go in...you must agree the meeting was important enough to all of us to justify that."

"But..."

"Let me finish, Carrie! I'd probably just left the house when you came. I did not make a mess. I was very careful."

They were both quiet, then Carrie thought of something.

"Did you look inside JoAnne's bedroom closet?" she asked, wondering if he'd realize that searching a clothes closet would seem ridiculous to anyone who really believed he was in the house looking for a meeting report.

He did hesitate, as if thinking over his reply, but simply said, "Yes, how did you know?"

"The door was open Sunday. I had looked in the closet and closed the door on Saturday."

"My mistake."

"Where did you get a key to the house?"

His voice rose again. "All right, Sergeant McCrite, I found the key under the flower pot. Any self-respecting burglar could have found that key in seconds. It's really an obvious hiding place. Knowing JoAnne, I'm surprised she didn't realize that."

Carrie decided not to comment on the fact that he wasn't supposed to know JoAnne very well, but there was still the problem of the EC notes. If Henry was so determined to use JoAnne's supposed request that he go over the notes with her as his excuse for being in the house, she would have to tell him the truth before he was questioned.

"You said JoAnne called you to come and help her organize her notes from the Environmental Commission meeting."

"Yes."

"Henry, there never *were* any notes! Sergeant Taylor called the chairman of the commission on Sunday. JoAnne never met with them! She couldn't have made notes."

He was silent, and the urge to shout at him bubbled

inside her again while she waited for his answer. She wanted
to make him tell her the truth, but how could she do that?
How could she tell him what she was feeling—what she
knew?

Finally he said, very softly, "Someone has lied then,
right?"

"Henry, did JoAnne really call and ask you to come
by?"

"Yes."

"It wasn't because of the notes, was it?"

He stared out the car window for a long time, but Carrie refused to break the silence or give him an out.

"I thought it was," he said finally. "That's what JoAnne
told me."

He is lying, she thought, surprised she could tell it so
easily in his voice, even when the post light by her drive
was the only light in the car, and she couldn't see his face.
Henry King hated lies, and he was a lousy liar. She wondered if she should act as if she believed him.

Before she could make up her mind, he went on. "You're
a very smart woman, very smart, but don't meddle in my
life. This is not any of your business, Carrie."

You have no idea, she thought, but swallowed her im-
patience with him and said, "Well, do we save you from
suspicion by letting everyone believe you were JoAnne's
lover?"

"No one who knew JoAnne—or me, I hope—could
possibly believe that."

Her eyes dropped to her lap. She was about to twist
the finger off one of her gloves.

"No one in the sheriff's department ever met JoAnne
Harrington, and would anyone else really be sure? They
must believe it."

This time his silence lasted a long time. She wondered what he could be thinking. He still didn't seem to grasp the fact that she had come up with a plausible way, maybe the only way, to get him out of an awful mess.

"All right, Sergeant McCrite, it seems you're in charge." His shoulders slumped, and he sighed.

She hesitated before she spoke. Maybe the lie was painful, but wasn't it for his own good? They had to go through with it.

"Okay, we agree then. I guess we're ready to go to dinner now."

As he started the car, Carrie was thinking, this will work. We're only lying to save him. Henry understands that.

But, she wondered, if that's true, why am I so miserable?

CHAPTER XI

Jason's blue Buick was already parked in front of the porch that ran along the width of the Booths' white frame house. Henry pulled in behind it, and since he had to walk around the car anyway, Carrie sat still and waited for him to open the car door for her.

She hoped that physical closeness and a smile from her would melt his frostiness. However, Henry stepped back as he opened the door, and since he didn't look at her, there was no reason to smile. She thought about apologizing for being so quick to organize a defense for him without any discussion, but she couldn't get the words out.

She stumbled on the porch step, and Henry reached for her arm, steadying her. She glanced up to see yesterday's sorrow in the shadowy lines of his face. Was it because she'd asked him to say publicly he was JoAnne's lover? Well, after all, that had once been true, and what other reasonable excuse could they offer for his fingerprints being in JoAnne's house? She thought she'd worked out a perfect strategy, and now... Oh, phooey! The man was just being pig-headed. He'd come to understand, especially if he found out she knew about his past.

Roger opened the door and greeted them warmly, shaking Henry's hand and giving Carrie a hug. At least he wasn't going to let the problems surrounding them get in the way of open friendship.

Jason was standing by the stone fireplace with the framed photograph of a cow in his hands. There were a number of similar pictures on the wall, each with a blue or red ribbon attached to the frame. Roger had evidently been showing off prize-winning members of his dairy herd. When Carrie and Henry came into the room, Jason put the photo down and came to shake hands awkwardly with each of them.

As soon as she could, Carrie left the men and headed for the kitchen. She needed the comfort of Shirley's quiet presence and the large room full of chintz and warmth.

Shirley was humming as Carrie came in, quite at ease cooking for guests. Of course, Carrie thought, she and Roger raised four children, so she's used to a crowd.

Shirley smiled from the stove and declined Carrie's offer of help. "I'm near ready. Just rest yourself there at the table. I reckon you've had quite a day. You look a bit peaked."

Carrie laid the book she'd brought with her on the counter. "I thought you might enjoy this. It's called *A Living History of the Ozarks*. The woman who wrote it, Phyllis Rossiter, traveled all over this area and tells about the beauty and history of lots of places near here."

Shirley wiped her hands on her apron and came to see the book. She touched it carefully, then picked it up and looked inside. "See," she said, "here's a picture of the bluff in Roaring River State Park in Missouri. It isn't too different from the bluffs around this valley. Roger and I took the kids to Roaring River a few times. Thank you. I'll enjoy seeing this." She put the book down and pointed to a chair. "Now, you sit there and rest."

The large round table had five places set, and the red and white checked cloth was almost hidden under dishes filled with food. There was a beef pot roast with carrots and potatoes, and Carrie also saw applesauce and a big bowl of cabbage slaw. As Henry had said, it sure wasn't TV dinners. Carrie thought of last night's meal, her Hungry HE-MAN Roast Beef Dinner, and started to laugh. Even the smell of this food made her giddy.

Whether she understood or not, Shirley smiled while adding a large bowl of gravy and a plate of biscuits to the loaded table, then she called the men. As she went to her chair, she gave Carrie a pat, saying, "We'll talk later, but let's enjoy this meal without thinking about problems."

Shirley directed Jason and Henry to chairs on either side of Carrie, and when they were settled, Roger bowed his head. His blessing ended by asking comfort for those in sorrow and included "those present around this table and all them who are absent."

Carrie added her own "Amen" after he had finished.

Conversation centered on everyone's children and, in Jason's case, on the new grandson in Ohio. Carrie wondered if Henry was thinking about Susan and baby Johnny. She learned that only one of the Booths' children was married, their oldest daughter, and that both Roger and Shirley were hoping at least one of their sons would eventually return to Walden Valley and take over the dairy farm.

"It's a shame to have to hire help when we have two

grown sons," Roger said, "but young folks today gotta try things out before they settle to the real world. Times past, they'd have stayed on at the farm or lived nearby."

"Now, Roger," his wife said gently, "you don't know that. They're good boys, and if it's right for any of 'em to come back, they will. If not, well, we'll just sell out some-day and move into town."

Silence fell on the group. Carrie supposed all of them were thinking about how things changed as people got older.

Roger broke the silence from his chair, which faced the window. "Sure is a peculiar amount of traffic on the road since we sat. I ain't been countin', but there's been lots of headlights out there. Wonder what's up?"

Everyone turned to stare into the darkness just as a car zoomed past, lights flashing across its top. Even at a dis-tance they could see the bounce of the lights as the car hit bumps and rocks. If there was a siren, which Carrie doubted since even the flashing lights seemed ridiculous on the little-traveled road, they could hear nothing inside the house.

"Seems to be headed toward the old deserted farm," Roger said.

Shirley stood up. "Well, it's none of our business, not yet, anyway. Let's move to the living room. I'll bring along coffee and cookies, I didn't make a fancy dessert."

"Cookies are my favorite dessert," Henry said as chairs scraped back on the worn vinyl floor.

Carrie decided she'd bake cookies as soon as she had time. Susan would probably enjoy them, and she could share a few with Henry.

"Well," Jason said when they were settled in a com-fortable half-circle around the fireplace. "So how much does anyone know for sure, and what has the sheriff found out?

Seems impossible someone could really kill JoAnne unless it was a hunting accident after all."

Everyone looked at Carrie. She cleared her throat. Here goes, she thought.

"This is what I know, and maybe Henry can add something since he's spoken with the detectives, too." She looked around at the group. "Have they talked to any of the rest of you yet?"

Jason, Shirley, and Roger all shook their heads.

Carrie explained minimum details of finding JoAnne's body and told about going to JoAnne's house "to take care of the cat." She didn't mention that the house had been searched carefully on Sunday morning before she got there, but only described the mess she and Detective Taylor and Sheriff Storm had found on Sunday afternoon. She said that, so far as she knew, the only thing missing was JoAnne's address book. She didn't add she'd missed it on Saturday.

She took a deep breath and went on. "They did tell me a couple of things they've found out. One of them is very important. JoAnne never went to any meeting with the State Environmental Commission. No one there had ever talked with JoAnne or even heard of her." She stopped and looked around again. She certainly had their attention.

"But," Jason said, "why? Well, what—" He sputtered to a stop.

Roger studied Carrie's face for a moment, and then he spoke, his words coming slowly as they followed his thoughts. "Didn't you tell us JoAnne was pleased and excited about somethin' when she talked to you Friday night? When the cat caused a mess, didn't she say she'd save the surprise fer Saturday's meeting? And wasn't it your thinkin', Carrie, that maybe she had some good news about the quarry?"

"Yes."

"Any hint about what it might have been?"

"None at all. She certainly acted like she'd have some good news for us at the meeting, though."

"Well, then, ain't it likely she'd found out somethin'? She'd got ahold of somethin' that she thought was big enough to stop the quarry and was gonna tell us all on Saturday. Wouldn't it be likely she didn't go see the environmental folks because she didn't think she needed to? And what if the quarry owner found out she could put a stop to him? What would he do about that?"

He halted, somewhat uncertainly.

Of course, Carrie thought, that's it, and I didn't see it! I didn't even think that JoAnne might have discovered something so very important on her own, but...kill her because of it?

Jason spoke her thoughts aloud. "I can't believe they'd care enough to kill someone..."

Henry said, his voice very low, "I know about a lot of people who have killed for much less reason."

"Well, then, whatever happened," Jason said, "we need to find out what JoAnne found out—if anything—though I'm certainly not saying you're not right, Roger. What you suggest does fit what happened. Doesn't anyone have an idea at all what she might have discovered? If she found it, surely we can too."

"She roamed this valley a lot," Roger said. "She even knew the caves and wasn't afraid to poke about in them. You know about that, Carrie. Didn't you go in some of the bluff caves with her? Couldn't JoAnne have found somethin' important there, way back in where folks wouldn't be apt to go?

"Guess we'll have to start lookin' around very, very care-

ful! I do recall hearin' talk there was Indian remains here in
the valley, even maybe a burial place. I know we still find
arrowheads around. Maybe we could get ahold of somethin'
those genealogy folks, or folks interested in history or savin'
Indian remains, would say needed savin', whatever it is.
Seems I read somewhere there's laws to do with that.
Shoulda paid more attention.

"Maybe lookin' at environmental stuff is the wrong
track to be on. I'm gonna start talkin' to all the old-timers.
I kin do that pretty easy and not even make the quarry
folks suspicious since," he grinned, "us hillbillies is a close-
mouthed lot. And besides, quite a few 'round here has Indian blood. Some may know more about the history of
this valley than we do. We've only been on this place forty
years."

Jason spoke up. "Carrie, do you really know something
about the caves?"

"Well, I have been in a few with JoAnne, but we didn't
see anything I think might stop a quarry, and I can't say
I'm anxious to go back in alone. Maybe Susan might enjoy
taking time for a cave crawl with me when she comes." She
avoided looking at Henry. He was probably too large to
squeeze in some of those caves anyway.

"And I can keep her baby," Shirley said. "I'd be pleased
to do that anyway."

"Let's get re-organized then," said Jason. "I'll go to the
historical society, the court house, and the county library
to see what I can find out about the history of this place.
Maybe a lawyer will know about laws that govern the dis-
covery of things like burial sites, but under the circumstances it might be safer for me to talk to someone in Bonny
instead of the lawyer in Guilford, especially if the quarry
people are around here. Has any of you ever seen the owner

or any of the rest of them close enough to recognize?"

They all shook their heads.

"I'll call Rob," Carrie said. "History, archaeology, and geography are his fields. Maybe there are some general laws he knows about."

Roger looked at Shirley. They were all getting excited, and his voice showed how he felt. "We'll start talkin' to old-timers here. Shirley can take the ladies. And we can easy walk over that abandoned farm. We just might lose a cow there. I kin get my lead cow Mary Belle to go with me just about anywhere, she's that tame.

"Carrie, let me know if you go into any of the caves, even with Susan. We oughta keep track of you if you're gonna go on quarry land. It might not be safe, though you could probably explain you're a spell...speel...you know, one o' those people who likes to study caves. But, maybe that's what JoAnne did too, so you got to be real careful!"

Henry nodded in agreement. "If Carrie and Susan are going there, I'm going too."

"Good idea," Jason said. "Now, shouldn't we get in touch with the Bruners?"

Roger's quick response, "No need to, is there?" surprised Carrie, but he followed up, "They're pretty busy right now. Jack has just got 80,000 baby chickens, and with this iffy weather, he sticks pretty close to home. They've also got a couple of steers that are doing poorly, accordin' to the vet, so there's plenty on their hands. Let's just see what the five of us kin do."

Roger cleared his throat, looked around, then went on. "Uh, any of you folks know how to shoot? Probably wouldn't hurt to think about that, especially you, Henry, if you're goin' with Carrie and the young lady to search the caves. I'm not sayin' there's a problem, but then, well, you never know." He stopped and gave a small laugh. "Just can't tell when you might see a copperhead, now, kin you?"

"I have a gun," Henry said, speaking the words so quietly that Carrie almost missed hearing them.

So he did have a gun, after all!

"What we got here is a rifle and a shotgun," offered Roger.

"Revolver, .38 Police Special," said Henry.

Roger looked at him. "Guess you got a permit to carry it?"

Henry nodded.

"Good, so you'll go with Carrie and Susan. Jason?"

"Never owned a gun, never shot one, never intend to."

"Okay," Roger said, "we got what we need anyway, and you won't be around where someone, some snake, might want to cause a problem. This is pretty important to all of us, and what happened to JoAnne sure puts a different light on the other side of the question and what they might do.

"Now then, does anyone have anything else to say?"

"Yes," Jason said, turning to Carrie. "You said the police told you a couple of things they found out that we didn't know. If one of them was the fact that JoAnne had never been to Little Rock, what was the other one?"

He would ask, Carrie thought. She glanced over at Henry, hoping he would say something, but he was staring into the fire. Oh, well, news about the fingerprints would get around eventually anyway, so why not tell it now and get it over with.

"Well," she said aloud. "They found lots of fingerprints in JoAnne's house. They'd already taken fingerprints from Henry and me, so they discovered pretty quickly that both of us had been in the house, and..." She hesitated, wondering if anyone was remembering that Henry and JoAnne had said they barely knew each other.

Jason's expression showed he did remember and had been quick to assume exactly what Carrie had planned. Just as quickly, she realized she wasn't pleased about it at all. This was her own fault, but then, what other story would have saved Henry? What else could she have done?

"Um, ah," she said aloud, glancing at Roger and then Shirley. It didn't look like they, at least, were imagining anything at all. They just looked attentive, waiting for her to go on—though she thought she caught a flicker of sympathy in Shirley's quiet brown eyes.

"Anyway," she continued, "JoAnne made it plain she didn't think much of most men, you know, so she didn't tell us that she and Henry had known each other for a long time. They sort of grew up together in Kansas City, so...well, it was natural his fingerprints would be in her house, and, um, they were." She paused, feeling like a school girl who not only didn't know the answer to a question asked by her teacher, but couldn't even remember what the question was.

I used to be able to tell any story without a problem, she thought. I should have taken more time to figure things out before I opened my mouth about this to Henry or anyone else. They're probably wondering why I'm telling the stupid story instead of Henry himself!

Shirley clicked her tongue and shook her head. "Well, we all have a lot to straighten out, don't we? Which makes me think, Carrie—when you're ready to put JoAnne's house to rights, let me know. I'd be pleased to help."

Carrie decided Shirley must be the kindest woman she'd ever known and smiled warmly at her. Then she looked at Henry again. Was there the hint of a twinkle in his eyes? He was probably just laughing at her discomfort.

"All right, then," Jason said. "When shall we get together again? How long before you all will have time to do some checking and looking? I can spend tomorrow doing my research in town. If Susan is coming Wednesday, Carrie, aren't you pretty busy?"

"Tomorrow morning I'm going to the lawyer's in Guilford to get legal things about JoAnne's estate started, then I hope tomorrow afternoon the sheriff will let me...us into JoAnne's house so we can begin to clear out the mess." She smiled at Shirley again.

"I'm to pick Susan up at the Fayetteville Airport Wednesday morning. She'll probably spend Wednesday night with me, and Thursday we hope to begin going through things at JoAnne's. Her husband comes Friday night, and the memorial service is Saturday morning. I don't really know how long Susan and Putt plan to stay after that."

"Well, then," Jason said, "why don't we leave everything open-ended, and I'll keep in touch with all of you to see how things are going. Let's don't talk about this outside our group for now. I'm sure we all agree with Roger on that. We already know we aren't going to get much help outside our own little group anyway, so talk won't help us, might even do harm, and," he hesitated, "could put one or more of us in the same danger JoAnne ran into. You all understand that?"

Before anyone could answer, a car roared into the yard. They sat in silence, looking at each other. Footsteps sounded on the porch floor, then someone began knocking.

"If the quarry owner is arrested fer murder," Roger said as he got to his feet, "then it'll stop things in a hurry, won't it? We may find out something about JoAnne's murder, as well as about whatever it was she'd dug up. But we don't want the sheriff to cut us off. Mostly now, we want to be free to find out as much as we kin about things. We should tell whatever we know that might help the sheriff find JoAnne's killer, but let's not be in any big hurry to say anythin' about our other plans. Sheriff 'n his people care nothin' about the quarry, one way or another anyhow. So, is it okay with everyone that we kinda work on our own?"

They were all nodding their heads as he reached to open the door.

CHAPTER XII

When Roger opened the door, Carrie heard a familiar voice say, "Mr. Booth? Sorry to interrupt your party."

That man should be on radio or television, she thought. What a voice!

The voice went on. "I'm Detective Sergeant Don Taylor of the Spavinaw County Sheriff's Office. I guess you know we're investigating the murder of JoAnne Harrington. I'd like to talk to you, and maybe some of the folks inside, if you don't mind. I saw the cars from the road. May I come in?"

"Sure, just come on in out of the cold," Roger said as he stepped back. "I'll be glad to talk with you. As fer the other folks, well, they're our company, just here fer supper, so you'll need to ask if they want to talk to you here. That's their say, not mine."

Taylor entered the room, hat in hand. Jason and Henry rose to shake hands as Roger continued, "This here's my wife, Shirley, and Jason Stack. Mr. Stack lives a mile north of the highway on the east side of Walden Road. I think you know Mrs. McCrite and Mr. King? Let's pull up another chair by the fire. Would you like some coffee?"

Shirley left to get coffee without waiting for Taylor's reply, and Roger pulled one of the kitchen chairs into the semi-circle around the fireplace as Jason and Henry scooted their chairs sideways to make room.

As soon as Taylor was seated, Shirley handed him a filled coffee cup, then put cream and sugar and a plate of cookies on the table beside him.

Carrie watched the sergeant with interest as he took two cookies, then blushed and said, "Thanks. I haven't had supper so this looks mighty good."

"Oh, my," Shirley said, "I can fix you a plate. We have plenty left over."

"No, thanks, ma'am."

Taylor's wistful look said he hated rejecting the offer. Probably, Carrie thought, eating on the job in front of witnesses...or suspects...is considered unprofessional. How could he ask us questions with his mouth full?

For the first time, she felt sorry for the man and wondered if he had a wife and, perhaps, children. She'd already noticed he didn't wear a wedding ring.

Taylor ate one cookie in two bites, swallowed some coffee, then set the cup and second cookie aside.

"Mr. Booth, Mrs. Booth—can you remember seeing any cars or trucks on the road out there, especially on Saturday morning, or even Friday night?"

Roger considered. "Well, I didn't pay any special attention. There's been a little more action since the quarry folks bought that farm at the end of the valley, and of course it's huntin' season. We get some traffic, mostly on weekends, fer that. I'm afraid I can't recall anything special though. Just trucks. That's what we see this time of year, hunters' trucks."

"Do you recall seeing Ms. Harrington's grey truck, maybe early Saturday?"

Carrie looked around the circle. Everyone was paying close attention. They've found JoAnne's truck, she thought.

Shirley shook her head, and Roger said, "Nope. Shirley and I worked together in the milkin' barn from about six o'clock until time to clean up and go to Carrie's. We didn't pay any mind to who was drivin' on the road."

"You didn't hear any vehicles?"

"Just heard cows and milkin' machinery," Roger said as Shirley nodded in agreement.

Taylor looked at the rest of them in turn. "Any one of you remember seeing her truck, or noticing other cars or trucks coming or going on Walden Road? I know Mrs. McCrite and Mr. King both live down in the woods far enough so they wouldn't see cars on the road—if they were at home. Mr. Stack, is your house the brown one on the east side? If so, you can see the road from your windows. See anything at all that you remember?"

"Our kitchen's in the back," Jason said. "My wife is away helping our daughter, and from about seven until time to leave for the meeting at Carrie's, I sat in the kitchen alone, reading and getting together an outline for the meeting. I did go out in the yard once for more firewood. Someone drove by quite fast then, come to think of it, but I didn't really look at them. I remember wondering who it might be, since it hadn't been daylight long and I didn't think a hunter would be leaving yet. I was sure it wasn't one of us." He swept his arm around the circle.

"What time would that have been?"

"Oh, 7:30 or so. I didn't look at the clock."

"Truck or car?"

"My impression now is that it was a truck. A car would have sounded different, and we don't see many outsiders on the road in cars. Mag and Jack Bruner live at the beginning of the road, and at least one of them would probably have been out checking on their chickens. Have you asked them if they saw something?"

"Yes. Jack Bruner was at his chicken houses, but doesn't remember seeing or hearing anything," said Taylor.

He stopped to eat his second cookie, and Carrie noticed that he glanced down at the plate of cookies by his elbow with something that could only be described as longing.

Shirley had seen his glance too, and she lifted her eyes to Carrie's and smiled.

"Well, now," Taylor said, "I do have some more questions for you individually, and I think they should be asked privately. Mr. and Mrs. Booth, would it be imposing too much if I asked if you have a room where I could talk with each of the folks here? It sure would save time. I'll need to talk with all of you eventually, and now might be easier, though I'm sorry to break in on your party."

"You can have the front bedroom," Shirley said. "We use it for an office now."

"That's fine. I appreciate your help. Will you show me that room then?" He turned to Carrie. "I'd like to talk with you first, Mrs. McCrite. Some things have come up since we spoke last."

Shirley disappeared in the direction of the kitchen, to finish cleaning up, Carrie supposed, and Roger led the way down the hall to the first room. There was a twin bed pushed against one wall, but the rest of the room did look just like an office, with a big oak desk and metal filing cabinets. Taylor pulled a chair up at one side of the desk for Carrie to sit in. He took the desk chair for himself, removed a pen and pad of paper from his pocket, laid them on the desk, and leaned forward, folding his hands on the desktop as he looked at her.

Carrie's heart began thumping. What was he going to ask? What would she say...what would the others say? Would their answers sound reasonable? Would Henry's?

Before Taylor could begin, Shirley pushed the door open and came to the desk, putting a plate of food and a glass of milk in front of the astonished man. She took a napkin and silverware from her apron pocket, laid them down, then left, winking at Carrie as she passed.

Don Taylor looked at the food, then at Carrie, and blushed. *He looks like he has no idea what to do*, she thought. Finally, he picked up the fork, speared a piece of meat and put it in his mouth, following with a carrot, a bite of potato, and a swallow of milk.

Carrie wasn't sure whether to talk or not, but since she couldn't think of anything to say, she sat in silence and stared at Taylor's reflection in the window behind his head. She decided the man couldn't be much older than Rob. Well, at least seeing him eat lessened her own nervousness even as it increased his.

She wondered what Harrison Storm would do if he came in right now, and she almost giggled, whether from nerves or humor, she really couldn't have said. Then she thought about Shirley's wink and felt better.

Taylor pushed the plate aside, took another swallow of milk, wiped his mouth with the napkin, and looked at her.

"When did you last see Ms. Harrington's truck?"

She considered. "Wednesday. I picked her up after I

got off work and we drove into Guilford for supper. Her truck was parked next to the house then, like maybe she planned to go someplace later. I didn't see her Thursday. That's when she was supposed to drive to Little Rock."

"And Friday?"

"We talked on the phone Friday evening, that's all."

"What time did you talk on Friday?"

She didn't remind him he'd asked her these same questions Sunday afternoon. "Around eight."

"Did she seem different in any way then? Notice anything unusual?"

"Oh, yes. She was excited." Carrie spoke slowly, remembering the conversation. "We're all doing research, trying to find some way to stop the stone quarry that's planning to destroy the valley. You know about that, and about JoAnne's plans to go to Little Rock. I assumed she was excited because she had good news about what she learned there. She was going to tell me, I think, until her cat dumped something over and she had to hang up. But before she did, she said she'd have a surprise for us at Saturday's meeting. Of course, you've found out she never went to Little Rock. Now we can only guess what her good news was."

"Any ideas at all? You think her news was about the quarry?"

"Yes, I do, and I haven't the faintest idea what it was. Maybe she talked to the quarry owner himself. Perhaps you should ask him."

"Yes, Charles Stoker. We haven't located him yet."

Taylor changed the subject. "Have you talked with Mr. King about his relationship with Ms. Harrington?"

She looked at her lap. "Not much." She wondered if Taylor thought she was jealous.

"Did you tell him we'd found his fingerprints in the house?"

"Yes."

"Did he offer an explanation?"

"Turns out they were old friends, but you'll have to find out about that from him."

He looked at her for a moment, and in the silence Carrie heard a noise, then realized she was tapping her index finger on the arm of her chair. She stopped, hoping he hadn't heard the tapping.

Taylor, relaxed now, took another bite of food, chewed, and swallowed. Then he leaned back in his chair and asked, "Have you had further thoughts about why anyone would have a reason to kill Ms. Harrington?"

"No, that is, unless it had something to do with what she discovered about the quarry—something that might stop it—and the owner or someone found out, and..."

"Hmmmm, yes. Tell me, are there plans for a funeral for her? I think the funeral home in Guilford called us."

"A memorial service only. Saturday. Her niece, Susan Burke-Williams, with her husband and son, will be here."

"The body has been sent to Little Rock for autopsy. If it's a memorial service, I don't suppose that will matter."

For just an instant, Carrie wanted to protest, "To us, JoAnne is more than just a body!" but instead she said, speaking quietly and looking at her lap, "I guess it won't matter, but Susan would be the one to say. She's coming Wednesday. She'll be staying at my house, since we can't use her aunt's house." She looked up at Taylor again. "Do you know when you'll be through there?"

"Should be by noon tomorrow. If your lawyer approves, you can have it after that. Sorry, it's a mess."

There was a pause.

"I've been thinking," Carrie said, "that you've found JoAnne's truck."

"We have."

"And?"

"It was in the barn on the abandoned farm. Someone drove it into the half of the building that's still standing."

Carrie decided it couldn't hurt to ask detective-like questions. "Any evidence in the truck?"

Taylor looked at her sharply, and she thought he might not answer, but after a moment he said, "It's quite obvious that Ms. Harrington was sitting in her truck when she was shot, then was removed from the cab and hidden in the camper shell, probably until early Sunday morning when she was moved to the hillside."

"Blood in the truck cab?" She was trying to be detached, to prove he couldn't shock her, and to push away the thought that it was JoAnne's blood they were talking about.

"Yes."

"Why do you think someone would go to the trouble of moving her?"

"We don't know." He looked at her. "Do you?"

Carrie ignored the question. She hoped he thought she was simply an old woman with a morbid curiosity.

"Fingerprints?" she asked.

"Yes, mostly inside. Ms. Harrington's, and yours, of course. There are one or two unidentified prints. We've sent to Kansas City for the niece's prints. I assume she's been in the truck?"

"Yes, and I've been in it with JoAnne lots of times. She and I were together a lot." Carrie stared at her reflection and Taylor's in the night-mirrored window behind him.

"Mrs. McCrite, you're sure you neither heard nor saw anything at any time over the weekend that seemed unusual, other than the Saturday morning shots, that is?"

She hesitated, then said, "Quite sure."

He rose. "Thank you, then. I'll talk to Mr. King next. Will you ask him to come in, please?"

Carrie didn't know what to say to Jason, Shirley, and Roger after Henry left the room. Then, remembering Taylor hadn't said she couldn't repeat information he'd given her, she told them about the conversation concerning the quarry and the finding of JoAnne's truck, and she said they were looking for Charles Stoker, the quarry owner.

"Think I'll ask Sergeant Taylor if he'll tell me what town Stoker lives in," Jason said. "It might help us. I'm glad they're checking up on the man, and it's good you could mention our suspicions about him without any fanfare, Carrie."

Henry was gone a long time. Conversation in the room had slowed to small talk by the time he returned. She looked carefully at his face, wondering if Taylor had asked him about his relationship with JoAnne, and what the answer had been. What was Taylor really thinking about Henry...about all of them?

Henry was frowning, but that might be just because this whole situation was difficult. She hoped he'd tell her what had been said later.

Taylor spoke only briefly with the other three, and then, after thanking Shirley for the food, he said good night.

When the sound of Taylor's car had died away, Jason looked around at the group and said, "Well, I found out Stoker lives in Ocalla. Did anyone other than Carrie learn anything that will help our cause?"

When they all shook their heads, he said he'd be in touch with each of them by phone no later than Thursday night. With that, Jason and Henry said their thank you's and rose to leave.

Carrie went to Shirley, looked up at her, and found she had to blink her eyes quickly several times. After a moment, she said, "I'll be really grateful for your help. I think we can work in the house tomorrow afternoon. How about one o'clock?" She had planned to add "thank you" but, surprised by her feelings, couldn't say more.

This time Shirley did give her a quick hug, smiled, and said, "Don't worry, we'll get it in shape, and it'll be nice to work together—the two of us."

Roger and Shirley watched from the porch until Henry and Carrie were in the car, then waved and returned to the warm house. The car started with a chug and rattle and bounced along, following Jason's tail lights down the lane toward Walden Road.

While Henry was concentrating on driving, Carrie's thoughts went back to Don Taylor's questions. Surely Henry would tell her what they had talked about. They couldn't suspect him now, if they ever had, since the presence of his fingerprints in JoAnne's house had been explained.

When they were out on the road, she began to tell him what Taylor had asked her, almost shouting to make herself heard above the noise from the car and the road.

Then she said, "I guess he told you about JoAnne's truck?"

"Yes, and that's a relief. It'll give them more to go on."

When he didn't offer anything further about what had been said while he was with Taylor, she asked, "You weren't ever in JoAnne's truck, were you?"

"No. No Henry King fingerprints there."

"Thank goodness. What do we do next?"

"I'm glad you asked."

"Yes? Why?"

"Because you have a tendency to make plans for folks

without their okay, or hadn't you noticed?"

"Oh." For just a moment, her lower lip moved out. Why didn't he understand? He really should be thanking her for helping him!

After the car was up the hill and settled into its regular whir and rattle, Henry said, "I think we do exactly as we discussed after supper. I assume you'll be busy all day tomorrow, and Jason asked me to go into Bonny with him to see what we can find out at the Court House and County Historical Society."

"Then will you call me tomorrow evening?" she asked. "I'd like to know what you learned. I hate being unable to help. Since I'm going to be at the lawyer's in Guilford anyway, maybe I can ask him about laws covering land use."

"I wouldn't."

"Why not? It wouldn't be suspicious. I'm going to be there anyway."

"Do you know him well?"

"No. Just met him when JoAnne signed her will."

"I think Roger's right. The less folks know about what we're seeking, especially in Guilford, the better. We aren't sure where anyone's sympathies lie yet."

They pulled up in front of Carrie's porch. "Can you come in?" she asked. "I'd like to hear more about what you and Taylor discussed."

"No, not tonight. I'm meeting Taylor at my house."

"But, why?"

"He needs to take my gun with him. It's the same kind that killed JoAnne. They want to make tests."

"Uh...your gun? How did he find out you had a gun?"

"He asked, and I told him, of course! Are you going to suggest that I should have lied about that, too?" His face, seen in the dim porch light, looked as hard as his voice sounded. "Or,"—he looked out into the night—"do you think my gun killed JoAnne?"

She felt as if he'd struck her, and she couldn't answer his question.

Just what would you say if you knew I had a copy of your daughter's birth certificate inside this house, she was thinking, and that I also have a note saying I'm not to tell you about it? Would you say I should be honest about that? What on earth would you tell me to do about that?

And the gun? Well, he had asked her the awful question, but hadn't provided any answers he surely must know she needed to hear.

How could he be so inconsiderate? Why didn't he understand?

Well, if he didn't, he didn't. She had no way to explain her thoughts to him now.

She heard her voice saying, "Call me tomorrow evening then," and, feeling like she'd been parachuting through a dark sky into unknown—and dangerous—territory, she went to unlock her front door.

CHAPTER XIII

Henry's gun.

A .38 Police Special. Carrie had no idea what that meant, but she supposed it was a gun policemen carried, and that JoAnne had been killed with a policeman's gun. Carrie only knew of one policeman, or ex-policeman, who might be involved in JoAnne's death.

A little before midnight, she decided that worrying about a gun was going to keep her awake all night.

She bounced from her left side to the right, facing away from the clock. Think about something else.

The gun faded into an image of JoAnne's dead face. *No!*

Why had she been angry at JoAnne? Why had she ever assumed JoAnne would go off without a thought for her cat or her house, leaving everything in the charge of faithful, pick-up-the-pieces Carrie?

If she managed to figure out who JoAnne's killer was,

Henry would respect that. He'd see she was a good detective...much more than a smart woman.

Honesty. Think about that. She was honest. Except when... Phooey! Well, think about...

Rob. She'd called him as soon as she got home. At least that conversation had been very satisfying. Rob had the knack of showing concern without too much anxiety. He offered to come right away if she needed him, though it was nearing the end of the semester. If she didn't need him immediately, he would, he promised, come for Thanksgiving.

Keeping her tone casual, she had asked if he'd like to bring a friend. He'd hesitated over that one and hadn't given a direct answer.

She wondered if her son assumed she'd be jealous of any other woman in his life. Hmpff, she'd always hoped for a daughter-in-law. Rob was thirty, but Amos had been thirty-five when he married her. There might even be a grandchild some day—a velvety baby to hold.

She thought about Susan and baby Johnny. Oh, goodness, she'd forgotten she needed to find a baby bed. She'd told Susan she'd get one. The problem was, where to borrow or rent it? She'd have to do that tomorrow, too.

She bounced back to look at the clock. Today.

Rob had offered a few ideas about what JoAnne might have discovered in the valley. Native American burial grounds or campsites were the most likely. He thought if quarry development had to be postponed while mandated anthropological or archeological studies were made, then the delay might halt the quarry completely.

"Mom, there are national laws now about protecting relics and burial grounds, such as the Native American Graves Protection and Repatriation Act. That only protects skeletal remains on Federal land, but many states have laws covering protection for significant Native American historical and religious sites on private land too. I'm not exactly sure what those are in Arkansas, though I plan to do some research on state protection laws next year. You might call the University of Arkansas and speak to someone in the anthropology or archeology department. They can help."

She hadn't asked Rob about a .38 Police Special. He knew nothing about guns. No matter what, she'd just call Henry in the morning and ask him about it. If only a policeman would have one...well, why hadn't Henry explained? Why hadn't he said, "Of course it didn't kill JoAnne!"

Suddenly a heavy weight punched into her, and Carrie jumped, crying out. She sat up in bed and looked down at an indignant cat who, it seemed, had once more been knocked to the floor by a flailing arm.

"Yowl," said FatCat, whose haughty posture showed just what she thought of this insufferable human behavior.

Carrie shook her head, her fright diminishing rapidly in the face of FatCat's ludicrous glare. She looked at the clock.

Almost eight o'clock! Goodness, she had fallen asleep after all. Her appointment with the lawyer was at nine. Would she have time to call Henry and ask him about his gun? It didn't matter. She was going to call him anyway!

After she'd put on water to heat for coffee, she picked up the phone, then put it back down. Exactly what would she say? "Tell me more about your gun" sounded ridiculous. "Why do the police think your gun might have killed

JoAnne?" sounded more sensible, but he probably wouldn't even answer that.

Drop it, she told herself. Who cares, anyway! The man obviously didn't care enough about...didn't want to share his information with...me.

With a twinge, she remembered that he'd asked if she thought his gun killed JoAnne, and she hadn't answered him either. Well, so what, let him think whatever he wanted about that.

She drank her coffee, took a banana for breakfast, and after checking the woodstove went to get dressed for town.

As she was driving the seven miles to Guilford, big flakes of snow began to fall, plopping against the windshield and frosting pasture grasses and treetops. Fortunately they were melting as soon as they hit the road. The radio said temperatures were rising and no accumulation was expected. That was fine with her since she hadn't time to put up with the problems a heavy snowfall would cause.

The business meeting with JoAnne's lawyer took less than an hour. Evan had been right when he said she could leave the whole thing in the lawyer's hands if she wanted to. The fact that he was the same man who'd helped JoAnne prepare the will might have had something to do with it, but he was very matter-of-fact about seeing to all the necessary legal provisions and having her confirmed as executor of the estate. He said under the circumstances he thought she could be allowed access to the house right away.

Before ten o'clock Carrie was on her way to the small Guilford grocery store. She'd promised FatCat a treat for her part in rescuing the box.

After looking at the large selection of pet toys, she decided she agreed with folks who wondered if humanity had lost its wits over cats and dogs. In the four-aisle store, half of one aisle was devoted to pet food and toys. That left three and a half aisles for, presumably, everything the store owner thought people were supposed to need. Absurd. Too often the store didn't have what she came looking for, and she knew why. No room.

She selected a stuffed rubber mouse called "Calico Bounce Toy" (catnip-scented) and a "Kitty Bangle," with white and pink beads and bells strung on an elastic band to be worn like a necklace. The card holding the bangle assured Carrie that now she would always know where her cat was. That wasn't a bad idea, but were bells going to ring if the cat was asleep in the middle of Carrie's down pouf?

Her next stop was at church. The potted plants inside the building were her responsibility, and it was time to water them. When she went into the nursery to tend the philodendron on the window sill, the row of baby beds stopped her. She looked at them thoughtfully, then went to the phone and called the nursery chairman. Ten minutes later she was on her way home with a borrowed baby bed in the back of her station wagon. So far the day was going rather well. She'd have time to clean the guest bedroom and set up the baby bed before she met Shirley at JoAnne's.

Before the afternoon was over, Carrie had decided that if at her age she needed a role model, it would be Shirley Booth. Shirley must have known how difficult facing this cleaning task alone in her dead friend's house would have been for Carrie, but she didn't mention it. The woman took everything in her stride, which Carrie could not have done. Shirley's calm presence and constant woman-talk made the necessary sorting and organizing of JoAnne's possessions possible. Without Shirley, Carrie didn't think she could have made it through the afternoon.

Shirley was even undaunted by the black powder left all over the house as a reminder that the detectives had tested for fingerprints. "We'll just treat it like it was soot from the fireplace," she said, and it was obvious she knew how to deal with that.

The two women chattered like teenagers, and when Carrie told Shirley about Evan's recent interest in her, Shirley had an explanation immediately. "The man's in love with you, pure and simple. He sees himself as the gallant cowboy ready to sweep the lady out of her troubles and ride off with her into the sunset. He thinks you need him now.

"Men want you to need them," Shirley said, looking sideways at Carrie as they wiped tabletops.

Evan in love with her? That certainly hadn't occurred to Carrie. She'd always thought Evan could only love himself, and thinking he might be in love with her made her wince.

The house was in order by four o'clock, in plenty of time for Shirley to get home and meet the milk truck. Engine trouble had kept it from coming that morning, and the driver had called and promised to be at the farm before evening milking began. Shirley needed to be there when he came, since their helper was taking the day off, and Roger would be busy tending the herd.

After Shirley left, Carrie wandered through the house, thinking about JoAnne and the complete lack of any clue to what she had learned that might stop the quarry. She sat down at the desk and decided to look at every single paper it held. She'd looked at things when she piled them back in the drawers earlier in the afternoon, but maybe some scrap of something had slipped by her.

Carrie thought about the reminder notes she often jotted on miscellaneous scraps of paper and decided JoAnne might have done the same thing. She doubted if the sheriff's men would have noticed anything like that, especially if the note seemed insignificant.

She began a methodical search, looking at the front and back of every piece of paper and envelope in the desk. When she came to the collection of mail that had been on the desk Saturday morning, she remembered the lawyer said she was supposed to take care of JoAnne's bills. She decided to check inside the envelopes, which had been slit open.

And there it was. A penciled note on the back of the electric bill in JoAnne's handwriting: "Head rights for minerals!!! Old farm, 6:30, morning."

JoAnne had probably pulled out the bill, then laid it aside and put the note on it later, perhaps when someone called.

Head rights was a term Carrie knew. In Oklahoma it meant each member of a Native American tribe benefitted from the sale or lease of something of value the tribe owned in common—kind of like shares. In fact, she knew an Osage woman who had inherited head rights for minerals on property in Osage County, Oklahoma. As a result, the woman had a very comfortable income from oil lease money that had been invested. But here? Carrie had never heard of head rights being allotted for minerals in Arkansas. She'd call the university first thing tomorrow and ask someone about it.

"Old farm, 6:30." 6:30 Saturday morning? That was early, but JoAnne had been an early riser, and she'd have needed to finish whatever this was before coming to the meeting at Carrie's.

Should someone be told about the note?

Henry and Jason had gone to town and would probably stay there for dinner. Roger was out with the herd, and Shirley was busy with the milk truck. No one to tell now. Later tonight, maybe. And, she'd take the note with her since it was on an electric bill she must pay.

For now, she might just drive down to the old farm and look around. It had been some time since she'd actually walked around down there, and she was curious as the dickens. The sheriff's men could have missed some important clue. Perhaps she could find out what it was JoAnne had discovered, and that would make everything clear. Whatever else it meant, wouldn't it prove to Henry King she was a very capable woman, one who could be trusted with information about his gun...or his life?

It would be getting dark soon. She'd have to hurry.

CHAPTER XIV

It wasn't until she was bumping along the lane to the old barn that Carrie remembered Roger's warning that no one should go to the proposed quarry site alone. For just a moment she slowed her station wagon, but then decided since she hadn't seen trucks or cars anywhere, and certainly no outsider would walk here from any distance, there could not possibly be danger. Just twenty-four hours ago men from the sheriff's department had been all over the place. No one would come here now. Except she would, of course, because she had a reason.

She parked her wagon by the remains of a corral fence near the barn. She could check the barn later. Probably Taylor and the others pretty much tore it apart after finding JoAnne's truck there anyway. But perhaps they hadn't looked as carefully in other places on the old farm.

She headed toward the foundation of the house, glad she had on heavy jeans and boots. The dry brush was tall in spots, though it had obviously been trampled, and the scattering of rocks and pieces of rusted metal would have made walking difficult in anything but boots.

The day had remained cloudy, but now the setting sun slanted through a gap in the purpling clouds and illuminated the naked chimney. The old bricks were a warm rosy color. JoAnne had told her they were made from clay dug near Walden Creek. Maybe a loose brick had fallen somewhere, and she could take it home and put it in the rock garden in front of her house. The quarry people certainly wouldn't care about a brick since they were planning to blast the place to bits anyway.

Attracted by the idea of saving one of the historic bricks, she started around the chimney, looking at the ground and wondering how many years ago the house had burned.

As she came to the old hearth, she nearly fell over a pile of rocks. Someone had been digging and, from the looks of things, very recently, since dirt on the rocks was damp. She looked around but saw no person and no tools anywhere. It was all right then. Whoever it was had gone.

She kicked at the pile, trying to figure out why someone would be digging, but all she uncovered were more rocks. Maybe she'd have time to come back with a pick and shovel tomorrow while Susan was tending to the baby and getting settled. Maybe Henry would come with her, or even, maybe, Shirley would keep the baby and Susan could come too. Carrie smiled, thinking of this prospect. At the very least, now Henry and Susan would get to know each other, even though Susan could have no idea of their real relationship.

She looked around again. The angle of a weak sunbeam highlighted a track of broken weeds and pasture grass that led toward the bluff and the trees along the creek.

Glancing at the sky, Carrie decided she had several minutes before dark. She headed off, following the rough path.

When she got to the creek bank, there were more signs that rocks had been disturbed. Could the quarry people have done it, making tests or something?

It was already quite dark in the shelter of the bluffs, and barred owls in the woods above her were beginning to call. Ordinarily Carrie would have called back, but she didn't have time now for a conversation with owls. When she was outside at dusk, she sometimes mimicked the owls, and they came to the trees over her head. Of course, she hadn't the slightest idea what the conversation was about and often wondered if the owls did.

She looked up toward the overhang that marked a cave entrance on the face of the bluff. Shadows accented a path slanting upward until it reached the overhang and the dark hole behind it. For how many centuries had people walked up and down that path? Anyone sitting on the overhang could see the whole valley, a good vantage point.

Sadly, if the quarry came, all this would be destroyed, blasted into oblivion to make nothing but gravel.

She began pushing piles of stone around with the toe of her boot, but, here in the shadows, it was almost too dark to see. Too bad she hadn't thought to bring a trowel and flashlight. She'd have to leave soon. In the country, dark meant no light at all unless there was a moon, and tonight clouds covered stars and a waning moon. She couldn't even see the Booths' farm lights from here.

A sudden rustle in the dry underbrush caused her to start, and her boot dug sharply into the pile of rocks she had been kicking at. Some nocturnal animal had come out to hunt for food.

She looked down and saw a curving shape near the toe of her boot. Surely not a shell, not here. She picked the curved thing up, brushed it off with her gloved hand, then took off a glove to feel. Smooth, with slight circling swirls. In the faint light it looked like a shallow bowl.

Her heart thumped. Pottery! That must mean some kind of Indian camp. She *had* found something important. She wrapped the bowl in a facial tissue and tucked it away in her pocket, counting on the heavy jacket to help protect it from harm.

She could no longer see her station wagon in the distance, but, more by instinct than sight, she headed back toward the old barn, first feeling carefully to be sure her key was still in the pocket of her jeans. As she walked back toward the barn, she thought she heard a metallic clink. She stopped to listen and decided it had been the sound of her wagon's engine cooling.

Everything was very quiet as she approached the old corral. The wagon was barely visible. Only a dark blob against the weathered boards of the barn revealed its location. She leaned against the driver's door, reaching in her pocket for the key.

She was just touching the key when a rush of movement came around behind her, and before she could turn, a dark fuzzy something had been pulled over her head, knocking her cap off and covering her eyes and mouth.

She was able to cry out, and the person behind her made no effort to stop her, realizing as Carrie did at once, that there would be no one to hear. Now her mouth was full of woolly fibers. She gagged, then choked, and took an involuntary, gasping breath. Whatever it was covering her head smelled awful.

The attacker grabbed her shoulders and pushed her,

front forward, against the curving side of the wagon. He leaned against her, using the force of his body weight to keep her immobile while he yanked her hands back and up. She cried out in pain as her shoulders twisted.

Now her hands were being tied with what felt like nylon fishing line. It was wound around each wrist, then between her hands and looped over and over before it was knotted. Carrie counted five knots and winced. The line was thin and had already cut into her bare flesh.

Repeatedly, she tried to kick backward at her enemy, but found that her weight was so off balance she could barely move her feet. When she finally managed one feeble blow, the man, because by now the pressure of his body against hers had made her certain it was a man, kicked her sharply in the ankle.

Her mind was racing, a survival instinct taking over even as she was being tied. Terror was her biggest enemy now. Oh, dear God! Why was the man doing this? She had been leaving, why had he stopped her? She shouldn't have come here alone! Why hadn't she listened...been more sensible...not so eager to rush into things? Oh, *why*!

She began to pray silently and tried to decide if she was afraid of dying. Then the man suddenly backed away from her, and she fell sideways. Her shoulder struck the hood of the wagon, but she could barely feel it. Her heavy jacket and whatever had been tied over her head did at least end up being a lot of padding, she realized, not without gratitude, as she slid to the rocky ground.

She lay still, trying to control her trembling body as a flashlight raked over her, and she listened to the man's heavy breathing. Maybe he would think she was unconscious.

One thing was sure—her attacker was strong, though he was much shorter and less bulky than Henry.

The man stood over her for a long time, and Carrie could hear his breathing slowing down. What was he thinking? Trying to decide whether or not to kill her? But why would he kill her? She couldn't think of a single reason. Certainly not because of a piece of pottery!

The man couldn't know she had it.

Just as she was thinking that, she heard him kneel beside her. He pushed her over on her back, sat on her legs, and began to search her pockets. He found the tissue-wrapped bowl first, and she could sense that he was inspecting it in the beam of his flashlight.

She heard him put it in his own pocket, then he began going through the rest of her jacket pockets, where he found only her glove and facial tissues, and finally her jeans pockets. It was hard not to shudder as she felt his fingers through the thin cloth of the jeans pocket lining.

The contact must have affected him too because he hesitated, not long, but long enough for her to be sure he was aware his moving fingers were touching her intimately through the light-weight fabric. What was he thinking? Rape? Did that happen to women her age? Oh, yes, yes, it did. She had read recently that rape was more often about power than it was sex, and then it didn't matter much what age the victim was...or what she looked like.

Now it was nearly impossible to control her body enough to keep it from trembling.

After a very long moment the man removed his fingers and checked her second jeans pocket. When he found the key to her station wagon, Carrie almost recoiled in terror as she thought of her purse on the seat, and her house key inside the purse.

Suddenly the man paused as both he and Carrie heard the roar of a truck engine in the distance and a horn tooting twice in quick succession. Her key clinked to the ground, and the man's feet pounded away as he ran to-ward—she concentrated, thinking of directions—as he ran toward the old barn. A metal door slammed, then a car—no, probably a truck—started, reversed, and raced past her, the tires coming so close that she could hear the spray of gravel they threw against her jacket as they picked up speed.

Then everything was quiet. Very quiet. The truck that had sent the man running was gone too. Carrie was alone.

She was lying on her tied hands, which was terribly painful, so the first thing she did was sit up, digging into the ground with her heels and lifting her upper body. A few movements of her arms and wrists told her that the more she tried to free her hands, the more the line cut, so she stopped struggling.

She tried to think which direction the station wagon would be. After deciding it must be behind her, she began bumping her rear end painfully across the rocky ground, scooting in what she hoped was the right way. She could stand and walk, but then she'd lose contact with the only reference point she could figure out with certainty—the ground that was beneath her.

After about five bumps and bounces she knew she must be going the wrong direction and stopped to think again. She was facing the wagon when she fell over, then he rolled her on her back, and...yes, she was going the wrong way...that is, she was if she hadn't bounced at an angle. Several more bounces brought her up against the front bumper, and, enjoying the small amount of heat still ra-diating from the engine, she sat still, leaning against the hard surface, thinking about what to do next.

If only she hadn't locked the car. But locking it was automatic when she left her purse inside.

Oh, no, thought Carrie. The car key! She'd heard it drop, and it would have been easy to locate if only she'd felt around before she moved. If she had it in her fingers, she could back up to the lock and open the door. Then there'd be somewhere to sit, somewhere to stay out of the cold. And, she could probably manage to honk the horn.

Carrie shifted as the point of a rock dug into her behind, and she tried to think where the key might be. She started to open her mouth for a real, no-matter-what wail, and, just in time, remembered the disgusting taste of her woolly mask. Well, at least she could breathe, there was that to be grateful for, even if her head covering did have an awful smell. The line holding it around her neck was tight, but the mask itself kept the ties from cutting her.

She sat in silence for a few minutes. Her hands were beginning to feel numb. She wiggled her fingers, trying to wrap her bare right hand in the gloved left one. She'd just have to find that key and get into the wagon! But she dreaded bumping back across the ground and wasn't sure of the distance to where the key had dropped. Oh, why hadn't the man tied her hands in front? Then she'd be able to crawl and feel. Did she dare leave the small but familiar comfort of her own station wagon and its waning engine warmth?

And how long would it be before somebody began to look for her? That was one problem of living alone. No one missed you for a long, long time if you got in trouble. Tears began to seep into the woolly mask. She thought of crying into Henry's big, wide chest.

"Carrie's the stoic." She could hear Amos saying it. "The stoic, the stoic." Oh, no, no, no!

Maybe searching for the key would help keep her warm.

She gave a determined shove against the bumper and began to bounce in the direction of the driver's door, wishing she'd worn heavier underpants and her long underwear. At least they would have been some protection against the rocks. She tried getting on her knees. That made moving easier, but the rocks felt even sharper on her kneecaps, where neither flesh nor clothing offered any worthwhile padding at all.

When she reached what she guessed was her original location, she rolled on her side and inched along, feeling for the key with her bare right hand.

In a few minutes she had to stop and rest. It was hopeless! But at least movement was making her warmer. She'd have to keep trying.

After a long time, scooting and feeling, she gave up. She wasn't going to find the key.

Wearily she made her way back to the station wagon and leaned against the door. She wiggled her fingers, trying to warm them. It was easier to wiggle now, because she could no longer feel the line cutting into her wrists.

She tried standing for a while, pushing her body up against the side of the wagon, but there was a breeze, and standing only made her colder. Finally she just sat in silence, her mind almost blank, until her head dropped forward and she fell into a semi-conscious doze.

In a troubled dream, Henry was scolding her for going to the old farm by herself. Well, she thought, he's right, and this time, I must tell him he is. I'll tell him right away!

She heard Shirley's voice saying, "Men want you to need them," and thought, Please, God, I need someone very badly tonight.

She jerked her head up and cracked it against the station wagon door. Wide awake now, she sat listening to a black night where not even owls talked to her and tried to control a body that was shaking violently with cold.

Chapter XV

Time ceased to have any meaning for Carrie. In between pondering the events of the past four days, she prayed, recited Bible verses, and sang hymns to herself. She was fighting panic as well as an urge to close her eyes and drift into unconsciousness, and she hoped keeping her thoughts active would help. She kept telling herself that she needed to be alert and aware of her surroundings. Yes, and wiggle hands, legs, feet, hands, legs, feet. So cold...

Think... She couldn't brag about being strong now. She just felt like crying and crying. Her life sure had changed. City housewives didn't get into this kind of mess!

Tears made her cheeks feel like ice, and she couldn't blow her nose if she cried, so she began saying the words of the 91st Psalm, learned in Sunday School so many years ago:

"He that dwelleth in the secret place of the most High shall abide under the shadow of the Almighty.

"I will say of the Lord, He is my refuge and my for-
tress: my God; in him will I trust.

"Surely he shall deliver thee..."

She stopped. Trust. *Oh, dear God, this can't be beyond
you! Almighty...all mighty, I will trust, and...that's all I have
right now.*

She had to stay alert, keep her spirits up.

Her thoughts went back to the pottery she'd found.
She knew what it was as soon as she felt it because of a
similar pot Evan had given to Amos and her a number of
years ago.

Evan often spent three or more weeks in Arizona during the winter, and one of his favorite activities was pot
hunting. Not the archaeology kind of hunting, the shopping kind. One year he had brought them a lovely little
black pot made at the pueblo of San Ildefonso near Santa
Fe. It wasn't by Maria, the internationally known potter of
San Ildefonso, but that didn't matter at all to Carrie.

She loved rubbing the pot's glossy surface. It had been
coiled rather than thrown on a potter's wheel, then
smoothed with a small wood paddle and with fingertips.
The surface looked quite regular, but those who touched it
and rubbed fingers around its circular form could find the
irregularities—something like the small irregularities in a
chubby baby's skin, Carrie thought. Indeed, the pot's surface did seem almost soft if you didn't rub too hard.

Carrie still had the San Ildefonso pot. She could picture it now, sitting on the bookshelf in the main room of
her house. She usually took time to run her fingers across
it when she dusted the shelves.

She was startled when she heard a small whimper and
understood that it was hers.

Would she ever dust that pot again?

She forced her thoughts back to more positive specula-tion. Of course, the piece of pottery she had found by the bank of Walden Creek wasn't black. It had been, the best she could tell in the dim light, almost rosy in color, some-thing like the brick in the old chimney. She'd have to ask Evan about the color. He'd be interested in what she'd found since he collected pottery.

Her attacker had taken the pot, so that probably meant it was very important. Was it proof there were once Native Americans living in the area, and would something to do with that stop the quarry? Carrie decided the man must have been the quarry owner since he didn't want her to have the pot she'd found on his land.

Her head jerked downward as she started to doze. She pushed herself upright and began saying verses from the 91st Psalm again:

"...shall deliver thee from the snare of the fowler, and from the noisome pestilence."

Here Carrie, without realizing it, switched to first per-son:

"He shall cover me with his feathers, and under his wings I will trust: his truth shall be my shield and buckler. I will not be afraid for the terror by night..."

Years ago, she'd resisted memorizing all those verses in Sunday School, but her teacher said she'd be glad some day. Well, Mrs. Butler had been right, she was glad now.

"Because...the Lord...is my refuge, even the most High, my habitation;

"There shall no evil befall me...

"For he shall give his angels charge over me, to keep me in all his ways.

"They shall bear me up in their hands, when I dash my foot against a stone."

Trust. Even here, even now. God was here.

Carrie began to feel warmer, calmer.

"...He has set his love upon me...I will answer him...he is with me in trouble..."

Trust completely, she thought, but why only now, in trouble? Why don't I do this all the time?

It hadn't occurred to her that her assailant would come back, not until she heard a truck engine in the distance.

The urge to stand and run was almost overwhelming, but where? Could she get to the old barn? How would she know she was really hidden if she couldn't see?

But she had to hide somewhere. If she could just get out of the awful head cover! The cord around her neck felt like it was getting tighter—it was almost choking her.

Under the station wagon! It would be a poor hiding place if someone really hunted her, but where else could she go? She might as well be blind. For her, there was nowhere else! If she lay on her stomach, she could use her toes to shove herself under the wagon.

She fell on her side, then flipped over on her stomach. Painfully she pushed forward until her body was under the wagon. Rocks banged her cheek as she turned her head to keep from hitting the metal frame.

The vehicle was coming very slowly. She wondered, too late, if her wagon was high enough for headlights to shine under it as they approached the farmyard. Well, she'd done the best she could. She had to trust. Had to.

She laid her head against the ground. He was going to kill her now...for no reason. She didn't know anything, she didn't, she didn't...her twirling thoughts skittered and screamed, then once again, she thought of God's presence and became completely quiet.

The vehicle came into the farmyard and stopped. Tears

melted into her mask. She prayed, *Please help me, oh, please,* and then, eyes shut, she waited.

Two doors slammed and a bright light hit her. Dear God, oh, dear God...he'll cover me with his feathers.

Then, she heard Henry's blessed, wonderful voice calling, "Cara! Carrie!" followed by Roger's voice saying, "Here, under the car," and two sets of feet thudding toward her. She heard Henry say, oddly echoing her own words, "Dear God." And, "She moved, oh, thank you, God!"

She heard both men kneel at the edge of the car.

There was silence for a moment before Henry spoke again, very calmly and slowly, "Carrie, can you hear me? Are you hurt anywhere?"

She heard her own voice saying, "No," and ignored the taste of the mask.

Hands reached her, touching her more gently than she thought possible. In a minute Henry was holding her against his familiar rough jacket while Roger cut the ties on her wrists and neck and murmured, "Look at that, would you!" to Henry. Then the awful woolly thing was off her head, and Henry was smoothing her hair with his big hand. He carried her to the truck like a child and held her in his arms while Roger drove away from the farmyard.

Finally, she managed to say, "My key," and Henry, who for some reason understood at once, said, "Yes, Roger found it in the dirt. I'll come get your car in a bit. First, let's take you to Shirley. She's waiting."

For a while things were a blur. Shirley helped her get out of her torn and filthy clothes and into a tub full of hot water. "May hurt," said Shirley, "but use that soap good on your wrists." Then Carrie sat docilely, wrapped in a flannel gown and robe that had belonged to one of the Booth girls, while Shirley smoothed salve on her wrists and covered them in gauze.

After putting on a pair of Roger's socks and Shirley's slippers, Carrie insisted she could walk just fine and flapped into the living room. She sat in front of the fireplace eating a bowl of stew with biscuits and applesauce and listened while Henry and Roger told their part of the story.

Henry had called her, as promised, when he got back from Bonny about seven o'clock. When she still didn't answer at 7:30, he would wait no longer and drove to Carrie's house, then JoAnne's. Seeing neither activity nor car at either place, he headed to Roger and Shirley's, where Shirley told him she had left Carrie alone in JoAnne's house around four. Then he and Roger began a search, and the first place that seemed logical was the old farm.

No one rushed Carrie into telling what had happened to her, but when Henry, who was sitting beside her holding the plate of biscuits where she could reach them, finished the account of what he and Roger had done, he asked if she felt like talking about what had happened. "I called the sheriff's office while you were in the tub," he said. "I should have called earlier, but seeing that you were safe and taken care of seemed more important.

"I haven't gone for your station wagon yet because I didn't want to risk destroying evidence. The man undoubtedly wore gloves, but maybe he dropped something or left a shoe print somewhere."

"His truck was hidden in the old barn," Carrie said. "He ran to it and drove off when we both heard a motor and horn in the distance. Did any of you see him leave? It was about dark."

"You must have heard the milk truck," Shirley said.

"The driver was still way off his schedule, thank the Lord, for it sounds like his truck is what scared the man away. I didn't see anything else. As soon as the milk truck left, I came right in the house to finish making the stew. I don't reckon Roger saw anything either since he was in the barn."

Roger shook his head. "Nope. Didn't. Sure am sorry. All the activity on this road, I'm goin' to have to put up a guard house out there."

"It must have been the quarry owner who tied me," Carrie said. "What was over my head?"

The two men looked at each other. Finally, Henry said, "JoAnne's stocking cap, the heavy red wool one with the rolled edge. He simply unrolled it.

"But," he added quickly, understanding as her eyes widened in horror, "she didn't have it on when she was shot. It smelled funny though. Did she get permanents or color her hair? Smelled like beauty shop stuff. Irena's hair smelled that way sometimes after she'd been to the beauty shop."

Of course, that was it, the funny smell! Relieved by the commonplace origin of her head covering and its odor, but puzzled by the cap's availability since the sheriff's men had searched the barn and surrounding area, Carrie said, almost to herself, "Wonder why he had JoAnne's cap." Then she dropped the subject and told the story of her ordeal, including her feeling that someone should return to look for evidence of more pottery before the quarry owner could come back and destroy it all.

"Maybe that's our proof, what JoAnne found," Roger said after she had finished. "I don't know what the man was doin' there, but it's possible he was huntin' around fer more pots as you say. Darn trouble is, this time of year, anyone can come and go around here without notice since there's so many hunters out. Lots of trucks from all over, and any one of 'em could be the quarry owner. The man wouldn't need to look at night, though, would he? It would make sense fer him to be on his own property during the day, but not at night."

"Jason and I did find out something very interesting today," Henry said. "We went to the court house in Bonny, and they gave us quite a surprise about that old farm, which was confirmed by the real estate agency that handled the sale.

"The farm property was inherited in equal parts by the five children of the couple who lived there when the house burned over forty years ago. The old couple died a few months apart, some five years after the fire, and the kids inherited. They didn't sell, and my guess is that at least one of the heirs didn't want to, because nothing happened until a couple of them were gone too. The remaining heirs put the land on the market then and it sold about ten years ago—to Mag and Jack Bruner!" He paused, but no one spoke.

"Maybe they bought it, thinking they might eventually settle in the valley, I don't know. But, anyway, the Bruners are the ones who sold the land to the quarry company."

Shirley and Carrie just stared at Henry, but Roger said in a low voice, "Hmmmm, sorta suspected somethin' like that way in the back of my head. Just felt it. That's one reason I thought the five of us should go this alone without the Bruners, though I didn't want to say so since I only had suspicions. The gal at the court house couldn't tell me who had sold the land when I was there. Maybe they didn't have the records done yet, or she just didn't know how to look.

"I've seen Jack down on the old farm quite a bit, and he's baled hay there fer several years. When I asked him about that, he said he was gettin' hay rights from the owner. Guess he was! But, I didn't think much of it since it's common to sell hay off unused land, and if the man didn't want to talk about it, well, I won't talk much about my business to others neither. Finally all the little things got me to thinkin', though, and I'm not surprised, though I didn't know enough to make any speech about it."

"Well, *I'm* surprised," Carrie said. "It's terrible! Why on earth would Mag want to be on our committee? Spy? That's ridiculous, isn't it, unless she was afraid we'd spoil the sale, and they'd have to give the money back."

No one had an answer. Just then a knock at the door told them someone, probably Sergeant Don Taylor, had arrived. Carrie looked at the clock. Her long ordeal had taken only three hours. It wasn't ten o'clock yet!

Sure enough, the resonant voice at the door belonged to Taylor. She wondered if he'd been spending a quiet evening at home when Henry called. She also wondered how many peaceful evenings Henry spent at home when he was a policeman. She tried to picture Henry sitting in a living room with a shadowy woman named Irena and couldn't.

Carrie repeated her story to Taylor, explaining in response to his question that her sole reason for going to the farm had been to see if she could find out what good news JoAnne had for them. She told him about the note on the back of the electric bill, which was still in her purse locked inside the station wagon. When he left, he said men were already searching the old farm. Henry went with him to bring Carrie's purse and station wagon back.

Evidently, quick checking of the wagon had told the detectives the man who tied Carrie left no marks on it. In less than an hour, Henry was back, ready to drive Carrie home. She insisted she could drive herself and, after squeezing her own boots on over Roger's socks and thanking the Booths with a fervor she certainly felt, she tucked her borrowed robe around her, threw her dirty clothing in the back of her wagon, and headed for home.

Henry followed close behind and got out of his car to walk with her to the door. He came inside without asking and insisted on going through every room to check windows and doors. "I think I should spend the night here," he said. "I can sleep on the couch."

"Goodness, no, I'm fine," she said, hoping she meant it but not really one hundred percent sure.

They sat in the two chairs by the woodstove, and Carrie found his presence quite comforting, even if she was fine.

It was wonderful to feel safe and warm again.

"When does Susan come?" he asked.

"The plane's supposed to be in at eleven."

"I think I should go to the airport with you. I can come along and drive your car. You've had quite an ordeal, after all."

Carrie was sure his wish to come with her had to do with more than her ordeal, but she didn't say so. She'd welcome his company on the hour-long drive to the airport, and the sooner he and Susan met, the better.

She asked if he didn't agree with her that they should do more looking on the old farm for pottery, or other evidence of Native American inhabitants.

"Yes, but I also told Taylor that there might be something of that nature. They'll keep their eyes open. If burial remains or anything else of historic significance is found, they'll notify the Arkansas Archeological Survey."

"Do you know if they've found out anything, any clue to who might have killed JoAnne?"

"Suspicions only, and Charles Stoker, the quarry owner, is on top of the list. Jason and I stopped in today and talked with Storm. He's a haughty sort of fellow, but very intelligent. He seems to be good at his job. I respect the man. He showed me the photographs taken where you found JoAnne. She was almost certainly put on the hill some time about dawn on Sunday morning. They could guess it from the fact you had seen a crushed frost flower under her hand, of course, but there was lots of other evidence. Did you notice that her clothing wasn't damp on top?"

"No."

"It wasn't, and the leaves under her looked like they had been damp with frost when they were disturbed, and so did those on the path down from the fire road. The photos showed that too. There was some general frost early on Sunday, and the leaves were damp for a while, but they hadn't been the night before, and they weren't later in the morning when you came along."

"Have they any idea why she was moved there?"

"No, but Carrie, it almost seems as if someone wanted you to be the one to find JoAnne. How many people know when and where you usually walk in the woods? Have you thought about how carefully the body was placed near a path that you—you and JoAnne—have made? Another thing, with her red coat on someone might have noticed her from a distance. Without it, well, you'd almost have to be on your path to see her. I can think of no other reason someone would bother to take off her coat.

"And you say she was put almost exactly where Amos was shot. Can you think why someone might have done that?"

"Goodness, no. It has to have been a coincidence."

"Who knows where Amos was found?"

"JoAnne knew, and I'm sure she told Mag because Mag walked with us occasionally, and once she asked me if it bothered me, walking past that place. Either of them could have told other people, and," she hesitated, thinking about it, "Mag could have told Charles Stoker, the quarry owner, couldn't she?"

"Does it bother you, walking there?"

"Not any more. I can't erase the memory, but it's all been way in the background—or was until Sunday."

Henry spoke slowly. "The thing is, there just doesn't seem to be any reason the body would be put in that spot unless it has a connection with you. It would have been so much easier to leave her in the truck. That's why I think moving her is connected—maybe it was done to frighten you. Otherwise, it makes no sense at all."

"Well, I don't see any purpose. If it has to do with me, the killer lost what he intended, because I don't get the point. Maybe the quarry owner just wants to scare the whole committee, including me. But, murder?"

An odd thought struck her. "Henry, did you think I killed her?"

"You had no reason to, did you?"

"No, I didn't, but you haven't answered my question."

He looked at her sideways. "Well, I certainly can't see you with a gun." His eyes were sad as he continued. "I do know you suspected me. You didn't answer when I asked if you thought my gun had killed JoAnne."

She didn't say anything, but the feeling of remorse must have been obvious in her face, because he smiled before he went on. "Sometimes reasons for murder and the person-alities of people who kill are about as far from what you'd suspect as possible—on the surface, at least."

"Well, I worried when Don Taylor wanted your gun. I spent half of last night sleepless over that. Tell me, what about your gun?"

"They needed to test it since it shoots the same type of bullet that killed JoAnne, but, of course, testing proved it wasn't the murder weapon. Storm gave it back today."

"I guess the gun is one only policemen would have?"

"No, it's fairly common. You could buy one."

When she looked startled, he said, "Oh, Carrie, I didn't think...a .38 Police Special...did you suppose only someone who was with the police would have one, someone like me?"

"Yes."

"I'm so sorry, I never thought..." He hesitated. "But I'm glad you cared enough to worry. It's been a long time since anyone worried about me like that."

How sad, she thought, and said, "Don't apologize. I do understand. All I was thinking last night seems pretty overblown now. Besides, you haven't told me yet how stupid I was to go to the old farm."

"You know how very dangerous it was."

He didn't say I was stupid, she thought, at least not out loud.

They smiled at each other, almost shyly, it seemed to Carrie. She knew she felt—suddenly and surprisingly— shy. Then Henry stood up and said, "I'm going home and get a few things, then come back and stay on your couch. Do you have a sheet to throw over it and a couple of blankets?"

"Henry, there's the guest bedroom."

"No, I saw you had the room ready for Susan and the baby. I spent lots of nights on the couch in my office at the police station. I can sleep almost anywhere after that. You go on to bed. I won't be long."

Carrie found a house key for him, let him out the door, and went to get a pillow and blankets. Then she sat in her chair by the woodstove wondering about head rights, and a piece of pottery, and why JoAnne's body had been brought to her woods.

Most of all, though, she was waiting for Henry to come back.

CHAPTER XVI

Carrie's furry slippers were silent on the hall rug as she walked to the door and peeked around the corner.

Well, that was no surprise. Henry was gone, and the blankets, pillow, and sheets were folded and stacked neatly at the end of the couch. He'd said last night he would go home to get ready for the drive to the airport as soon as he awakened. It was actually a relief to find him gone. She needed to be alone with her thoughts this morning.

FatCat rose from her down pillow as Carrie came into the room, angled her legs back and forth, yawned, then trotted over to help inspect the wood stove. She sat down at the edge of the stone flooring, looked up, and said, "Yowp," which Carrie interpreted as an affirmative comment.

Yes, she agreed with the cat, it was nice. Henry had refilled the wood box and got the fire going.

The clock said 8:30. She'd overslept again. Twinges from

various places on her body had awakened her during the night, and, once awake, she got so involved in fretting over her circumstances that she couldn't go back to sleep.

Most of all, she was upset because the stiff backbone she'd depended on all these years seemed to have collapsed. Even Amos's death hadn't broken through her usual ability to maintain at least a surface calm. So what was wrong now?

Was it simply that, for the first time in her life, a man had hugged and comforted her and then had carried her out of danger like a child?

Well, she thought, the fact I was in danger was my own fault. I needed help, Henry came, and that's why things are all going backwards. Be grateful, and then forget it.

It wouldn't happen again.

In the quiet room she imagined she heard Shirley's voice: "Men want you to need them." But how would a woman who didn't have a man get along in life if she crumpled the minute some difficulty appeared? Women *had* to be strong on their own. Collapsing in tears never helped solve things.

"Want you to need them." Did that mean you just let them think you needed them? Well, she was incapable of pretending she was helpless. You couldn't let a man take over your life or you'd lose your independence—she and JoAnne had agreed on that.

Henry and she were good friends, that was all. She didn't dare want anything more.

Besides, she'd told herself during the night, she was perfectly safe now, in her own home, lying under her pouffy comforter. Henry was sleeping just down the hall, though of course she didn't really need a guard.

Then—alone in the dark—she shivered with the icy

chill of the night's terror and thought of Henry's arms around her, carrying her out of danger, taking her to safety and warmth.

She'd turned on her side and started to curl up, pushing away thoughts of being close to Henry, but her bruised knees complained, so she straightened her legs.

All right. She had needed someone last night. She'd been stupid, going to the old farm alone. It was too late to change what had happened. Now what she needed was to put the night behind her and move on.

If she succeeded in helping find JoAnne's killer, it would still prove her strength and capability to Henry, and to her family and friends. She had to remain strong. Her very life here in the woods depended on it. She couldn't give in to masculine ideas of mushy female weakness.

And, she realized as she lay in the dark, she had the advantage of information and insights that others didn't.

For one thing, Henry's suggestion that the attacks could be directed at her personally was impossible. She knew that, even if he didn't. Henry would be looking for a connection, and she already knew there wasn't one.

So, what next? Might as well make plans, since she couldn't sleep.

JoAnne had wanted her to know about Susan's background and saw to it she found out. She also made sure Carrie would feel duty bound not to tell Susan, but there should be some other way to bring father and daughter together.

Well, of course! JoAnne had never said or written she couldn't talk to Henry about his daughter. She would start by doing that, find out what he knew, what he'd done so far. Something would work out.

The quarry. It must be stopped. They had to draw a

line somewhere, before this entire part of the Ozarks was logged, blasted, and paved. Most people just didn't care enough and wouldn't wake up in time. The five of them were probably closer to learning JoAnne's secret than they knew. They'd surely find whatever it was—they had to.

And, most important, they would find out who killed JoAnne. The best prospect was the quarry owner, Charles Stoker. And if they caught him, that solved two problems. How could a convicted murderer build a quarry anywhere?

She'd figure out a way to meet and talk with Stoker. She was sure she'd feel something, recall some little thing that she'd noticed about him last night. But would anything she remembered be a real help to the sheriff? Henry could tell her that. He would know if a victim's memory of little details worked as evidence.

Comforted by what she considered her well-thought-out plan for action, Carrie finally fell asleep.

So now she was up and ready to deal with whatever Wednesday was going to bring.

She went to the kitchen and fed FatCat. Carrie hoped the cat had elected to spend the night in her own bed and not with Henry on the couch. At least she hadn't tried her already well-established nightly routine of trouncing around on Carrie's bed until, after repeated removal and loud admonitions, she finally retired to her pillow-padded basket in the cabin's main room.

Carrie was just finishing a bowl of cereal when she heard a car and peeked out the window. Henry was back.

She rinsed her dish quickly and went to the door.

"Good morning," she said. "I'm running a bit late, but was just going to get dressed. Thanks for fixing the woodstove. I'm not sure I could do it yet."

"You're welcome. I was hoping I'd get here in time to

put fresh bandages on your wrists before you were all dressed. I think it'd be best if you put on everything but your shirt, then got back into your robe and let me do the bandaging. Or, um, do you need help getting dressed?"

"Oh, no," she said, "but I may be a bit slower than usual. While you're waiting, would you mind calling the university and see if you can locate someone who's able to tell us about state laws governing Indian remains? Rob said probably the anthropology or archeology departments. You might ask them about head rights too. Do they apply here?" She pointed. "The phone book is in that drawer."

As she was leaving, she thought of something else and stuck her head back around the corner. "I wonder if we should bring Jason up to date?"

"Already have," said Henry, as he picked up the phone book.

Getting dressed wasn't easy, but finally everything went together, and she was ready. She put her robe back on, rolled the sleeves up, and stuck gauze, tape, and scissors in the pocket.

Henry was still on the phone when she got back to the main room.

She crawled up on a kitchen chair and, so he wouldn't have to stoop while fixing her bandages, turned, sat down on the table top, put her knees together primly, her stocking feet in the chair, and waited.

She heard him thanking someone, then he came and began telling her what he'd learned as he unrolled the gauze.

"Talked to a professor of anthropology who does archeological evaluation for the state. There was a law passed in 1991 that prohibits desecration or commercial use of skeletal and other burial remains found on either public or private land. But after studies are done and artifacts taken care of, original plans for use of the land can normally be continued. The professor also said he'd never heard of head rights being applied here.

"I'd guess that whatever we might find could serve as a nuisance and delay for the quarry owners, but wouldn't necessarily stop their plans. And it's very curious JoAnne wrote down the term *head rights* if it doesn't apply at all. Maybe someone just told her it did."

He stuck down the last piece of tape. "There, you're fixed. Your wrists look good. The cuts are closed, and there's no evidence of infection."

She was paying no attention to her wrists. "Well, if Charles Stoker is a murderer and we prove it, then that'll sure stop the quarry, won't it? I was certain I'd found a solution when I saw that piece of pottery, but now it looks like we just have to work doubly hard to convict a murderer. I'd like to meet Stoker. Maybe something about him would remind me of the man who tied me up last night. Would doing that help prove his connection to JoAnne's murder?"

Henry didn't answer her question. Instead, he said, "Oh. I haven't had a chance to tell you yet, but Taylor called this morning and told me they talked to Stoker and he says he was hunting Saturday and Sunday. Alone. He says he didn't kill any deer so didn't go to a check station. They don't know where he was last night yet. His wife says he was gone for a couple of hours, but he didn't tell her where he was—or she didn't care enough to ask. He'd left for the Missouri quarry when Taylor called this morning. By the way, the drive from Stoker's home to our valley takes about thirty minutes. Taylor timed it Monday."

"Hmmm," she said. "Well, it sounds like finding remains of any historic significance won't help much, but if that's the case, why did he steal my piece of pottery?"

"*Whose* piece of pottery?" asked Henry, and she bit her lip in frustration.

"All right, I guess it was on his land, but I've seen pottery of that sort before, and I like it. If it won't be any help stopping the quarry, he probably knows that already."

"Oh, it might be some good. Taylor told me if the deputies or one of us do find anything significant, then construction and blasting have to be halted while any remains of archeological significance are studied and identified and proper disposition is made. All of that, of course, is what your son and the professor have suggested. It's possible such studies might delay the quarry owner's plans long enough that he'd want to go elsewhere.

"I called Jason this morning and told him about what happened last night and what we'd learned. He thought we should try to locate an alternate site for the quarry, one that wouldn't ruin a valuable natural area and probably wouldn't involve the study of Indian remains. Then, if we do find something of significance in our valley, Stoker might be persuaded to put the quarry at the new location. Jason's going to start looking this afternoon."

"Um, yes... Oh, no, FatCat, shame on you!"

FatCat was busy batting her Kitty Bangle across the kitchen floor.

"So that's what I heard last night," said Henry.

"Oh, dear, I am sorry. Did she keep you awake? I bought her that necklace thing because the card said the little bells would help me keep tabs on where she was, but she's one female who hates jewelry. At least she hates that. She pulls it off, and I've already stepped on it two or three times. She hasn't played with it before, though."

Carrie grabbed the Kitty Bangle and stuck it in a drawer.

"Guess it wasn't such a good idea after all. I have a lot to learn about cats." She leaned over to offer a chin rub to FatCat, who purred and went to wind herself around Henry's legs.

"Didn't keep me awake. I heard it before I went to sleep and wondered if your mice were playing games."

Carrie giggled at that, and Henry looked at his watch. "We'd better go."

"I'll be ready in a minute. All I have to do is put on my sweater, jacket, and hat, and I'd like to take time to call the center. I said I'd check in every day."

The quick phone call told her that everything was running smoothly. "Thank goodness this is our quiet time of year," she said as she led the way to the garage.

Carrie's new resolve made her determined to quit side-stepping awkward issues, so, after they were on the expressway heading south, she said, "You still haven't said what you were really doing Sunday morning. You know what I did. Isn't it fair for me to know what you did? Maybe, between the two of us, we have more helpful knowledge about this mess than we think we do."

"Yes, that's possible," he agreed, then was silent for so long that Carrie thought he wasn't going to share information with her after all.

Finally he said, "At the time, I felt I couldn't tell you what really happened. I hope you'll understand.

"I had decided I'd walk toward your house, see if I could find any of the frost flowers, and be at your place in time to surprise you so we could come out together. I walked straight through the woods to the old fire road and crossed the hilltop along it before I came downhill. It's a wonder I didn't run right into the killer.

"JoAnne was already on the hillside when I got there. It only took a second to realize nothing I could do would help her, so I went on to her house. That's why you didn't see any path coming sideways across the hillside from my house. I never walked that way.

"And I can't tell you the reason I searched her house. Please bear with me. It isn't because I don't trust you, and I know how odd it must seem, but, believe me, Carrie, it has nothing to do with you and nothing at all to do with JoAnne's murder.

"JoAnne and I did know each other a long time ago and she had some...important information that involved both of us. I had begged her to talk with me about it, and she finally said she would. That's why I went to her house Saturday morning, and why I was so surprised when she was gone.

"She had papers involving what we were going to talk about, and as soon as I saw she was dead, I wanted to find those papers. Not for myself. If others find them, then an innocent person might be hurt.

"Am I making any sense at all? It was the dumbest thing in the world to search that house, especially without gloves on, but I wasn't thinking clearly. I was too...bothered. Searching did no good anyway. I didn't find the papers or any hint where they might be."

After another long silence, he continued. "I hate to involve you, but perhaps the papers are in her safe deposit box. Is Susan going through that with you? Maybe you could check before she..."

His voice cracked. "I can't say more, I just can't."

When Carrie looked at Henry and saw the grief on his face, her racing thoughts straightened and found resolve.

It was time.

"Henry, don't worry. I have Susan's birth certificate and the papers you signed. They're hidden at my house."

The car swerved, then steadied. He pulled over to the side of the expressway, turned the motor off, shifted in his seat, and stared at her. "How...how long have you...?"

She told him everything then. After she had finished, they sat in silence until she said, "We still can't tell Susan, can we?"

"I...no. We don't dare. Not only have we vowed not to, Susan may not know she's adopted. I had hoped, selfishly, I admit, that JoAnne would eventually tell her, but she said she'd made very sure Susan would never know, and was also certain Susan would never have anything to do with me if I tried to make contact on my own. Can you see why I didn't want just anyone to find those papers and hurt Susan some way? Carrie, there were times when JoAnne wasn't easy to get along with."

"That may be a gentlemanly understatement," she replied as he looked at his watch and pulled back on the expressway.

They drove in silence for a few miles, then Henry said, "Of course, no one on Sheriff Storm's staff knows any of this. When Taylor and I talked Monday night at Booths', I did go along with your story that I spent lots of time at JoAnne's house because we were lovers. Taylor and Storm seem to have easily accepted that." His laugh was almost a snort. "I suppose some older men would find that flattering. I'm afraid I don't. It embarrasses me.

"And we never were...lovers, I mean. There was only the once. We were both adults, of course, in night school. I was taking a law course, she was in a psychology class, and all the other students seemed so much younger. We got to talking in the Student Union one night. She asked me about my work, said she'd like to know more for a paper for her class. I was flattered. We went to her home, both drank some, and then...it was all so stupid, so dumb!"

Carrie studied his profile. She could see how even JoAnne might be attracted, especially when Henry was—what? Thirty-five? And now it was still the same. She couldn't deny it, no matter how hard she tried to put the thoughts aside.

She turned to stare out the window. Could JoAnne have thought of sex with Henry as a psychology experiment? No—no birth control! And she got caught!

Henry was quiet for a few minutes, then asked, shyly it seemed to Carrie, "What's Susan like? I've never even seen her. I've never seen my own daughter! I guess I could have tried to find her, could have seen her on a school yard, or leaving work, or something, but I decided it would be easier if I never knew what she was like, if I just tried to forget she existed. It didn't work. I don't think there's been a day since I found out JoAnne was pregnant, went to see her, and she and her parents said I'd never see the baby, that I haven't thought, and wondered."

"She's a lot like JoAnne," Carrie said.

In response to his frown, she rushed on, "Oh, I mean very intelligent and very determined. But Susan is a softer person. She has a tenderness that JoAnne wouldn't have acknowledged in herself, assuming she had it. Susan has JoAnne's sense of humor, though, and her strength. She doesn't share her aunt's, uh, mother's—oh, golly, that's too unnatural—JoAnne's distrust of men. She is married, after all, and has a son."

He allowed himself a tiny smile. "Is she pretty?"

"Nice looking. Not what I'd call pretty, but you'll have

to decide for yourself. She has JoAnne's dark hair and olive skin, and," she looked over at him, "your brown eyes."

"What's her husband like? You've met him, haven't you?"

"Yes, and I like him too. He's rather quiet, wears thick glasses, no taller than Susan. Looks intelligent, and I think he is. He's some kind of accountant. I'm sure you two will get along."

"Have you seen her baby?"

"Only once, and he was very tiny. In fact, I barely saw him then because he was sleeping. I really don't know what he looks like now, he must have changed a lot. JoAnne had a photo of the three of them that was taken about three months ago. It was on the table in the living room. Did you see it when you searched the house?"

"I saw it. It wasn't too clear. I was tempted to take it, though."

"You should have. It's missing now. I don't think I mentioned that to you, and I didn't bother to tell Taylor. Such a little thing. I didn't see it when I was in the house with Taylor and Storm, and Shirley and I didn't find it either. It's weird, but I guess whoever tore up JoAnne's house took the picture with them."

"Expensive frame?"

"No. JoAnne got it at Wal-Mart."

He frowned. "Odd."

"Yes, I suppose so. But, we began talking about Susan, and you didn't say where you went after you searched JoAnne's house. I guess you didn't go home."

"No. I climbed back up to the fire road behind JoAnne's house and followed it north. You could tell someone had driven along there recently, but there would be no way to know if it was a hunter, or JoAnne's murderer, or both.

That road actually comes out by the barn on the old farm.
I should have told Roger, by the way, because he didn't act
like he or Shirley knew the road is still passable. It's open
all the way down to the old farm and then goes west along
the creek. When the water's low, you could drive out of the
valley right next to the creek bank. You wouldn't have to
drive past Roger and Shirley's house at all if you didn't mind
a bit of rough travel and had four-wheel drive. By the way,
I didn't take time to go into the old barn, though if I had,
I'd have found JoAnne's truck."

Carrie was busy thinking, trying to remember sounds
from the night before. "You know, I was pretty disoriented
by then, but it's quite possible that the man who tied me
left that way. I wonder if knowing about the road really
helps us, though. Other than meaning anyone who knows
the way can get to the old farm unseen, it tells us no more
about JoAnne's murderer."

"It might. What if the person Jason saw leaving Saturday morning actually was the murderer? It means that person probably didn't know the fire road continues along the
creek and out of the valley. The quarry owner would surely
know about it."

"Oh, yes, I see that. Wish I could recall which way the
man drove off. I can't picture it clearly enough now, but
maybe it'll come back to me later. Tell me the rest—you
evidently went back to JoAnne then."

"Yes. It hadn't occurred to me that you would go out
before you talked with me, and my walk had taken longer
than I expected. When I got back and found the radio
right there by her, I felt awful. That's something I will never
forgive myself for. I could have spared you that."

She thought once more of Henry's comforting hug
when he came to her Sunday morning. It made her eyes

wet now as she remembered it. She couldn't seem to stop
how she felt, but it was frightening to be so vulnerable.
She'd cried more this week than she had since she was a
child. She'd heard Susan cry over the phone. Henry shed
tears. Weren't tears always a sign of weakness? JoAnne never
cried, of course, but if Henry could cry, well, then... The
man certainly was confusing her.

Aloud she said, "Yes, but maybe we're stronger friends
now because we both...found her. And I think I'd rather
have seen JoAnne there than have to imagine it later. Don't
forget I went to Amos very soon after he'd been shot. It
wasn't nearly so bad with JoAnne."

She saw the airport sign. "Look. There's our turn-off.
Henry, tell me how you think I should explain you to Susan. I know it was logical for you to help me drive today
because of that awful thing last night, but should I explain
anything more? Because of Susan, I'm sure you want to be
with us as much as possible, and there has to be a reason."

He laughed. "Simple. Just tell her I'm your 'significant
other.' That term covers everything."

"Oh," said Carrie. "Significant other. Yes. I'll tell her
that."

There was one more thing. She asked it. "Did Irena
know—about JoAnne or the baby, I mean?"

"No," he said, "she never knew. I couldn't have told
her, and not just to protect Susan, or because of JoAnne's
parents, or the papers I signed. How could Irena ever understand, or forgive me? And...I was ashamed."

"Not anymore, Henry," she said. "Let it go now. I'm
not saying I don't think what you and JoAnne did was
wrong, but I also see how much you both suffered because
of it. It's been over thirty years now. You're about to meet
your daughter, and she's innocent. You can't continue with

anything that would punish her, so doesn't that mean it's time to stop punishing yourself?"

She paused to catch her breath, then plunged on. "Remember last night you thanked God when you found me alive? God is love, the Bible says, and love forgives. Accept that now, before you meet Susan, and go forward."

She stopped, wondering if she'd said too much, and how he would take it. Then she looked out the window. "Oops, I believe we park to the right. And that's our door. We go in there."

"Not a minute too soon," said Henry. "We'll have to hurry to meet the plane. And," he continued, speaking so softly and with such a sense of awe that she almost thought she imagined hearing him, "my daughter and my grandson."

Before they got out of the car, she noticed that he took time to wipe his eyes.

CHAPTER XVII

As Carrie watched Susan walk down the concourse, she realized that, even if Henry had come to the airport by himself, he should have known at once who Susan was.

Not because of how Susan looked. Because of how baby Johnny looked. He was a miniature Henry. That possibility hadn't occurred to Carrie.

She was so sure both Susan and Henry would notice it immediately that she was unable to say anything at all.

Johnny had Henry's square jaw and Henry's mouth with the upper lip that was just a bit too large. There was a miniature Henry nose. The baby, riding securely in his backpack carrier, looked over Susan's shoulder with Henry's wide-spaced brown eyes.

Now what, thought Carrie.

Now nothing, it seemed, at least not from Henry, who stood silently behind Carrie as Susan came toward them, her eyes searching the crowd for a face she recognized.

Finally, Carrie was able to say, "Susan, here," and the young woman rushed to her, bending awkwardly for a hug. Johnny, surprised by the sudden tilt forward, started to cry.

After Susan had lifted the baby out of the carrier, speaking softly to him until his protests subsided, she looked up and blinked at Henry, her face showing the wisp of a smile, before she turned back to Carrie.

Well, carry on, thought Carrie.

"Susan, this is my friend, Henry King. He's a neighbor and came with me today to help out. Henry, this is Susan Burke-Williams."

There was a moment's silence before Henry said, "Ms. Burke-Williams," and reached around Carrie to hold out his hand.

"Oh, for heaven's sake," responded Susan, "it's Susan, and if you're a friend of Carrie's, I'll call you Henry. I hate formalities!" She turned to Carrie, suddenly very formal, in spite of her words. "I have some things checked. I couldn't manage everything and the baby too. I brought a carrier that works as a car safety seat, if we need it."

"Thank goodness," said Carrie. "I didn't remember that part. Luggage pick-up is this way."

Nobody's saying anything, thought Carrie as they headed away from the passenger area. Surely they noticed, but then, what could anyone say about it?

"My, what a surprise, Susan, but your baby looks like me."

"Well, yes, isn't that odd, but I do notice that he does."

I suppose it's possible Henry wouldn't see it, she mused, but Susan must!

After the luggage was stowed in the back of the wagon, Henry helped fasten Johnny in his safety seat next to Susan. As soon as he and Carrie were settled, he headed the station wagon toward the expressway.

For a few minutes, no one spoke. Grief is like that, thought Carrie. You worry that whatever you say is only going to make things worse.

Just then, Susan solved the problem by saying, "I guess they're really sure Aunt JoAnne was murdered? That it wasn't a hunter?"

"I think so," said Carrie, "but maybe Henry would be better at explaining it to you. He understands about evidence and guns. He used to be a police detective."

Carrie wondered if she should mention that Henry was from Kansas City, but said nothing and turned toward the back seat. "He lives across the hollow back of me. You remember Mrs. Foster? She's gone to stay with her daughter, and he's renting her house for now. She hasn't decided if she wants to sell.

"Henry's been very helpful through all of this. You'll understand when you hear what's happened. But, Susan, are you sure you want us to talk about it? Some of it's really awful."

"Won't I have to hear it all sometime?" Susan asked. "You might as well tell me what you know. Reality can't be worse than things I've imagined since Sunday."

Henry spoke up. "They believe your aunt was killed with a gun most hunters wouldn't have with them. It was a .38 Military and Police, commonly called a Police Special, and that's a handgun, one meant to kill or injure people. JoAnne evidently left home in her truck to meet someone on Saturday morning about 6:30. She left a note that mentioned the time, 6:30, and we assume it referred to a meeting. She drove to the barn on the old farm in the valley. Do you know where that is?"

"Yes," Susan said. "And I've been reminded of the area every time I talked with Aunt JoAnne recently, because of the quarry."

"Well, someone did meet her there, in the old barn, and that person shot her while she was sitting in her truck."

In response to Susan's gasp, Henry went on quickly, "She died instantly. We're...they're sure she had no idea what was going to happen. The killer stood outside the driver's window of the truck, probably talking with her, and she wouldn't have seen the gun until the last minute. There was absolutely no sign, according to the sheriff's department, that she tried to escape or struggled to get away from anyone."

"Oh," Susan said, very quietly. "And then...?"

"The person put her body in the back of the truck, under the camper shell. The sheriff's department says they have no idea why, but I think, and possibly they do, that the killer knew approximately how long it takes a body to stiffen after death and didn't want it to be in seated position in the cab of the truck. It looks like the killer wanted her body lying down, which may mean that what the person did later, moving her to Carrie's hillside, was already planned. When the killer moved the body to the back of the truck, he—or she—probably got blood on their clothing, but there wasn't any usable evidence on or around the truck. No fingerprints."

Susan broke in. "You said he or she, does that mean a woman could have killed my aunt?"

"It's physically possible. JoAnne was tall, but not heavy, and even though the killer did pull her from the cab and take her around to the back of the truck, most women could have managed it since it was only a short distance.

"Your aunt was wearing her red coat, which has since disappeared, and her red stocking cap was somewhere around, but she didn't have it on at the time of her death. We, uh, found it later and it had no blood on it at all. Her coat and purse are still missing."

"So that was Saturday morning," Susan said. "What happened next?"

"JoAnne was left in the truck through the day and overnight. Of course, a passer-by could have found her there. Just looking in the cab of the truck would have told anyone, in daylight at least, that there was something wrong because of the blood, but the killer probably knew there wasn't much risk of that. The old farm is on a dead-end road, and no one would have any reason to go to the barn. On the side toward the road, the barn looks like it's falling down anyway. Only the south side is still pretty firm. There are often hunters in the area this time of year, but it's likely if any of them saw the truck, they'd think it was one more hunter's truck and leave it alone.

"Early Sunday morning, the killer returned before daylight and moved the body to his or her vehicle, probably a truck. The ground was hard, and there were no prints of any kind. Then that person drove up the fire road to the hilltop back of Carrie's house, dragged the body downhill, and put it in almost the exact place where Carrie's husband, Amos, was killed five years ago."

"Oh, my," Susan said. "This hasn't been easy for you, Carrie. But, why there? It seems the whole story involves more than Aunt JoAnne. It's all so crazy."

"When we find out why," said Henry, "then we'll likely know who."

An unmistakable sound came from Johnny's half of the back seat.

"That reminds me," Susan said. "I didn't want to bring

bulky packages of diapers, so I only have a few with me. Can we please stop somewhere and buy diapers?"

Susan insisted on going into the Wal-Mart in Rough Creek by herself, so Henry and Carrie sat in the car listening to a conversational babble coming from the back seat. The fact that the voice was light and tiny and there were no recognizable words made no difference. The noises had the tone and inflection of human language.

"He seems like a very bright baby," said Henry, looking over his shoulder. "You said he was six months old. He's almost talking, isn't he?"

"Not yet. He's copying the sounds he hears. I imagine he thinks he's talking, and undoubtedly Susan and Putt talk to him a lot."

"Does he go to day-care while she's at work? Too bad she can't stay home with him."

"Well, yes, but in this case it works out rather nicely. The company she's with, the home office of a brokerage firm in Kansas City, has child-care facilities right in the building. She can go there during breaks to nurse the baby."

Henry was still watching Johnny.

"Cara?"

"Um?"

"Am I imagining it, or does that baby look just a bit like me?"

"No, you aren't imagining it. He looks so much like you that it's embarrassing. I've been wondering what to do or say about it."

"Do you think Susan noticed?"

"I don't see how she could miss it. But then, since she'd have no idea of any connection, maybe she just passed it off as a coincidence."

"We can't say anything."

"I suppose not."

Both of them fell into a thoughtful silence, and Carrie noticed the baby was quiet too. She glanced over her shoulder and saw that he had fallen asleep.

Henry also looked at the sleeping baby, then said, "You may be wondering why I was willing to go ahead and describe how JoAnne was killed to Susan. You said it earlier, and she did just now, and you're both right. When a tragedy like this hits, knowing what really happened is better than imagining. It's best to hear the facts told in an unemotional way, face them, deal with it, then get on with your life. I saw that over and over when I was with the department."

"Yes, I understand," said Carrie.

She looked toward the store entrance and said, "Here comes Susan."

They turned to watch her as she started toward them.

"Cara?"

"Yes?"

"I think you don't see her the same way I do, maybe because you're a woman. She's very pretty."

As Susan's slender blue-jeaned legs swung across the parking lot, Carrie had to agree with him. The dark, shiny hair, cut to the level of her chin, swayed as she walked, and her oval face, though sober, was flushed becomingly.

The orange jacket she wore accented the warmth of her olive skin.

"Yes, I agree," said Carrie as Henry got out to open the door. "She's very pretty."

"There," Susan said as she bounced into the back seat, bringing a rush of cold air. "We're fixed for a little while at least. Thanks for stopping. Now you can tell me the rest of what's going on—what you've found out about the quarry owner and all of it."

So Carrie talked the rest of the way home, with Henry adding comments here and there, bringing Susan up-to-date on everything that had happened in Walden Valley since Sunday.

"Do you think Carrie's in some danger?" Susan asked Henry, as he repeated his speculations about why JoAnne had been brought to the big tree beside Carrie's walking path.

"I just don't know, but everything about this worries me. There are so many peculiar things that we have no explanations for yet. The sheriff's department has suspicions about Stoker, the quarry owner, but so far they have no proof of anything. The bullet that killed JoAnne was stuck in the wall upholstery of the truck cab across from where she was sitting. It was stopped by the metal wall. But, though Stoker owns several guns, none they found at his house could be the murder weapon. It would have been easy to dispose of the gun, though. Easy for him, or anyone else. It could be anywhere in the tri-state corner—in Arkansas, Missouri, or Oklahoma—and that's a pretty big hiding place. It could lie in some hollow for years without anyone seeing it."

"Carrie, I'm not letting you out of my sight the whole time I'm here," said Susan. "I'll protect you from any more of what happened last night. We'll stick together now.

"It does sound like there might be something worth finding in those caves, though. Going to search them sounds like fun but under the circumstances a little scary too. I don't think the two of us should go alone. I think Henry should come along."

"I'd insist on it," Henry said.

As they headed down the lane toward Carrie's garage, Susan said, "Oh, look, there's FatCat, come to say hello."

Carrie stared at the cat, who was sitting upright on the porch watching them.

"But she doesn't go outside," Carrie said. "JoAnne never let her out, and I don't. She was inside the house when we left. She didn't get past us, did she, Henry?"

"I don't think she could have," he said. His words sounded clipped and tense.

He didn't put the station wagon in the garage, but pulled up in the drive, asked Carrie for her house key, and was out before she could unfasten her seat belt. He scooped the cat up with one hand and unlocked the door with the other.

Henry didn't open the door at once. He came quickly back to Carrie and said in a low voice, "Take the cat, then get back in the station wagon, and lock the doors. Be ready to drive immediately. I'm going inside. You stay here with Susan and the baby. If anyone comes out of the house but me, or I'm not back in five minutes, don't get out. Go for help."

Carrie had no time to protest. He pushed the cat in her arms, opened the door to the house, and was gone.

Chapter XVIII

For a while all Carrie could think of was that, without hesitation, Henry had rushed into what could be danger and, once more, it was her danger. Her house...her danger. But why her danger? Why here? Why!

She tried to settle her thoughts...to pray for Henry's safety, which should be the most important thing at the moment.

"Men want you to need them."

Shirley—wonderful, warm, mother-woman Shirley—had said it, but her words were only half of Henry's idea.

"People need people," he'd said. Well, children needed adults, and less fortunate ones needed help, but she was strong by herself! She would stand on her own feet!

As she began a prayer, a phrase from Second Corinthians 8:14 came to her: "...that there may be equality."

Funny thing to come to mind now. Bible passages now should be part of her prayer for Henry, but, there it was.

Equality. Sharing. Helping each other. But how could she prove her ability to be independent when troubles like now came up and she needed help, time after time?

In Kansas City, they said Henry had lost his nerve. But what about now? He had rushed into her house so quickly that there was no chance for her to say anything at all, either of encouragement or protest. He'd just done what he must do. Was that simply his training taking over, or was it concern for her life and home as well? Whatever it was, it took plenty of bravery, plenty of nerve.

Equality. Everyone had a role to play out at any time...a God-given role. Like now? Yes, like now.

In spite of her fear and confusion, Carrie suddenly felt a peculiar sort of peace.

She heard Susan move in the back seat.

Whatever was happening, whatever the danger, it had begun to touch Susan too. Until this moment it seemed right for Susan to come here. But was it safe?

Susan moved again, a quick, nervous bounce. Finally, she said, "I can't stand this! Don't you think we should check? Surely he could have looked through the house by now."

Susan's young life probably wouldn't yet understand what Carrie was thinking, so, without taking her eyes off the front door, she said, "He needs to know we're safe in the car. He's trained to deal with things like this. He will be all right."

I hope I really believe that, she told herself, still watching the door.

"Well, if I didn't have Johnny with me, I'd be in that house right now," Susan said.

Maybe I should be, Carrie thought.

Susan shifted nearer the car door, another quick bounce.

"Does he carry a gun?" she asked.

"No, no, he doesn't, not anymore."

Just then Henry reappeared.

"Someone was in the house when I opened the door," he told them as Carrie got out of the car, "but he's gone now. I only caught a glimpse as he jumped off your deck, but I think I might recognize him again. Funny, I know he saw me too, and he'd made no effort to get away until he did. I don't think he was expecting me to be the one who came in the house."

He hesitated for a moment, then said, his words coming slowly, carefully, and almost without expression. "I'm thankful you and Susan weren't here alone."

"I...I am too."

"I took a quick look around. Nothing seems disturbed, other than the glass in the door to your deck. I'm afraid it's smashed."

She stared at his sober face. "But why? *Why?*"

He shook his head and went on. "I'm sure I interrupted whatever was intended. I've called Taylor. He's on the way, and until he arrives, we'll stay out of the main part of the house and not touch anything. They'll search the woods, of course, but the man will be long gone, and there will undoubtedly be signs that a vehicle has been using the old fire road again."

Carrie was no longer frightened. She was furious. "This is outrageous! What's more, it makes no sense. As soon as we can, when we're all fed and Johnny is settled for his nap, we've got to talk, and think, and decide where among all this craziness something does make sense."

The first thing Carrie did was shut FatCat in the laundry room with her basket, water, toys, and litter box, hoping a quick back rub was enough apology. Then, while Susan tended to the baby and Henry carried in luggage, she looked around quickly and checked to see if JoAnne's box was intact. It was. Henry was right. There was no sign anything but the door had been disturbed.

She called her insurance company and the patio door company from the kitchen, then began work on the soup she'd planned for lunch—an easy combination of canned tomato soup, chopped frozen tomato from her summer garden, celery, onions, and basil, combined with quick rice and a dash of hot pepper sauce. Cold baked ham would do for meat. She couldn't manage more now.

In a few minutes, Henry appeared in the kitchen. "Susan's settled and feeding the baby. I'll clean up the broken glass after Taylor's through. Your door was smashed with a big rock—it's still there. It would have been very noisy, so the intruder knew you were gone. I'll go get plywood to put up after Taylor leaves, though I hate to leave you alone now."

Carrie finished brushing garlic butter on a pan of unroll-and-bake french bread and put it back in the oven. "Don't worry about the plywood," she told him. "The glass people are coming right away. They were available, and the insurance company says it's okay under the circumstances."

She lifted the soup pot lid to stir, then wiped steam off her glasses. "Henry, do you think there's any danger for Susan and Johnny? If so, I'd like to put them on a plane back to Kansas City. But first, maybe the three of us working together can make some sense of all this. Let's talk and combine all our ideas and knowledge of JoAnne. I'd think we had a lunatic on our hands, except, well, it seems focused toward a few of us fighting the quarry, doesn't it? If so, Susan should be safe."

"I don't see how Susan could be in any danger," he

said, "but I plan to sleep on your couch again tonight, and I don't think it's a good idea for her to move to JoAnne's house tomorrow. I believe in sticking together."

The lunch was a success. Both Susan and Henry assumed she'd spent hours creating the soup, and her salad made with strawberry gelatin, frozen strawberries, and whipped cottage cheese was always a hit. Dessert was Sara Lee cake.

They were just finishing the meal when Taylor appeared at the front door. He greeted Carrie cordially, but showed no interest in asking her more questions. She'd decided if he did, she was going to spice things up by inventing something exotic. The man already knew more about her than most of her friends and family.

Carrie introduced Susan, then left her with the men and went back to the kitchen to finish cleaning up. Taylor evidently didn't have much to ask Susan, because in a few minutes she re-joined Carrie in the kitchen. They made fresh cups of coffee and sat at the table while Carrie described her visit to the lawyer and the preliminary plans for Saturday's memorial service. Susan approved the plans and agreed to a meeting with the lawyer on Friday.

They heard the front door shut and in a minute Henry was with them. "I pulled the drapes over the door," he said. "That'll have to do until the repair people come."

"Anything new from Taylor?" Carrie asked.

"No clues as to who broke in, which isn't surprising, and he also said they haven't found any helpful evidence or any more pieces of pottery on the old farm. They located Stoker, and he says he was at a club with friends last night. They're checking on that. I suppose the man could create an alibi by getting his friends to lie for him. But, as you know, Taylor's pretty good at smooth-talking with folks and finding out more than they planned to tell.

"I told him that both you and I would like to see Charles Stoker, especially since I got a glimpse of the man who broke in here. Maybe they'll plan a line-up."

Carrie made another cup of coffee, and Henry sat. She'd noticed he wasn't too big for her kitchen chairs after all. Not larger than life, she thought. Just a big man!

She pushed a pad of legal paper out in the center of the table and said, "Now, let's think. What do we know?"

The phone rang. "Oh! Well, you two think. Excuse me."

It was Mag Bruner. "Hello, Carrie. It's awful about JoAnne. I know you two were close, and this is especially terrible for you. Tell me, are there plans for a funeral?"

Carrie told Mag what was planned and remembered to be polite, since Mag had a right to be thought of as innocent unless something came up to prove she wasn't.

"Is there anything I can do? Cook? Will there be family coming in?"

"Just JoAnne's niece and her husband and their baby."

"Let me bring you a chicken casserole. That's easy to store and warm up. And an apple pie and salad? How about it? I'll bring it over Friday evening before suppertime."

"Mag, that's very nice. It would help. I haven't much time to cook right now."

"It's done then. Carrie, look, I talked to Jason today, and he told me...well, I need to explain lots of things about that quarry land to all of you."

Not sure what to say, and not knowing how much Jason had told Mag, Carrie simply answered, "As you can imagine, things are kind of on hold for now, but Jason will be in touch with all of us, I'm sure. Thanks for offering food."

Carrie returned to the table and had just finished repeating Mag's conversation when the phone rang again.
She left Susan's dark head and Henry's grey one bent over
the legal pad and went to answer the phone.

"Hello, Carrie. How are you? Is Susan there yet? Any
new clues about the death of your friend?"

It was Evan.

Reminding herself that patience was a virtue, she assured him she was fine and answered questions about her
plans for the week. When she returned to the table, Henry
said, "We couldn't help overhearing part of that. Someone
sure is interested in knowing everything that's going on in
your life. Sounded like a boyfriend."

Henry was just joking, but she made a face, remembering Shirley's words about Evan being in love with her.
"Hardly. It was Evan Walters. Ever since Amos died, he's
felt a certain responsibility for me, I think. He read about
JoAnne in the Tulsa paper and has been calling to make
sure I'm all right. It's getting rather tiresome, but I'm trying to be nice to him. After all, I guess he's just showing
kindness. He's single and spends lots of time alone. I do
think he has too much time to worry."

Susan had lifted her head to look at Carrie. "Evan
Walters from Tulsa? Stock broker? Oh, my, I'd forgotten.
Aunt JoAnne told me he's the one who was hunting with
your..."

Carrie interrupted her. "Yes. Do you work for Michaels,
Nelson, and Tolby? I never asked JoAnne the name."

"Yes, I do," Susan said. "I'm in Cash Control. Is Evan
Walters your broker now?"

"No," Carrie said. "He was, but I transferred everything to the office in Bonny when I moved. I saw no need
to leave anything in Tulsa at all."

"Good move," said Susan, looking at her thoughtfully for a moment before turning back to the legal pad.

"What we've been doing," Henry said, "is identifying what we know and what we need to find out or figure out to fill in the pieces of our puzzle. Here in this column is what we know. Mostly it's the times various things happened and where they happened. We began with Friday night when JoAnne told you she had good news. We've included everything up to the break-in here today. All the times are written in as near as we know them. On this side, Susan is writing the unknowns and peculiarities about each event. So far, nothing even looks like a pattern, except...well, do you see it? Susan and I agree. You've been touched by this too many times."

"Maybe so," agreed Carrie, "but would someone try to scare off the whole committee through me just because, like JoAnne, I'm a woman alone? It doesn't make sense. JoAnne's death would have scared me if it was do-able, and I sure don't have any information that would bother anybody.

"Haven't I just been in the wrong place at the wrong time? I've tried to think about what it might have to do with me since you first suggested it last night, Henry, but I can't figure anything out. And, couldn't the break-in just be a burglar we scared away?"

"I don't see it that way," he said, "but let's tackle other unknowns."

"Go farther back in time," Carrie said. "I think the first big unknown is where JoAnne was on Thursday, because she'd have to have believed she'd learned something that would stop the quarry by then, since she didn't think it was necessary to go to Little Rock. Don't we agree on that? But still, what was she doing on Thursday?"

"She didn't mention Little Rock or any good news to me Thursday night," Susan said. "We didn't talk long. She talked fast—like she was excited—but that was normal."

"I believe she was doing quarry research on Thursday," Carrie said. "But what, and where? *Where was she?* And how did Charles Stoker find out what she knew, assuming she was killed to stop her from telling us. I sure wish now I'd tried to call her before I left for work Friday. I didn't because I thought she might have been up late getting back from Little Rock."

"And then the murderer called her Friday, and she made that note," said Henry, thinking aloud.

"Taylor has the note," Carrie explained to Susan. "It was on the back of the electric bill that came in Friday's mail. She must have been on the phone when she wrote it. That's what I would do, jot a note on the nearest paper if I didn't expect the call and didn't have a note pad handy."

She paused. "Well, that's something. She probably didn't expect the call. Maybe she set the 6:30 meeting time herself so she could find out whatever it was before the quarry meeting at my house later."

She continued. "The note said, 'Head rights for minerals,' and had three exclamation points like she was excited, but was doodling while she listened. Then, 'Old farm, 6:30, morning.'"

"And," Susan said, looking at Henry, "you say these head rights don't apply here as far as anyone knows?"

"Yes."

"Well, why that term then?"

They were silent until Carrie said, "To get her to the old farm. Most of us knew she loved mysteries. But," she added thoughtfully, "Stoker didn't know her that well."

Susan said, "Who'd use the term 'head rights'?"

"Anyone who's studied Oklahoma history," Carrie told her, "or someone with Indian heritage. And I just remembered, Mag Bruner is one-quarter Osage. That's the tribe with mineral head rights in Oklahoma. Oil money, though she wasn't in on it."

"Mag?" Henry said. "How'd you find that out?"

"We talked about it a long time ago, when she learned I was from Oklahoma. Mag joked about moving back here to her old hunting grounds.

"Ancestors of the Osage people were in the Ozarks long before there was a United States. Caves here that were used from about 8000 to 1000 BC by people we call Bluff Dwellers were used later by the Osage, who lived all over this area. They gave up their claim to most of the Ozarks Plateau in a treaty with the United States signed in 1808. But they continued to hunt in the Ozarks for a number of years after that. That's what Mag was joking about."

"Goodness," Susan said, "you know lots of history."

"Part of my job," Carrie explained. "You'd be surprised what tourists want to know. And besides, I'm interested because Bluff Dwellers could have lived in our caves, though no one has ever found evidence of that here."

"We really have to look in those caves in the valley," Susan said. "We might find something wonderful."

"So," Henry said, thinking aloud, "Mag knows the term head rights and could use it in a way that would sound sensible to JoAnne, though I think she would have had a hard time convincing JoAnne to meet her at such an odd time and in that place. JoAnne would wonder why they couldn't just talk at home or go to the farm at a more reasonable hour. Or for that matter, why Mag didn't simply give the whole committee the information."

"But Mag could have told Stoker or someone else,"

Carrie said, "and that person could have called JoAnne. I even doubt JoAnne would have known Jack's voice on the phone if he was the one who called. JoAnne would have been surprised to see one of the Bruners in the old barn, but it wouldn't have frightened her. She might not have known Stoker or person X, but if she was expecting to meet a stranger, then that probably wouldn't have frightened her either. She'd think of it as just another adventure."

"So, Stoker could know the term too," Henry said.

"Yes, there are many ways he could learn about it. But, assuming someone used that term to lure JoAnne to the valley, we still have to figure out why. Why did they kill her? Was it to stop her from sharing what she had discovered—or what they thought she had discovered?"

"Well," Susan said, "I could tell from my phone conversations with her that she was really obsessed with stopping the quarry, so I'm sure she'd be eager to follow up on anything that might get it stopped.

"But, though she talked about all sorts of things she was checking on, she never hinted that any one of them was more promising than another. I think I'll write down everything I can remember that she said to me concerning the quarry. Maybe you two will see something in what she told me that I don't.

"And, what about the piece of pottery?" continued Susan. "Could that mean something, and could Aunt JoAnne have known about it?"

"I must admit I'm anxious to get back to the creek bank and look around," Carrie said.

"Hey," Susan said, "do you suppose we could put Johnny in the carrier and go to the valley this afternoon—at least for a short walk to the creek bank? We don't have to work on Aunt JoAnne's things right away, do we? I would like to stop by her house—to be sure everything is okay, you know. But what about going to the valley after that?"

Henry, who had been silent and thoughtful through all this, said, "Since the killer only attacks one person who's alone, a trip to the valley should be perfectly safe if we go together and stay close to each other." He looked at Carrie. "In daylight at least."

"I'll never go there after dark again," Carrie said. "And it sounds like you think all this is caused by a single person and not a group of people working together."

"More than one person could know about it, but I believe only one person is actually doing the dirty work. Two people could have carried JoAnne to where she was found, for example. They wouldn't have needed to drag her."

Carrie shuddered, thinking about the man who had attacked her. She had not wanted to admit he was the one who murdered JoAnne, but she'd known he must be.

Aloud she said, "Yes, I see. But go on."

"Someone does need to double-check that creek bank since Taylor and his men didn't find anything. From what you say, Carrie, the pottery was nearly the color of the rocks. It might be hard to see unless you know exactly what you're looking for."

"Oh, drat," Carrie said. "I forgot I was going to ask Evan about that! He does know quite a bit about Indian pottery. Some pots in his collection are rosy color, and he might know who made something like them in this area. I think I'll call him back, tell him I was out walking and found a piece of pottery, and describe it to him."

"While you're doing that," Susan said, "I'll begin trying to recall for Henry all that Aunt JoAnne said to me about the quarry and see if it gives him any ideas."

Carrie dialed Evan's office number, gave her name, and

asked the receptionist if she could speak with Mr. Walters.

"He's away from the office," the woman said. "May another broker help you, or may I have him return your call? He's keeping in touch."

"No, I'll call later. My schedule is uncertain," Carrie said, thinking that Evan hadn't mentioned not being at work when he called. She wondered where he was. Too bad she hadn't remembered to ask him about the pot when he was on the phone. Well, she'd just have to wait.

And, something about the pot had bothered her when she first saw it...a memory. She was trying to recall her impressions when the knocker interrupted her. She went to the door to find that the men had come to replace the broken glass. After showing them where it was, she left them to their work and returned to the kitchen.

Henry and Susan were studying the legal pad again.

"Here," Henry said, "look this over and see if JoAnne told Susan anything that isn't familiar to you."

Carrie read the list carefully. There was one new thing. Susan said JoAnne had asked her Thursday night if she knew how long charcoal drawings lasted.

"Are you sure that's what she said?" Carrie asked, "and that it had something to do with the quarry? It sounds like something to do with art."

"Yes, I know, and it's possible it had nothing to do with the quarry. Sometimes she did change subjects rapidly. But we'd been talking about the quarry when she asked. She didn't explain anything more about it, though. She just dropped the subject. It was almost like she wanted to surprise me too. And that was the last time I talked with her."

Susan stared out the window, swallowed a couple of times, then went on. "One reason I remember is because I thought, Oh, golly, she's going to have me going to the Art

Institute to find out about charcoal drawing."

She was silent again, still looking out the window. Then she cleared her throat and turned back to face them, ignoring the wet streaks that had dripped down her cheeks.

They all bent their heads to look at the yellow pieces of paper scattered on the table.

Suddenly a baby's cry broke the silence.

"I hope those men are through fixing the door soon," Susan said. "I think Johnny's ready for an excursion to the valley, and I know I am. Let's put our hiking clothes on!"

She pushed her chair back and went to get her son.

Chapter XIX

Everything was peaceful at JoAnne's house and in perfect order, just as Shirley and Carrie had left it.

Henry offered to hold the baby, who sat quietly on his lap, staring up with wide eyes that so closely resembled Henry's. The three of them waited in the living room, leaving Susan to walk through the house alone.

Carrie was wondering when Susan would put the house on the market. The idea of new people living in JoAnne's house was going to take some getting used to. In a few years, the connecting path she and JoAnne had worn through the woods would grow over, and there would be no outward sign left of the friendship that created it.

As they got back in the station wagon, Carrie suggested they stop in at Roger and Shirley's before going on to the old farm. "We should say hello. They'd like to see you, and she did offer to keep the baby tomorrow afternoon."

Carrie looked at her bandaged wrists. "Besides, Mon-

day night Roger said it would be a good idea if he knew
when any of us were going to the old farm, and he was sure
right about that!"

When they got to the Booths', they found Roger and
Shirley in the barn tending a cow and newborn calf. Shirley
washed her hands and came, arms out, to hold the baby.
As she took him, she glanced quickly at Henry's face but
said nothing.

She's noticed the resemblance, Carrie thought.

Henry and Roger began talking about the old fire road,
and the three women leaned against the wooden railing,
watching the new calf.

Susan said, "I wish Johnny was a bit older. He'd love
this, wouldn't he?"

Roger turned toward them and said, "Well, bring him
back in a year or so. I kin always use an extra hand."

Susan nodded as she took the baby from Shirley. "I
may do just that. We'd both like to come back."

"I'll plan to see the little fella tomorrow afternoon then,"
Shirley said. "Bring him by any time. But check in with us
when you leave the valley today, too."

"Yes, ma'am!" Carrie said.

Henry parked the wagon near the old chimney, and Carrie
went to look at the disturbed piles of rock while he brought
over the spade and trowel.

"I doubt there's anything here," she told him, "since it
had been pretty thoroughly dug up when I came yesterday
evening. Let's go on to the creek."

"This is so beautiful!" Susan said when they reached
the creek bank. Johnny, enchanted by a bird that had flown
from a nearby bush, chortled a delighted assent from his

baby backpack.

Sun sparkled on the rock ripples in the water, water-cress swayed in the current, and crawfish and minnows could be seen going about their business near the rocky bottom.

"This doesn't look like a place of evil," Susan said, "and how could anyone bear to destroy it? Thinking about that makes me want to cry. It looks like something that *should* be named Walden! I'll bet Walden Creek's name has lots to do with a man named Thoreau!"

"Nope," Carrie said. "It has lots to do with a man named Walden. He settled in the valley before the Civil War. You and Johnny enjoy a look around, but please don't get out of sight."

"It doesn't seem anyone could ever be in danger here," Susan said as she walked out on a gravel bar. Squatting carefully so as not to tip Johnny over, she picked up a fossil rock. "Do I dare say, 'Oh, look at this'? I suppose by now you've seen this sort of thing many times."

"Yes, but I'll never get over the 'oh, look at this' stage," Carrie replied as she sat down on the creek bank and began poking about with her trowel.

Henry was shoveling carefully in the disturbed area where Carrie had picked up the piece of pottery. They didn't talk, but there was plenty to hear: the rasp of rocks on metal, delighted exclamations from Susan, burbling sounds from both the creek and Johnny, and the continuing ac-companiment of various bird calls. Occasionally one of the Booths' dogs would bark in the distance, and once they heard a brief moo chorus from cattle in the nearest pas-ture.

The sun was warm on her back, and soon Carrie found she was day-dreaming of nothing in particular. Her pok-

ing in the rock piles became lazy and undirected, and when
Henry came to sit on the bank beside her, she smiled at
him without speaking. It's a sunny, happy sort of afternoon, she thought, as he leaned toward her and his lips
brushed her cheek.

"Should have brought a blanket to sit on," he said. "The
rocks feel pretty cold."

"Not to me," Carrie said, "and you can credit winter
underwear for that. This is a good antidote to last night.
Susan is right—it is hard to think of evil here."

A small rock slide cascaded down the side of the bluff,
and they both looked up.

Henry was instantly alert. "Wonder what caused that?"
he said. "I should have thought about the possibility of
someone being up there."

When neither of them heard or saw anything more, he
changed the subject, though Carrie noticed he was still looking toward the top of the bluff. "It seems as if your piece of
pottery was one-of-a-kind, and I can't imagine we'll find
pottery in the caves after all these years, even if there was
any in the first place. Hate to say it, but this may be a wild
goose chase. I'm sure Susan will enjoy seeing the caves,
though, and I admit I'm looking forward to it. Are they
miniatures of the big caves with fancy formations that you
pay to see, or are they just rocky holes in the ground?"

"Some of both," she said, "but I won't describe them
now. I don't want to spoil tomorrow's surprises."

"How do we get to the entrances?"

"It's easiest to drive in from the other side. The old
track that turns off just before the Booths' leads to the top.
There really isn't anyplace we can cross the creek here right
now, though it's possible in summer when the water is lower.
You can also get across down around the bend where the

creek drops underground for a short distance, but it's a rough hike back. So we always climbed down the bluff face from the other side. The bluff slopes enough in several places to allow for fairly easy climbing up or down."

She pointed to a diagonal path leading from the top of the bluff about thirty yards downstream. "That's an entrance. And over there, a path angles up toward the overhang above us, which has a large cave opening that's quite easy to get to. It's obvious lots of people have been in that cave in recent years, and there probably isn't anything in it worth finding now. The overhang offers a terrific view of the valley, though.

"There are sink holes leading into the caves from up on top of the bluff and big rocks everywhere. That area is fenced, and once you're inside you have to be careful where you walk. I don't know how deep the holes are or how to get down in them safely. Often you can't see the bottom. It's a bit scary, but I suppose a real spelunker could drop in with a rope and head lamp."

"Maybe we should bring some kind of rope tomorrow, just in case," Henry said as he reached for her hand and leaned back against a tree trunk.

The next thing Carrie knew, Susan was saying, "Boy, you two are sure relaxed. Some pair of explorers you turned out to be!"

"We're still recovering from last night's adventures, young lady," Carrie said as Henry got up, brushed off his behind, then pulled her carefully to her feet, avoiding her wrists.

"I'm having a wonderful time," Susan said, "but I'd like to get back to the house before my office in Kansas City closes. I need to check up on some unfinished business.

"Tell me," she asked, "is there some kind of road up there over the top of the bluffs? I heard a car leave while you two were, uh, relaxing, but I hadn't seen anyone or heard anything before that."

Carrie glanced at Henry. He frowned and said, "A deer hunter, I suppose. We thought someone might be up there."

She wondered if he felt the same reluctance she did about sharing their paradise with any stranger. At least they'd heard no shots, and surely there could be no danger this near the Booths' in broad daylight.

He smiled then and changed the subject. "I'll treat you ladies to a dinner in town," he said as they headed back toward Carrie's station wagon.

"You're on," Susan said. "Can we go to that catfish place you told me about?"

Henry, in a repeat of the light-hearted mood of Saturday night, kept both Susan and Carrie entertained with his pompous Southern Colonel routine during dinner, and the mealtime flew by as they laughed and ate.

Johnny fell asleep during the return ride, and Susan put him in bed as soon as they got home. Carrie made cups of hot spiced cider, and the three of them settled around the woodstove, drinking cider, talking, and asking each other questions. Susan was curious about their life in the woods, and Henry and Carrie wanted to know more about Susan's job in Kansas City, since neither of them understood the inner workings of a brokerage office.

"It's a fairly new job for me," Susan explained, "and I took over from a woman who retired after many years in the same job. At times it's been hard getting acquainted with the various offices Mabel had handled for so long.

Most of them still ask how she is. All I do is handle money, really. Take care of checks and transfers for a certain group of offices. The Tulsa office is one of mine, though I wasn't with the firm when you had your account in Tulsa, Carrie, and, of course, all our work is strictly confidential."

Carrie laughed. "I'm sure the small amount Amos left wouldn't be worth talking about anyway. So you deal with Evan Walters? Do you talk with him?"

"Occasionally," Susan said, "but we communicate more through the magic of technology."

FatCat, who had been curled on Carrie's lap enjoying the attention of her stroking hand, decided it was time to play. She jumped down and trotted off, returning with an old cotton sock which she dropped in front of Susan, inviting a jump and bat game. After a few minutes of that, she turned away and disappeared down the hall again.

"More toys coming," Carrie said. "Sometimes I think she acts more like a dog than a cat, but I've been told Siamese can have some doggy traits, and I'm sure she's part Siamese. She is a very intelligent cat."

Susan nodded, then turned to Henry and asked, sounding a bit cautious, "What's being a policeman like?"

He didn't side-step the question, as Carrie thought he probably would have only a week earlier, but began to tell what she guessed must be tales of the lighter side of police work in Kansas City.

FatCat trotted back into the room with the toy she had chosen and, undoubtedly since Susan had already proven to be a willing playmate, went to her and put it at her feet.

"Oh, no, not that," Henry said, looking at what FatCat had brought in. "She's found that necklace you got for her."

Carrie stared at the object FatCat had dropped, then

sat very still, watching Susan and wondering if she should feel horror. She didn't. She felt a wonderful relief. She didn't know how FatCat had dug the thing out but, however it had happened, the whole matter was now out of her hands. Maybe one of her prayers was being answered.

In what seemed like slow motion, Susan bent, reached out, and picked up her own infant ID bracelet.

"Where are the bells?" Henry asked into the silence.

He's never seen a baby's hospital bracelet, thought Carrie.

Sounding embarrassed, Henry asked, "Isn't that, what did you call it, the Kitty Bangle?"

"No, no, it isn't," Carrie said. "FatCat's necklace, which looks very much like that, I realize now, is still in the kitchen drawer."

"It's a baby's hospital bracelet, fancier than they have these days," Susan said.

Henry didn't say anything, but Carrie could tell he was still completely in the dark about the significance of what the cat had brought in. She knew without question, though, how hard Susan was thinking, and how difficult her next words would be to say. But this was Susan's struggle. Carrie couldn't have spoken if she'd wanted to.

And it was as if Henry was no longer there.

Susan looked at her. "You know?"

Carrie nodded.

Then Susan began to talk, slowly, dreamily, as she turned the bracelet round and round in her hands.

"When Mom and Dad were killed, I wanted to know. Before, it hadn't really mattered, but then..."

Henry's whispered gasp brought him back into Carrie's awareness, but Susan still didn't look at him.

"I was twelve when they told me I was adopted. They

said they didn't know who the...who my birth parents were or where they were. They just said they had located me through a maternity home in New York. They told me I was the special treasure they had found. That's about all they said, and back then I wasn't even curious. I loved Mom and Dad and knew they loved me. I didn't need to know more."

She looked at Henry then, and tears were running down her cheeks, but he was leaning forward with his wrists on his knees and hands folded, staring at the floor.

"It was pretty easy, you see, especially since I knew what state I'd been born in. There are organizations... So I found out and got a copy of my birth certificate. What I don't know is...is how it happened...what happened. I know who. I just don't know why." She stopped and looked at Carrie with an appeal that Carrie couldn't face, and, like Henry, she dropped her eyes.

Susan said in a very small voice, "Would Aunt JoAnne ever have told me? I was always afraid to ask her..."

She stopped then, leaned back on the couch, and turned her head away, covering part of her face with one hand. Her tears were coming quickly and so silently that, when Carrie saw that Henry was still staring at the floor, she wondered if he even knew Susan was crying.

Well, she thought to herself, I don't care what he thinks of me now. It's time to do what I must do, no matter what.

"Henry King," she said, "your daughter needs you."

Then Carrie McCrite stood up and walked out of the room.

CHAPTER XX

Carrie, accompanied by a cat who looked very much like she was grinning, headed for the laundry room to check on things. It was obvious at once that, during her confinement in the small space, FatCat had decided to remodel her sleeping basket. The down pillow was on the floor, mattress ties were pulled loose, and the plastic bag Carrie had hidden under the mattress cover was chewed open. One of the pink booties was shredded. Fortunately, the other bootie and dress were still intact.

"Good cat," Carrie said, rubbing FatCat's head. "I'm sure Susan won't worry about losing one bootie, considering the outcome." The cat blinked at her in an owl-wise way.

After disposing of the plastic bag and raveled yarn, Carrie laid the dress and remaining bootie on top of the dryer to give to Susan later.

Then she went into her bathroom, unwound the gauze

on her wrists, and got out of her clothing. It was easier to take everything off than it had been to put it on. She dawdled through a long shower and, as she was drying, looked at the clock. So far she'd used up almost an hour. Surely Susan and Henry had come to some sort of under-standing—if only Henry wasn't too tongue-tied. She put on her nightgown and robe, picked up gauze, tape, and scissors, and padded back to the living room.

Father and daughter were sitting on the couch talking, their heads tilted toward each other. Both of them had propped stocking-clad feet on her low oak table. They looked up at her and, in unison, moved their feet to the floor.

Carrie laughed. "Goodness me, how guilty you both look. I almost hate to admit I put my feet on it, too."

Well, now! Susan looked rather teary, but she was smil-ing, and Henry was smiling too...no tears. In fact, he looked like he'd just won a million dollars or been given a Nobel Prize. Probably, Carrie thought wryly, things are going to work out just fine for them—but it was the cat that did it—not me.

Oh, well, results were what mattered. Mostly.

"Guess you two are getting acquainted? I do hate to disturb, but, Henry, could you re-wrap my wrists? And, since we have a busy day tomorrow, perhaps we should all turn in?"

Susan smiled at her. "Yes, Henry and I understand each other fairly well now, though we still have about thirty years to catch up on. But Carrie, how on earth are we going to explain us to your friends?"

"That is a question, isn't it? I'd say wait and just see what comes up. I wouldn't be surprised if Shirley has al-ready noticed the resemblance between your son and Henry.

She won't say anything until you do—she's too kind, but then, most people are. It is a heart-warming story, sort of a reunited family thing. Everyone loves those. And, you know, I do think you'll be able to talk about it easily. People here like Henry, they like you, and..." she looked at Henry, whose lips were twitching peculiarly, "there have been hints that JoAnne and Henry were once...connected."

"Problem solved," Susan said as she winked at her father.

Carrie was up early the next morning feeling decidedly cheerful. At least one thing had turned out even better than she hoped, though there were still big problems facing them...problems like a quarry and a killer in Walden Valley.

She had been thinking about the killer before she fell asleep, realizing lots of puzzle pieces were popping around in her head, and she surely should be able to make some sense of them. She just knew she was capable of figuring out who JoAnne's killer was, unless, of course, it really was a hunter, or some stupid, random thing, which didn't seem plausible now. If only she had noticed enough and could think clearly—make sense of it all.

Detecting, it seemed, was mostly about doing research, noticing things, and figuring out what it all meant in a logical way. If only her head would cooperate by sorting out all the unconnected events and make them connect. Logic was a skill she was still developing.

She heard Susan murmuring to Johnny when she went past the guest room door, and she wasn't surprised to find blankets and pillow neatly stacked on the couch in the main room. A note on the kitchen table said Henry would be back at 8:30 to escort them to JoAnne's house and make sure all was in order there before he left them to their work. He would come back at 1:30 so they could go cave exploring.

On a whim, and hoping Susan would be a while, Carrie dug out her own unique recipe for oatmeal pecan bars.

Stick of margarine, one-fourth cup dark corn syrup, half-cup sugar, tablespoon molasses, two and a half cups oatmeal, pecans. She had all that. She turned the oven knob to three fifty, melted the margarine in her big pot, stirred in the sugar, corn syrup, a blob of molasses that looked about like a tablespoon, and the oatmeal. After lining an eight-inch square pan with greased foil, she spread the gooey stuff in it, added pecans on top, and stuck it in the oven. Then she repeated the recipe to make extra for Henry.

Thirty-five minutes later, Carrie was taking the first pan out of the oven when Susan appeared, carrying Johnny balanced on her hip. "Sure smells good in here," she said.

Carrie explained what she was doing, and Susan said, "Can't we have those for breakfast? Oatmeal is oatmeal, after all! Johnny's trying oatmeal, too. We've started him on mushy things, but he's not at all sure he likes them."

Unwilling to wait for the bars to cool, Carrie lifted the foil out of the pan, turned the mixture over on a plate, and scooped off two large-sized portions. She and Susan drank orange juice and ate warm cookie bars with forks while Susan tried to convince Johnny that cereal from a jar was what he really liked best.

"Come on, son," she said, poking a small spoon toward Johnny's tongue-blocked mouth. "Yum yum. Oh, phooey, Johnny, you're a real mess."

Carrie took a tiny piece of cookie, checked it to be sure there were no nuts, and put it in the baby's mouth. His eyes widened as he mashed the new something with his tongue, and both women laughed when he turned toward Carrie and opened his mouth again.

"Oooh," Susan said. "We've got to get out of here before you spoil him. But," she added as she took another bite of her own cookie, "I must admit he's got discriminating taste. Have you ever tried that baby cereal? Yikes, it's almost tasteless!"

Carrie cleaned up the kitchen while Susan finished packing Johnny's toys and the portable bed, and they were ready by the time Henry returned. Carrie handed him a sack of cooled and cut cookie bars, and hid a smile as Susan informed him that Johnny liked them, so they should surely be appreciated by his grandfather!

It was clouding over and, as they went to their cars, Henry told them snow was in the forecast again.

"Too bad," Carrie said, "but it won't make any difference as far as the caves are concerned. They stay at fifty-eight degrees year round and will feel comfortable to us since we'll be warmly dressed anyway."

Henry had borrowed Carrie's key to JoAnne's house, and as soon as they opened the door, it was obvious he had been over earlier to start a fire in the woodstove. There was also a supply of split logs in the wood box for Carrie and Susan to add to the fire during the morning.

Several empty cardboard boxes were stacked in the living room. "They were left from when I moved here," Henry said, "and I thought they'd help."

He spent a few minutes playing with Johnny while the women began work. Then, after making sure Carrie locked the door behind him, he drove away.

The task was sad, but not overwhelmingly so, since Carrie wanted to remain cheerful for Susan and, she suspected, Susan was doing the same thing. They did talk about Susan's birth and, after some thought, Susan agreed with Carrie that JoAnne probably never would have found the need to uncover their mother-child relationship.

During the morning Susan excused herself and went to JoAnne's bedroom for another call to her office.

She must have a very important job, Carrie thought.

When Susan returned, the two of them puzzled about what had been stolen from JoAnne's house. "All I missed," Carrie told Susan, "was JoAnne's address book, the picture of you with Putt and Johnny, and a birthday card JoAnne had ready to send me. They seem peculiar items to steal, don't they?" Susan had no answers to that question but did explain the duplicate address book. JoAnne and her sister had address books alike. Susan's mother never used hers, so Susan gave it to her aunt after her mother's death.

At noon everyone, including Johnny, was ready to stop. After making sure the fire was burning down safely and the door was locked, the women got into the station wagon and went home for lunch.

While they ate, Susan brought up Evan again. "Carrie, it seems there have been questions about his honesty as a broker. Some of them go back ten years. His U-4 file, a record of complaints, has several incidents in it. So far, nothing has been proven, but it's possible something could be very wrong. The National Association of Security Dealers keeps a pretty close watch on any evidence of cheating among brokers, no matter how slight, though lots of times people do make complaints that aren't valid at all.

"There've been no recent incidents, and since I took over the Tulsa account I've been watching Evan Walters pretty carefully. I'm sure he realizes that, so he's probably walking the straight and narrow.

"When I called my office yesterday, I asked the Compliance Department to look further into his accounts and tell me more about your and Amos's account. They told me this morning that your husband's name was in Walters's U-4 file. Amos McCrite had registered a complaint on behalf of an estate he was representing just before he died. He never followed through, and the matter was dropped. I asked about the dates. It's possible he never followed up on the complaint because he was killed before he could. Our office didn't know he'd died and assumed the matter had been settled to everyone's satisfaction when they heard no more.

"They've found no irregularities in your own account up until the time your husband's assets were transferred to you. It looks like Walters could have cheated you then. Do you remember anything about the papers you signed for him at that time?"

Carrie was finding it difficult to take in what Susan was saying. "No, he just put a stack of papers in front of me, and, since I knew—well, thought—that Amos had trusted him, I did too. I didn't ask about anything. And, of course, Evan himself was tied up in the mess of proving Amos's death was accidental, and everything was so awful."

Susan sighed. "Yes, I can certainly see that. One of the forms you signed may have been a third-party release. It would have given Evan Walters control over at least a portion of your holdings and allowed him to put them in a fictitious account. Nothing is definite yet, but I'm sorry to say this is possible, and I wondered if you have ever had any reason to question his handling of your money, or if you remembered your husband saying anything about the mishandling of funds in the estate he was representing at the time he died?"

"No, I don't," Carrie said, remembering how little Amos had talked about business matters. "But I can't believe Evan would cheat me. In fact, Shirley just said Tuesday the man acts like he's in love with me."

Susan was quiet for a minute, then asked, "How did he feel about your move to Arkansas? Did he approve?"

Carrie thought about it. "No, maybe not, but he's been very protective since Amos died, so that didn't seem odd."

"Carrie, you couldn't stay in Arkansas if you didn't have enough money to take care of your expenses, the building of this house—all that. It's possible Walters thought of that. It's none of my business, but how did you manage?"

Carrie shrugged. "I had money from selling my Tulsa house, and I got a job after I moved here. There was a little money from Amos, and I had some savings. After Rob was in high school, I went back to work at the Tulsa City-County Library. I didn't make a lot of money, but it was all my own. Oh, after Rob went away to college, I did send him money now and then, but I saved some too. There's Social Security to help, of course. I'm doing okay."

"Well," Susan said, "we'll keep an open mind about Evan Walters, but I thought it was time to tell you about all this and make sure he wasn't some kind of, uh, special friend. You know, if he did cheat you and we prove it, he will have to pay you back, and it may be a lot of money."

"Oh, my," Carrie said. "I've felt sorry for Evan for years. He's always been so alone." She frowned. "But I wonder now if there's more under the surface with him than I suspected."

The two women sat in silence. Carrie had no idea what Susan was thinking, but, almost before she could fit information about cheating together with what was going on in her own mind, some intuition about what Evan had done, and might be doing now, made her feel dizzy and sick.

Susan noticed at once. "Are you all right?"

"Um...you say Evan realizes you might suspect...are keeping a watch on his financial transactions?"

"Yes, he'd be awfully stupid if he didn't know the company was keeping an eye on him."

Now Carrie began to put her thoughts into words and was barely aware she was speaking aloud. "And he knows you're JoAnne's niece. And, when he calls, and I can't think of things to talk about, I've talked and talked about JoAnne, and all of us, and the quarry. Oh, dear God!"

Susan was staring at her. "Are you thinking...Carrie, it can't be. You're scaring me."

"Maybe...maybe...evil people aren't always 'the other.' Maybe they're someone we know. Or someone we thought we knew." There was another space of silence before Carrie continued, still thinking aloud. "But then, what if I'm leaping to conclusions? How do we find out for sure? What am I going to do about that? I could be all wrong, very, very wrong!"

Susan's eyes were wide and frightened. "You must be thinking of something else, something more than this cheating, even if that could mean big money for you and serious trouble for Walters. You can't decide he's a murderer on that alone, can you? So, what is it? What else is it?"

"There's the pottery bowl," Carrie said as her door knocker banged, "and the fact I've known Evan for almost thirty years."

For another minute of silence, both of them ignored the knocker, then Susan said, "We've got to ask Henry's help, find out what to do about this."

"No, we can't! I mean, I'm not sure...what can we really

tell him? I have no facts yet. It's just that what you said fit with other things, and all of a sudden I wondered..."

She spoke rapidly, rushing her words over Susan's protests. "I'll call Evan tonight. Remember, I was going to tell him about the bowl—ask him if he could help me identify it? I'll start with that. He'll have no idea I suspect anything. I'm sure I can guide the conversation and learn something more. Besides, I need time to think about this logically and sort things out. We can't involve Henry, at least not until after this evening! If I am wrong, well, Evan has had enough trouble in his life already."

"Yes, I see," Susan said, "it would be bad to make a fuss if what you suspect turns out to be wrong. And, if you think you can find out something tonight..."

They looked toward the hall with a start as they heard the door open and Henry's voice saying, much too loudly, "Carrie? Susan? Everything all right?"

Carrie had forgotten she'd given him a door key.

"Yes, we're in the kitchen," she said, then whispered urgently to Susan, "We can't say anything yet. I might be making a terrible mistake. I have to be sure."

Susan hesitated, then nodded slowly as Henry's heavy hiking boots clumped into the room.

After they left Johnny with Shirley, Carrie directed Henry toward the end of the valley away from the old farm. For a while, his car climbed steeply, then they turned back along the plateau above the valley, bumping along a barely discernible two-track lane.

A light snow was beginning to fall when, carrying flashlights, they left the car and walked through an area of the plateau that was filled with sharp outcrops, sink holes, and scattered boulders. Finally, the three of them stood together at the edge of the bluff.

"What a beautiful picture," Susan said as they looked out over a valley frosted with snow.

"Are you still game to go?" Carrie asked Henry. "Will your car be a problem if the snow gets heavy?"

"Shouldn't be," he said. "It's done fine in worse weather than this and, besides, they didn't predict much accumulation."

"Careful, the paths may be slippery," she said as she led the way over the top of the bluff. "There are several cave openings here, and JoAnne believed they were all probably connected somewhere deep underground. I thought we'd try the largest one first, the one JoAnne called Carrie's Cave. Many of the passages get too small to squeeze through before you go very far, but there are some interesting things we can see anyway, and the going isn't that difficult."

The path wasn't slippery, just a bit wet, since the ground was still warm from yesterday's sun. In a few minutes, they reached the opening Carrie had chosen and, leading the way, she stooped and went in. "Careful of your heads," she directed. "It's pretty tight for about twenty yards after we get past this first room."

The air in the cave felt warm after the cold outside. They crossed a plain rock room, then the passage narrowed, and before long they came to a small underground lake which filled the bottom of the oval tunnel. "Watch me," Carrie said, as she spread her feet on either side of the water and, steadying herself with her free hand, straddled the two-foot-wide pool and moved forward.

"How lovely," said Susan, who was just behind Carrie. They had reached an area where the beams from their flashlights showed delicate dikes and terraces growing out of the water between their feet.

As they moved farther back in the tunnel, they could see where human hands had broken off the points of stalactites that had once dripped, icicle-like, from the ceiling.

A little further along, Carrie said, "Remnants of the Ugly American," indicating a discolored beer can.

"Slob," Susan said.

Henry's voice came from somewhere behind. "Did you say this opened up soon?"

"Just another few yards," Carrie promised.

The tunnel turned and, after climbing over a pile of loose rock, they slid down an incline and finally stood erect in a circular room about thirty yards across. Thin sheets of calcite hung above their heads like delicate cream-colored draperies. Henry pointed his flashlight up into what looked like unending space.

"Wonders underground," Susan intoned solemnly as the three of them looked up. Henry's flashlight showed that in places the deposits were thin enough to be translucent, and fold after fold seemed to glow from within. "It's incredibly beautiful," Susan went on. "This can't be destroyed. Johnny must be able to bring his children to see this someday! Oh, Carrie, what are we going to do!"

"This is part of what our fight against the quarry is about, and I wanted you to see it first. I think it's one of the prettiest places in all the caves here. Look over there. There are tunnels leading off this room in several directions. JoAnne and I never went farther than this. We were afraid we'd get lost, but maybe we'll want to explore some of the tunnels now, especially since there are three of us."

"I'll get the rope out of the car," Henry said. "If we have it to help mark our path, we can't lose our way. Then we can work in a relay system, with me out front, and you two spaced so we'll always be in touch. Shouldn't we be safe, Carrie? This rock looks solid enough.

"I do hear water falling into what sounds like a lake somewhere down that passage. I'm in favor of exploring the dry tunnels first. Anyway, I think it's worth a try. Do you two? Are you both all right so far? No claustrophobia? No big doubts?"

They both shook their heads.

"Good. Shall we look farther then?"

"Sure, let's," Susan said. "Since Carrie and I are smaller, one of us should be first down the tunnels."

"I'll get the rope," Henry said. "We can talk about who goes first later. We may find something worthwhile yet."

Carrie's hopes began to rise as they headed back toward the entrance with Henry in the lead. If he felt hopeful, she could too. Maybe they would find something to stop the quarry after all!

Henry had just started out onto the path and was turning to help Susan, who was behind him, when three loud cracks echoed through the cave. Before Carrie had time to do more than duck, Susan had fallen back against her, and Henry was lying on the path. She could see him quite clearly. There was blood running down his face.

CHAPTER XXI

Rifle!

Ice crystals of fear shot through her, and with them came one clear memory after another.

Oh, dear God. She hadn't listened, hadn't understood the danger.

Her silent prayer was instant and frantic.

She ducked again and shut her eyes as two more bullets hit the stone just inside the cave opening, sending sharp chips flying like shrapnel. Then she raised her head and began to slide toward the mouth of the cave, struggling to get to Henry with the weight of Susan's body still on top of her. Henry was where...the rifle...could reach.

Susan moved, then pushed herself sideways, rolling away. Free of the encumbrance, Carrie crawled rapidly toward Henry. "Are you all right?" she asked Susan, without looking at her.

"Yes, just a bump, but Henry...look. He pushed me

out of the way so quickly...even before I could think. Oh, look at the blood! Oh, Carrie! Pray he's not...not..."

They scooted side by side to the opening, reached for Henry's feet, and tugged him away from the path just as another bullet hit next to them, spattering rock chips.

Carrie, who had always thought women's screams were melodramatic nonsense created by scriptwriters, screamed, "Stop that!" as she and Susan pulled Henry into the cave.

For a moment, everything was very still as Carrie, blinking her eyes to stop the tears, reached for Henry's hand. "Please, God," she whispered, "I know now, but don't let me be too late!"

Susan said, "He's breathing."

With her free hand, Carrie pulled a wad of facial tissues from her pocket and began to wipe at the blood on Henry's face, trying to see where it was coming from, while Susan brushed at the wet snow in his hair.

"He's lost his cap," Susan said.

Suddenly, miraculously, Henry opened his eyes.

He said, quite clearly, "Wish I had a camera."

"*What?*"

"A camera. I'd like a picture of your faces to keep. No man deserves so much concern. But don't worry...don't think it's much. Must have just sliced my forehead...lucky." His eyes went shut again.

Carrie and Susan stared at each other, then Carrie began, "Henry, what should I...?"

He squinted his eyes back open, took the tissues from her hand, and held them to his forehead. "Nothing. I'll be okay. Right now it just smarts." He slid against the cave wall, pushing his body up enough so he could look them over. "Are you both all right?"

"Just a bump on my head," Susan said. "That's better

than being killed. Otherwise, we're both okay. But why is that maniac shooting at us?" She looked at Carrie, her eyes questioning. "Who is it? It can't be the quarry owner. He'd be crazy, trying to kill all three of us just to protect his stupid quarry. It's too much to be believed, and Roger and Shirley will hear him anyway."

"Roger won't," Henry said flatly. "I talked with him this morning. He broke a tooth and went to the dentist. He didn't want to leave, but I convinced him we'd be fine. Shirley's alone, and the snow may muffle the shots enough that they sound like a hunter in the distance. Besides, she wouldn't leave the baby, though she might call someone if she realized there was trouble."

Susan's voice trembled as she said, "That man wouldn't, he wouldn't hurt Johnny or Shirley, would he?" She bent her head and dug in her pocket for a tissue.

Carrie noticed that Henry wasn't attempting to sit upright. She was trying hard not to show how panicky she felt, and it was a good thing Susan couldn't see the worry in Henry's eyes as he said, "Oh no, he'd have no reason to."

Each of them was very quiet for a few moments, then Henry reached under his jacket and took out his gun. "Well, at least the person down there can't get close to us without putting himself in danger, but right now it's kind of a standoff. We can't get out either."

Susan said, her voice still quivering, "I can't believe I ever said this couldn't be a place of evil."

Carrie was thinking her own thoughts, but she heard Susan, and said, "This place is not evil. Places aren't."

There was another space of silence, while Carrie thought once more about the piece of pottery, a missing photograph, and a birthday card.

Finally, Henry said, "I spoke with Taylor this morning.

I don't think that's the quarry owner out there. He's supposed to be in Bonny talking with Sheriff Storm and Taylor right now."

Carrie lifted her head. She could have prevented all this. She hadn't been clever at all, and now Henry and Susan were in terrible danger, and it was her fault. All her fault.

She looked at Susan, apologizing silently, because she had said they should wait, should be sure. This danger was something she alone had brought on them. Susan's returning gaze showed she knew...and was afraid.

Then Carrie said aloud, speaking to Henry, "That piece of pottery never belonged here. It came from Arizona. He put it here as enticement for JoAnne. That's why he was in the valley Tuesday night. He came to pick up his pottery, and maybe other props he'd left behind until the sheriff's men were gone from this area, and it was safe for him.

"Oh, no *wonder* he took that bowl away from me. I've been incredibly stupid. He probably thinks I recognized it immediately. I should have. I've sat in his office holding it while Amos and I talked with him.

"He was in my house Wednesday when we got back from the airport, and he thought Susan and I would be alone. Thank God we weren't."

She continued, forcing herself to say it all. "You see, Henry, I have a hard time talking with him on the phone. It's a struggle to make conversation, so I told him all about the quarry and how hard we were working to stop it. I told him how much it meant to JoAnne. I even told him about JoAnne's niece.

"That made it easy for him. He knows a lot about Native American history. He could easily fake a story for this area, especially with props, say he was from a museum, say anything to convince her he could help win the fight against the quarry. And, of course, he knows about head rights. He's part Cherokee and very proud of that.

"JoAnne was so eager to find anything to stop the quarry that she wasn't cautious at all, just drove right into that barn, out of sight of everyone but him. I guess we'll never know all of it, not that it matters now, because the end is the same." Her voice broke. "He always was a good salesman. He can be very charming."

Henry had his eyes shut again, and Susan was silent, not looking at her.

Tears filled Carrie's eyes. "Susan put the puzzle pieces together. She told me he could have been cheating clients all these years and has probably cheated me. I didn't figure out fast enough how seriously he would take a threat to his safety, or the danger to his scheme from anyone who suspected the truth. He thought Susan would tell JoAnne he cheated me, or perhaps had already told her. That's probably why he's been so attentive to me recently, checking to see if I was reacting to any such knowledge.

"If JoAnne was dead, then the link between Susan and me was destroyed. And she'd come here, to an isolated area he knows very well. He's removing threats, you see.

"But he had no idea what Susan looks like. That's why he stole the picture Sunday. He must have gone to JoAnne's house first on Saturday morning, after...after he killed her. He was searching to see what she might have learned about him from Susan. You interrupted him when you got there, and all he had time to take was the book with Susan's address in it. When you knocked on the front door, he must have left by the back door, leaving it unlocked.

"Then he came back Sunday and made a more thorough search. He found nothing that would incriminate him, but he took Susan's picture and the birthday card. Maybe he thought the envelope with my name on it held information about him.

"You were right all along," she said, looking at Henry. "It has everything to do with me, so I must talk to him."

Henry's eyes were open now. "No," he said, "you will not. Eventually someone will miss us, or he'll give up, or...I have the gun, and there are a dozen bullets. It only takes one."

"But that's what I can't deal with," she said, "and you shouldn't have to. It's my battle."

"It's ours. He killed JoAnne. He attacked you brutally."

"And he's shot you," she said, looking at the blood-soaked tissues he was still holding to his forehead. "Henry, I can't live with knowing I put you in a situation where you may have to kill again. I've seen too much killing already, so I can imagine what you've had to face all those years in the police department. And what about the danger to you? How will you reach him?"

As if for emphasis, two more shots hit inside the cave opening, and they all flinched.

"He's on a higher level now," Henry said. "Perhaps up on that overhang. We'd better move away from the entrance."

He shifted slowly, then looked straight at her. "You mean it's Evan Walters out there? If I understand you then, Susan is in as much danger as you are."

"More danger. And now you can see why it's my fault."

She turned back to Susan. "Evan always has been sensitive to what other people thought of him. As soon as he knew you suspected he was cheating clients, then you can imagine what that did to him, especially since what you might uncover could destroy his reputation and livelihood.

Oh, Susan, I am so very sorry. I could have prevented all this."

Susan's eyes were wet, but she spoke calmly. "You didn't know about his dishonesty until I mentioned it, and by then, Aunt JoAnne had been dead for several days."

Henry said, emphasizing each word carefully. "Evan Walters is the only, the *only* one causing this. No one else is to blame."

Carrie was still looking at Susan. "He wants to keep you from exposing him, of course. As soon as he understood that we were both connected to JoAnne, then you became dangerous to him as Mabel what's-her-name in the same job never was. My fault...I told him about you.

"He isn't honest himself, so he couldn't believe you wouldn't rush to tell JoAnne about your suspicions, whether you had any proof yet or not. I'm sure he assumed when you did tell her that she'd tell me.

"Well, he's right about that," Carrie continued heatedly. "JoAnne would have told me and would have taken me by the ear and rushed me to Tulsa to confront him face-to-face."

She was tempted to cry now and snuggle against Henry's broad chest, but she didn't. She stuck her chin in the air and said, "I've got to do something! We can't just sit here waiting to be killed. I've got to talk with him."

Henry said, "It won't work. If he's unstable, you have no idea what he might do to you."

"Shirley says he's in love with me, so he wouldn't hurt me. And what if you did manage to kill him? Can either of us risk what that might do to the rest of our lives?" Tears were running freely down her face now, but she raised her chin firmly, meeting his troubled eyes.

Susan cleared her throat. "Maybe there's another way.

What if we find one of those other openings to the cave, a sink hole maybe? Then at least one of us can get to the car and go for help."

They sat thinking. Finally Carrie said. "Then I'm the one to go."

Another bullet hit just inside the cave opening, and Henry picked up his gun.

Carrie grabbed at his arm, but he pushed her hand away and said, "I'm not going to shoot at him. I couldn't get close without getting my own head blown off. That's a high-powered rifle, and he's higher than we are and can see the entrance to this cave quite clearly. But I do think he should know we're armed. That might make him hesitant about coming closer. It might keep him on that overhang. Put your hands over your ears." He pointed his gun at the cave opening and shot out over the valley.

The sound of the shot was just dying away when Carrie heard Evan's voice calling her name.

She started to answer, but Henry shook his head and asked in a low voice, "Is that Walters? You're quite sure now?"

She nodded.

Henry called out, "She was hit by a ricocheting bullet. She's unconscious. Who are you? Why are you shooting at us? We need to get help for her."

Evan was silent for a long moment, then said, "I saw you two together yesterday, Mister Boyfriend. If you want to help her, then you and the young lady should come out with your hands empty and in plain sight. I can take Carrie out in my truck if she needs help. She needs me, not you. I'll take care of her."

Another silence, then Evan said, "Put her out on the

ledge. I want to see her."

"We're afraid to move her," Henry said.

Carrie tugged at his sleeve and whispered, "Susan and I are going to see if we can find another opening. You stay here and keep his attention. That way he won't be able to leave the overhang."

His arm reached for her, and he pulled her to his side. "Cara, I don't want you to risk it."

"If I don't, what then? He'll shoot either you or Susan on sight, and you're the only one who knows how to handle that gun. I don't think he'll hurt me even if he sees me, and he isn't going to see me. It sounds like he was the one up on the plateau yesterday, though, if he's seen us together enough to call you my...boyfriend. He wouldn't have thought that simply by getting a glimpse of you in my house. That's why he wasn't in his office. He was here, breaking into my house and spying on us. I'd already told him Susan and I planned to look through the caves. If he heard us talking on the creek bank yesterday, then he found out when we were coming here, and that you'd be with us."

Evan's voice came again. "I've got explosives." He laughed. "I'll shut you in the cave, just like Aïda and Radames. Isn't that romantic?"

"Oh!" Carrie said. "Henry, let *go* of me. What else can we do? What if he really does have explosives? There is no other way out now. We can't chance waiting until Roger gets home or Shirley calls for help. Susan will come back to you as soon as we find an opening I can use."

This time Henry didn't try to stop her. He handed her the car keys and awkwardly tightened his arm around her for a moment. After giving him what she hoped was a strong, confident smile, she got to her feet.

"God go with you," he said in a gruff voice as she followed Susan into the tunnel. She didn't look back. She didn't want him to see her face.

CHAPTER XXII

The first two tunnels off the cave's main room were dead
ends. Carrie crawled along each of them as fast as she could,
not caring that she was tearing holes in her coat and slop-
ping muck all over herself. One of the tunnels continued
beyond where she could crawl, but there was no hope—
she couldn't get through.

She was sweating from exertion when she backed out
and re-joined Susan in the central room for the second
time. "There's no opening there either," she said. "I'm going to have to try that tunnel with the water sounds coming from it. Pray it works."

The tunnels were all above the level of the floor where
they stood, and there were few toeholds, but Susan helped
push and boost Carrie for a third time, and she started off
toward the sound of rushing water.

"Don't take time to come back if you find an opening
where you can get out," Susan said. "Just bang a rock against

the cave wall three times. That way your voice won't carry to the outside if you're close to an entrance. I'll signal back when I hear you. I'll pull myself up and wait here in the opening so I can be ready to come if you need my help. Be careful. That water scares me."

Everything about this scares me, Carrie thought as she crawled into the darkness, holding the flashlight in one hand and balancing awkwardly on two knees and the other hand. But there was no hope for it. She just had to find a way out, and only this way was left.

She could tell she was heading downhill, farther into the earth, which meant, she thought, that an opening to daylight would be very unlikely. Water sounds were getting louder, echoing along the passage where she was crawling. It was wet everywhere, and the rocks above her dripped constantly. She was glad her jacket was waterproof, at least where it wasn't torn. In places the tunnel was so narrow she thought her clothing would be pulled off before she could push her way through the rough passage. She was driven forward, however, by a frantic desperation and the feeling that she was now responsible for seeing that Evan didn't kill Henry and Susan.

Finally, the cave began to open up again and, creeping forward, she came to the edge of nothingness.

She could hear water roaring far below, and she turned her flashlight down into the abyss. The light disappeared in a misty blackness that had no bottom at all.

She didn't feel cold, but she was shaking as she pointed the flashlight around the area, trying to see what to do next. The ledge supporting her weight was narrow, but it continued along one side of the chasm to what looked almost like steps on the other side.

There was no way she could force her body to crawl

out along that ledge.

But she had to. She had to keep trying. Her own stupid determination to prove she could figure out what others (especially Henry) couldn't had put the three of them in this terrible danger. She had to keep trying now, even if it all ended right here.

Please, God...

She swallowed her terror and got down on hands and knees again, feeling her way carefully along the stone shelf, creeping forward around the horrible void and its invisible rushing water.

A dull boom echoed through the cave, and she froze as a piece of ledge under her broke off and disappeared into the roar below.

Her right leg swung free in black air and she moaned, gasping for breath. Fast-forward prayers filled her thoughts, meeting fear so overwhelming that it pressed against her body, pushing her toward the pit.

Fighting against the downward pull, Carrie battled to get her leg up and her weight away from the break—teetering on the edge, gasping, moaning, while impossible ages passed. The heavy hiking boot she was wearing turned her foot into a deadly threat. That, plus the force exerted by the drop of her leg, was going to be too much to fight against.

No!

She couldn't give up.

The sound of rushing water seemed to be getting louder and louder as she prayed:

"Give angels...charge over me...help me..."

Henry and Susan...she...had...to...make...it.

Carrie panted short bursts of air and struggled to roll on her back—away from the break—hoping the turning of her body would help lift her leg. More chips from the ledge fell away as she rocked there for an eternity, organizing strength, and willing her body to roll backward.

At last, breathless and weak, she fell against the wall on the inside edge of the shelf, not daring to wonder if it would hold her weight. Lying there, exhausted, she heard words: "I...have sent my angels..."

In all the years to follow, she'd never know if she'd actually heard a voice or if the words were simply in her thoughts, but it didn't matter.

The next thing she was aware of was Susan's terrified shout, "Carrie! Carrie!"

"I'm all right," she called back as soon as she could speak.

She began inching forward again, lying on her stomach and pulling herself along the wall toward the stone steps. Thank goodness she hadn't dropped the flashlight.

When she reached the end of the ledge and could sit on the bottom step, she stopped, leaned against the stone wall, and waited for the pounding in her ears to quit. She tried to breath deeply and evenly as she used the flashlight to investigate what did seem to be rough steps. They looked like they had been chipped with some sort of tool, and black stains on the ceiling over her head could be, she imagined, soot from torches. Perhaps it was fantasy, but it looked like humans had worked here, chipping steps to water that must have once flowed at this level and had, eons ago, worn the ledge that was now behind her.

She had to stoop as she climbed the steps, but they went up steadily until she stood in another room, dry and almost warm. She turned her flashlight toward the walls and gasped. The charcoal drawings!

They were everywhere, graceful, curving black lines.

She saw what looked like a cow...no, a buffalo or something similar, and a funny bird. That must be a drawing of a fire, probably a campfire, and those could be people. For a moment, she forgot even Henry and Susan as she took in the pictograph-covered walls.

When she finally turned her flashlight toward the floor, she saw footprints in the powdery dust. It was easy to recognize the tread print of JoAnne's hiking boots—she knew it well. And, there was another shoe, narrow, with a smoother sole. The print was no larger than JoAnne's.

Evan. He had small feet for a man. This could be where JoAnne was last Thursday, and she'd been here with Evan. Then JoAnne had already met him when she went to the barn on Saturday. He must have called Friday to say he'd found something more...something to do with head rights that would also help halt quarry construction.

Evan had been leading JoAnne in a deadly game. He had undoubtedly been in Walden Valley more than once last week, toying with JoAnne, perhaps even trying to find out if she knew anything about stock brokers who cheated people. But why had JoAnne listened to a stranger, and a man at that?

I know him, she reminded herself. He can be charming.

Oh, JoAnne—she almost cried it aloud—when you did choose to trust a man, why did you have to pick the wrong one! Caring so much about saving this valley meant you weren't careful enough for yourself.

But then, Carrie realized, I trusted him too.

It was a very unsettling thought.

Shining her flashlight across the room, Carrie saw a narrow slit in the wall on the other side and went toward it, following the footprints. It looked like the slit contin-

ued for at least ten yards. Was the blackness less intense at
the end of it? She shut off her flashlight. Yes, there was a
slight softness in the black ahead of her.

Of course, there would have to be another entrance.
JoAnne, much taller than Carrie and at least twenty pounds
heavier, couldn't have made it through those tunnels and
across that awful ledge, and she doubted Evan would try it
either. If they had used this opening, then she could too.

She hurried back down the steps, found a rock, and
banged it against the wall of the cave. Almost as soon as
the echoing sound had died, she heard three responding
bangs from the passage on the other side of the abyss.

Good, now Susan would go back to Henry. The rest
was in Carrie's hands. They'd get out of this yet!

She slid into the narrow passage, following it to another fissure that turned off at an angle. The end of that
was blocked by what looked like a rock slide, but light was
definitely filtering through at the top. When she got close
enough, she saw that weeds and clay were clinging to some
of the smaller rocks on the pile. They had evidently been
pushed there recently to block the entrance.

Thankful that her gloves were still mostly intact, Carrie shoved and clawed at the rocks. At first it seemed she
wasn't going to be strong enough to move them, but finally the top few began to slide away from the opening.
Scrambling up, she burst out over the rocks into clean air
and open sky, almost like a rabbit with a weasel behind it.

Except the weasel was in front of her.

He was sitting on a large rock by the opening. "You're
looking a bit disheveled, Carrie," Evan Walters said.

He couldn't have missed the sharp intake of breath or
her look of horror, but she steeled herself quickly and said,
"My goodness, Evan, how you startled me. Golly, yes, I

must be a mess. Crawling through caves is not a tidy occupation, fun though it may be."

She'd surprised him, taken him off guard. He cocked his head on one side and looked at her thoughtfully.

The gun he held was like Henry's. She turned her eyes away—this was the gun that had killed JoAnne—but turning away didn't help, because that's when she saw the rifle and two beer cans on the rock near him.

Beer cans? Was Evan drinking?

For a moment he seemed embarrassed, as if he realized that a friendly meeting wouldn't include two guns.

"I'm glad you've come back to the Ozarks, Evan, but you're certainly the last person I expected to see today."

She took off her gloves and hat to brush at her hair.

Keep it up, she told herself. He isn't sure of himself now. Keep him confused, off-balance. And be nice!

"My goodness," she said, unable to stop the quiver in her voice, "I've gotten rather muddy, and I've torn my coat, too. I'm glad the snow has quit at least. Come back to my house with me, Evan. I'd like you to see it, and I do want to change into dry clothes."

"Are you going to leave without your boyfriend and Susan Burke-Williams?" he asked, staring at her face. "Funny, but they thought you'd been shot. I did too until I heard you say very clearly that you were all right."

She attempted a laugh. "How ridiculous. We were exploring. I don't know where they got to. Well, never mind, it won't matter since you're here. I'll just leave the car keys and a note for them and we can go to my house in your car. And, the man with us isn't my boyfriend. He's Susan's father."

Evan spoke quickly. "You said Susan's parents were dead."

"Her adoptive parents. Henry is her birth father."

Again, he cocked his head sideways and looked at her.

"Evan, can we go? I'm getting awfully cold. Where's your car? I can hardly wait to show you my house."

Maybe I can get him away from the valley, she thought. Then Susan and Henry will be safe.

"Were you looking at the pictographs?" Evan asked. "I found them when I was exploring here several years ago. Never told you and Amos about it, just covered the opening and walked away. They were my secret. I showed them to your friend JoAnne last week, though."

He shrugged. "Too bad about her tragic death. I really liked her. She was impressed by the pictographs, and also by my story that the Osage people still hold mineral rights to this land. I told her that meant even limestone rock." He laughed. "Oh, JoAnne and I were going to stop the quarry. She enjoyed talking with a representative of the Cherokee Nation from Tahlequah, Ok-la-ho-ma!" His bottom lip drooped in a momentary pout. "She appreciated me like you never have, Carrie McCrite. She was a woman to admire!"

Carrie struggled to hide the rage that was boiling through her whole body and ducked her head so he wouldn't see her face. She pushed her lip out, not because she wanted to mimic Evan's pout, but because using that gesture of defiance gave her a small bit of courage.

His voice droned on. "JoAnne was smart...lots of fire. She listened to me, and she was so excited about surprising all of you. I was very, very sorry she had to die. She had more fire than ten of you, Carrie. Hated most men, she said. Didn't trust them. But she trusted me."

He was watching her closely. "JoAnne and I would have made a good team. I saved the red cap to remember her by, then had to use it on you. Too bad you got in the way.

"You understand that JoAnne knew too much about me and my private business. I'm sure her death bothered you. I thought it might frighten you right back to Tulsa! But still, it was too bad. I really did like that woman."

Evil, Carrie thought. Evil! Cold! Cold and cruel. "I liked JoAnne a lot myself," she said, still looking at the ground.

Evan gestured with the pistol. "Let's go then. We have a bit of a hike. I don't want your friends to see us, not yet." He laughed, but his voice still sounded hard.

"Carrie, I watched all of you together yesterday. I saw him kiss you."

He waved the pistol toward the beer cans. "It seems my hands are going to be busy with two guns, so you'll have to carry those for me. We don't want to leave them behind, though I have more stored in the cave. They're full of explosives, you see...a little surprise."

She stared at the cans. Explosives? Did he mean dynamite? Then, what would happen if she picked them up and threw them straight at him...would that kill them both?

"What's the matter, Carrie? Frightened of a couple of beer cans? Can't have that. *Pick them up.*"

She looked at him, saw the coldness in his eyes as the pistol waved toward her, and reached out slowly to pick up the two cans. They had black tape on top and what looked like candle wicks hung over the sides. The rifle was still on the rock too. Could she...? But Evan pulled it quickly out of her reach and, using the attached strap, slung it over his shoulder.

He gestured. "Let's go down the path." His voice was mocking, almost a sing-song. "Be careful. Don't stumble, Carrie. No telling what a shaken can of beer will do!"

"Evan, please. What are we going to do? You're frightening me."

"Yes, Carrie, I intend to. When we get down, you're going to stand in front of the cave and convince Susan and her father they'd better come out and join you. What happens next will depend on you. All you have to do is call them and get them to the opening. Then...I'll have you to myself, and we'll be ready to leave." He laughed. "This is going very well, better than I hoped. Move faster now. We don't want the hillbilly down the valley to bother us. He could come home any time, I suppose. We won't have to worry about that bony hillbilly hag, though. I took care of her."

Carrie gasped and felt as if the breath had been knocked out of her. Dear, gentle Shirley! The baby!

"Evan, you didn't hurt them. You couldn't."

He pouted at her again. "Oh, don't worry. I got in the pump house and cut the electric wires to their water pump. When she came out to see what was wrong, I locked her up in there." His voice changed to ice. "She's...not...the enemy."

"The baby, Johnny!"

"Oh, Carrie, stop fretting. You never used to fret. He's still in the house, was asleep in his bed when I looked."

His voice became dreamy—far away. "All that dark hair...I touched it...soft...that's why I didn't shoot yesterday...didn't want to hurt the baby. From on top of the bluff, I couldn't be sure I wouldn't hurt him. He was in the carrier, too close to his mother. Have to finish this whole job at one time and get away. Couldn't risk messing up yesterday. Now, Evan Walters is going to disappear. Do you want to disappear with me, Carrie? I have enough for two." He grinned, staring at her face, then the icy voice came back. "No? Well, bad luck."

The gun jerked toward the trail. "Come on, we've got to do this before they figure out I'm no longer up on that overhang." He chuckled, but it was an empty, bitter sound. "This is fun—bossing Amos McCrite's woman."

She whirled at him then, raising both arms, swinging the beer cans up and over her head, and hurling them toward his face with all the strength she could muster.

She missed him completely. Evan leaned sideways—almost lazily, without losing his balance or his hold on the guns—and they missed his head by two feet.

By the time they hit the path, Carrie had turned away, shrinking into her body, waiting for the explosion and for death.

There was no explosion, simply a dull metallic clunk. Evan was still chuckling as she turned in astonishment to see that one of the cans had broken open, spilling a trail of black powder on the rocks. The other one was rolling harmlessly toward her.

"Maybe you do have some fire in you after all, Carrie. That's not bad, not bad at all. But I must teach you about explosives. This stuff won't blow unless you light the fuse. You don't have any matches, do you? I thought not. Pick up that can and get going. You're wasting my time, and I won't stand for that."

For a while, she moved like a robot, seeing nothing, hearing nothing. All she knew was that she was stumbling down the bluff in the direction indicated by Evan, who touched her back every few moments with the pistol barrel.

Then she was aware that they were crossing the creek bed in the dry area beyond the curve. Now, trees and rocks would mask them from the cave opening, and Henry and Susan couldn't see them until Evan meant them to. She was not going to do what he wanted. She simply wouldn't call out to them. He couldn't make her do that. He'd have to shoot her first and that, at least, would alert Henry.

But what good would it do to resist him? He had the explosives...the guns. She had to think, to clear her head of the rage and fear that were distorting reasoning.

Dear God...God, help me, show me what to do.

Now they were in the old pasture below the mouth of the cave, still shielded from sight by trees. As if led by a will other than her own, Carrie collapsed on the ground, laying the beer can aside as she fell. Her body went as limp as a rag doll's; she would not go any farther.

Evan swore and began yanking at her. She bit her lip to keep from crying out as rocks bounced under her and he tugged at her arms.

Her weight must have been too much for him, because suddenly he stopped. "I'm not going to risk hurting my back again over some fool woman. You and JoAnne...too heavy. Get up."

Talk to him again, she thought. Get him to talk.

"Where's JoAnne's coat?" she asked.

He certainly hadn't expected that question. "Why? Do you want to wear it? I put it down one of the sink holes on top of the bluff, together with her purse. You could see that coat from too far away. I wanted to save the special privilege of finding her for you. The woods are evil, Carrie. The only safe place is the city."

"I like the woods, Evan. I always have, you know that. Finding JoAnne didn't change the way I feel. Amos's death didn't change it either. Their deaths had nothing to do with trees. They didn't spoil my woods for me."

She was watching him carefully when she mentioned Amos.

"Shut up," was all he said, looking back toward Roger and Shirley's pasture.

She hunched over, pulling her knees up under her chin. As she started to bow her head over her knees, she was aware of movement in the distance.

Evan had seen it too. Evidently something had broken a fence in the end pasture, or maybe Evan had cut the wire himself. A large mass of cows was moving toward them, grazing as they came, their noses brushing down through dry grass and melting snow to pull at green sprouts underneath.

"Evan, it isn't worth it. Please stop this. Nothing is worth killing for. These are real, living people."

He turned back to her, ignoring the cows. "It isn't any different from killing a deer, Carrie. You should know that. Amos was killed like a deer, wasn't he?"

He paused, then showed the hideous smile again. "I even shot a deer Saturday morning. Had to play like a hunter since there were hunters in the woods. Didn't dare arrange JoAnne on your hillside then. That's when I saw him, just standing there. An eight-point buck. Best hunting kill I ever made. His blood covered up hers. After that, I was free. No one could touch me. I was just out hunting."

The cows were moving closer in a huge compact clump, and Carrie stared at them, fascinated. From her place on the ground, they looked larger than life, and they were definitely heading toward the creek. Possibly they were thirsty. As she watched them, she suddenly felt like giggling. That huge cow in the lead was getting quite close.

"Get up," Evan commanded. "We have important business to take care of."

When she continued to sit, he poked at her with the

gun and said again, "Get up, *now.*"

Feeling quite light-headed, she did giggle, and then laughed out loud, not even noticing that Evan's face was growing red with anger and that he was lifting his gun to point right at her head. "Oh, Evan," she said, gasping now with wild, out-of-control laughter, "I do like cows."

The large cow brushed against her, then lifted its head and mooed loudly, bellowing in her ear. Evan seemed startled and looked toward the sound for a moment. Carrie ducked her head quickly and rolled under the cow's belly, coming to rest against a pair of heavy boots. Shirley stood up, leveled a shotgun at Evan's head, and said, "I'd drop that gun right quick if I was you, Mister."

Chapter XXIII

Instantly, a whirlwind of activity erupted from the middle of the dairy herd. Harrison Storm's voice rose over the whirlwind, and Carrie realized there were several men in black hidden among the huge black and white cows.

Mary Belle began to graze again, her own part of the mission completed. Carrie stayed seated on the ground near the cow with her head tucked over her knees. She could hear the soft ripping of grass and the cow's slushy swallowing noises. She concentrated on that, trying to shut out everything else that was happening.

Don Taylor's voice was suddenly quite close, talking calmly to Evan. Carrie kept her eyes down and tried to close her ears, to think of anything other than this moment, this place.

Then Shirley's arm came around her shoulders. "He's gone now," was all she said as she lifted Carrie to her feet, hugging her tightly until the awful shaking stopped.

After a few minutes of silence, Shirley asked, "Are Henry and Susan all right? Shouldn't we go find them?"

Carrie opened her eyes carefully and saw that Don Taylor was back, standing next to Mary Belle. His hand stroked the big cow's neck, over and over, and his own eyes looked as gentle and soft as the cow's.

"Those explosive things...the beer cans," she began, but he stopped her by raising a hand.

"They won't do anything now. Can you tell us where King and the niece are? Are they up in one of the caves? Are they hurt?"

She nodded, then changed her mind and shook her head, thinking of what could have happened, and didn't. "Henry was only slightly shot, and Susan was more or less bumped, but they'll both be all right, really," she said, and wondered why Don Taylor smiled.

She turned to Shirley. "Johnny?"

"He's fine. Jason's come to baby-sit. He's the only one I could call in such a hurry. At least he knows which end to put a diaper on, though he's probably fit to be tied right now, wondering what's happening."

"Then," Carrie said, feeling more like herself, "let's go get Henry and Susan." She looked at Taylor and pointed toward the creek bank. "I know which cave, but they can't cross the creek here, and Henry may need some help."

She hesitated as her thoughts went, once more, to the day Amos had died.

"Harrison Storm was sheriff five years ago, wasn't he?" she asked Taylor. "I need to talk with him. He'll have records of a hunting death, and I think Evan..." She bit her lip and stopped, wondering how she could explain, but Taylor simply nodded and accepted her request without comment.

She forced her thoughts back to the present. It was

time to take care of those who were here now.

"You'll need to go meet Henry and Susan on top of the bluff," she told Taylor. "Henry's car is up there. The road to the top turns off just before you get to the farm house." She handed him Henry's key ring.

"Deputies will get the cows headed back into your pasture," Taylor said to Shirley. "And, if you like, they'll give you a ride home. It's a good thing your idea worked. I don't know how we'd have gotten close to him otherwise. You know your cows. They're as tame as kittens."

"'Specially Mary Belle," Shirley said, "and she'll lead the herd back easy. The dogs would do it, but I penned them up, afraid they'd give us away. I'd like to stay with Carrie, and I don't think she'll want to walk clear to the house now, so I'm glad for your help. Tell someone to just head Mary Belle toward the break in the fence and the rest will follow. I put out a rope to tie across where we cut the wire. That'll do 'til we fix it better."

Carrie spoke up. "He, uh, left more of those beer can things up in the overhang cave. Henry can point out where."

Taylor ducked his head in silent acknowledgement, then turned to Shirley again. "Guess it's okay if I bring them both down to your house, unless, of course, we find King needs to go to the hospital." Without waiting for an answer, he turned and headed for one of the cars that had appeared in the pasture.

The two women started toward the creek bank. As they walked, Shirley's arm dropped around Carrie's shoulders.

God bless her, Carrie thought. God bless all my friends.

The sun was just breaking through the clouds when Henry, with Susan holding his arm, appeared in the cave entrance in response to Carrie's call. Evan had been right. Henry would have responded to her voice, even in the face of danger.

"It's finished," she shouted. "Johnny, Shirley, and I are just fine. Don Taylor is on his way up the bluff road to meet you."

Carrie could see Henry's face quite clearly, even though she'd left her glasses with Susan before she crawled away into the cave tunnels.

He was smiling.

She shouted again. "We've lots to talk about."

Shirley laughed out loud and then said to Carrie, "Boy, I'll sure have some talking to do when Roger sees what I did to the wall of our pump house. I set up some work for that man, what with breaking out the pump house wall and cutting the pasture fence. Whoo-eee!"

"I think Jason and Henry will help fix things, and I'll help too," Carrie responded as she watched Henry and Susan begin a slow climb toward the top of the bluff.

CHAPTER XXIV

"A rather nice Thanksgiving weekend," Carrie said, as Henry turned to help her over the last pile of rocks. "It's a good thing the weather is warm. I've ruined every heavy jacket I own. I need to go shopping."

Behind them several voices echoed from the pictograph cave. Everyone there seemed to be having a fine time discussing how an artist from so long ago had created drawings with soap weed brushes dipped in a slurry made of what they thought was nothing more than clay dust, pounded charcoal, and water.

Rob was there with his friend Dr. Jane Gallant, who had turned out to be an art historian, not a painter.

Abner Hill, a lawyer from the Native American Rights Fund, had arrived on Friday, and there were three people from the history and archeology departments at the University of Arkansas and the University Museum. Carrie was quite worn out over being impressed at the array of knowl-

edge crowded into the little cave. Everyone but Mr. Hill
was Doctor somebody. Well, her son wasn't really Dr.
McCrite quite yet, but she'd noticed that he was holding
his own in the scholarly discussions and that the others
listened to him with attention and respect.

It was a relief that the archeologist from the National
Museum of Natural History and his associate from the
National Museum of the American Indian, both part of
the Smithsonian, weren't coming until next week and that
Rob would still be here to help guide them.

But enough was enough, and no one had noticed when
Carrie and Henry slipped quietly away through the narrow slit in the rock and out into the late November sunlight.

"It's sort of overwhelming, isn't it?" Carrie said as they
found a large flat rock and sat so they could look over the
whole valley. She leaned against Henry's side, bent her knees
to rest her feet on the rock, and remembered, only briefly,
that Evan Walters had been sitting in the same place just a
few days ago.

"Charles Stoker certainly seemed overwhelmed," Henry
said. "I'm not sure he even knows what the Smithsonian
Institution is, but when Jason said Washington, DC, and
then told him about the alternate quarry site... Of course,
money talks too, and Jason has a way with people who
have money. He already has two foundations interested in
taking part. Now the valley will be safe, and it was mostly
your doing. After all, you found the cave, and you and
Shirley..." He hesitated. "Well, things that needed resolv-
ing got resolved. That should more than take care of your
contribution toward saving Walden Valley."

Carrie didn't remind him that Evan, and then JoAnne,
had really discovered the cave.

"It is satisfying," she said.

After a few minutes of silence, Henry continued. "I understand why you don't want to talk about it yet, but I hope you can remember what happened here only as a time of great bravery. Yours, Cara, your bravery, your courage. Do you even begin to know how I feel about that? I've been with many brave people, and I can still hardly believe you did what you did. Can you think only of the courage and let the rest go?"

She looked up at his face, wondering, and saw first somberness, then the hint of a smile as he went on.

"If we were in the police department together, I'd fight hard to have you as my partner."

"Oh," was all she could manage to say in response.

Courage. Yes, maybe she did know what that word meant now. Someday she would tell him all about it, and what it had been like, and he'd be the only one she'd ever tell the whole story to, because he was the one she could trust to understand and say the right things, the healing things.

Then she might invite him to go to church with her on a Wednesday night, when she could stand up and tell about her prayers and how things had worked out.

She didn't doubt now that Henry would go to church with her, and she didn't care whether their coming into church together would signify some kind of commitment to each other or not. It was all right.

She almost chuckled out loud. Courage. And what she'd wanted to prove to him, and to her family, was that she could be independent, and strong, and clever. Oh, yes, Carrie McCrite, be honest—you wanted to impress this man, you really did. And look what happened!

The rock was sun-warmed, and the peace of the valley

was working its magic again, making her feel quite lazy. She yawned and looked out at the scene in front of them.

The view was spectacular. Bits of red color remained here and there in maple, sumac, and dogwood leaves. In the distance she could see tiny figures among not-so-tiny black and white cows. Roger and Shirley were introducing Susan, Johnny, and Putt to "the girls." The Burke-Williamses, too, had chosen to be outside on this glorious, sparkling day.

"What have you decided to do?" Carrie asked, turning her head to look up at Henry again. "Are you going to move?"

"Hmm. Well, I can't really feel settled where I am, since Mrs. Foster may decide not to sell. If I live in Susan's house and pay rent to her, they'll be able to keep the house and have a place to stay when they come for visits. Putt told me yesterday he wished they could move here eventually and bring Johnny up in the special place two of his six grandparents chose as home.

"But then," he said, as his brown eyes turned somber, "there's something to be said for privacy, and quiet, and independence, as you have reminded me. So what do you think I should do?"

"I think," she said, shutting her eyes and leaning her head back against his shoulder, "if it gets too noisy when they come for a visit, you should walk down the path and sleep on my couch. Or—" her voice was fading as the sun's warmth moved gently through her body—"you might even use the guest room."

The End

ABOUT THE AUTHOR

Award-winning Arkansas writer and journalist Radine Trees Nehring and her husband, photographer John Nehring, live in the rural Arkansas Ozarks near Gravette.

Nehring's writing awards include the Governor's Award for Best Writing about the State of Arkansas, Tulsa Nightwriter of the Year Award, and the Dan Saults Award, which is given by the Ozarks Writers League for nature- or Ozarks-value writing. The American Christian Writers named Nehring Christian Writer of the Year in 1998, and the Oklahoma Writers Federation, Inc., named her book, *Dear Earth,* Best Non-Fiction Book and her novel, *A Valley to Die For,* Best Mystery Novel.

Research for her many magazine and newspaper features and her weekly radio program, "Arkansas Corner Community News," has taken the Nehrings throughout the state. For years Nehring has written non-fiction about unique people, places, and events in Arkansas. Now, in her mystery novel, *A Valley to Die For,* she adds appealing characters fighting for something they believe in and, it turns out, for their very lives.

OTHER BOOKS BY ST KITTS PRESS

PO Box 8173 ► Wichita KS 67208
888-705-4887 (toll-free) ► 316-685-3201
FAX 316-685-6650
stkitts@skpub.com ► www.StKittsPress.com

The Voice He Loved by Laurel Schunk

"...a masterful tale that reaches into the inner workings of a bruised and battered psyche, while keeping the plot moving at a breathless pace." —*The Charlotte Austin Review* (reviewed by Nancy Mehl)

Black and Secret Midnight by Laurel Schunk

"Beth Anne's appealing child's-eye view of the world and the subtle Christian message should make this appealing to fans of Christian and mainstream mysteries." —*Library Journal*

"Beth Anne is at times touchingly naive..." —*Publishers Weekly*

"...a memorable picture of racism that is variously stark and nuanced." —*Small Press Book Review*

"...a good look at racial relations in the south...with a mysterious twist." —*The Pilot* (Southern Pines, NC)

"The story is so gripping that I worried [Beth Anne] would be killed before the end."
—*Murder: Past Tense* (The Hist. Mys. Apprec. Soc.)

"…Schunk's adult novels are serious, skillfully crafted works."
—*nwsbrfs* (Wichita Press Women, Inc.)

"…a light in the darkness and a novel to sink your teeth and your heart into."
—*The Charlotte Austin Review* (reviewed by Nancy Mehl)

"…a great regional mystery that will excite fans with its twists and turns."
—Amazon.com (reviewed by Harriet Klausner)

"…skillfully mixes a story of segregation in the South and deep, dark family secrets with the plot of Shakespeare's 'MacBeth' in a very unique way."
—DorothyL (reviewed by Tom Griffith)

"MacBeth and mayhem in the 50s. What a mix! I love Ms. Schunk's characters, and I remember the milieu all too well. It was the era you love to hate, beautifully brought to life."
—Sandy Dengler, author of *The Quick and the Dead* and *Hyænas*

"Indicative of life in the South in the 1950s when racism and bigotry were around every frightening corner, *Black and Secret Midnight* is a great mystery with plenty of foreshadowing, clues, and red herrings to keep you reading far into the night."
—Linda Hall, author of *Margaret's Peace*

Hyænas by Sandy Dengler

"Highly recommended."
—*Library Journal*

"…a terrific murder mystery and a work of unique, flawless written exploration of prehistoric antiquity."
—*Internet Bookwatch* (The Midwest Book Review)

"Dengler has crafted a masterpiece. *Hyaenas* proves that there are still new slants to the mystery genre."
—*The Charlotte Austin Review* (reviewed by Nancy Mehl)

"For anyone who wants something a bit different with their mysteries, *Hyænas* is the answer, hopefully with future novels starring Gar and company."
—Amazon.com (reviewed by Harriet Klausner)

"...I had a hard time putting the book down when I needed to do some work."   —DorothyL (reviewed by Tom Griffith)

"Dengler is masterful at creating characters that come alive in any era."   —Pat Rushford, author of the Helen Bradley Mysteries

Death in Exile by Laurel Schunk

"What could have been a straightforward Regency romance is elevated by apt social commentary in this offering from Schunk..."
        —*Library Journal*

"Schunk is a good writer who has a good grasp of story and character."   —*The Pilot* (Southern Pines, NC)

"This beautifully written Regency novel...will throw you into another time, and you won't want to leave."
        —*The Charlotte Austin Review* (reviewed by Nancy Mehl)

"Laurel Schunk is a masterful storyteller."
        —*Murder: Past Tense* (The Hist. Mys. Apprec. Soc.)

Under the Wolf's Head by Kate Cameron

"The gardening tips seeded throughout the narrative are a clever ploy, echoing the inclusion of cooking tips in the ever-popular culinary mysteries..."   —*Publishers Weekly*

"Plenty of gardening filler and allusions to inept local law enforcement lighten the atmosphere, as do the often humorous sisterly 'fights' and the speedy prose."   —*Library Journal*

"You'll laugh at the sisters' relationship and grow to love the two women just as Callista's plants grow through her loving care."
        —*GRIT: American Life & Traditions*

"Schunk in the past has tackled child abuse and racism; her first gardening mystery provides a message about ageism and the value placed on elderly lives..."   —*Norwich Bulletin* (Norwich, CT)

"Highly recommended."   —*The Charlotte Austin Review*
                                          (reviewed by Nancy Mehl)

"...a wonderful new release..."
                    —About.com (reviewed by Renie Dugwyler)

"...evokes in the reader an understanding of the atmosphere of a small town, where everyone is important and interesting."
          —*The Bookdragon Review* (reviewed by Richard Royce)

"...a quick and pleasant read..."
                    —*nwsbrfs* (Wichita Press Women, Inc.)

"Kate Cameron brings this murder mystery to a finale, murders solved, villains implicated and captured, with the added bonus, protagonist Callie Bagley discovers new love in her life."
          —James D. Yoder, author of *Black Spider Over Tiegenhof*

Shaded Light by N.J. Lindquist

"...a cozy that will delight fans who appreciate solid, modern detection."   —*Publishers Weekly*

"Detailed characterization, surprising relationships, and nefarious plot twists."   —*Library Journal*

"A very good novel by an accomplished writer."
                                          —*Rapport Magazine*

"This most enjoyable novel is written in the style of Agatha Christie...Follow the clues to a bang-up ending."
                              —*The Pilot* (Southern Pines, NC)

"...an admirable first outing for a pair of detectives readers will look forward to hearing from again."   —*The Mystery Reader*
                              (reviewed by Jennifer Monahan Winberry)

"With any luck, we'll see more of Manziuk and Ryan in years to come."   —*The Charlotte Austin Review* (reviewed by PJ Nunn)

"This excellently plotted novel is the first in a projected series of Manziuk and Ryan mysteries."   —*I Love a Mystery*

"Paul and [Jacquie] make a fabulous team as their divergent personalities harmoniously clash to the benefit of the reader."
                    —*Internet Bookwatch* (The Midwest Book Review)

"A cozy reminiscent of the best Agatha Christie had to offer."
                    —*Midwest Book Review* (reviewed by Leann Arndt)

"...a well-plotted crime novel that should appeal to all those who especially like this sub-genre."
                    —*The Bookdragon Review* (reviewed by Gene Stratton)

"...a fast paced book that was really hard to put down."
                    —About.com (reviewed by Lorraine Gelly)

"...we are treated to varied and carefully delineated characters that hold our attention, to good, uncliched, lucid writing, and to a well-sustained pace as we try to match wits with the detectives."
                    —DorothyL (reviewed by Ginger Watts)

"...a page-turning, keep-you-up-all-night mystery where the murderer isn't revealed until the very end."
                    —Linda Hall, author of *Margaret's Peace*

"...an excellent mystery in the classic sense — a who-dunnit in the tradition of Agatha Christie, but for the 21st century."
                    —Joan Hall Hovey, Author of *Nowhere To Hide*

The Heart of Matthew Jade by Ralph Allen

"...a compassionate view into religious, familial and romantic love..."
                    —*Publishers Weekly*

"Fabulous!"   —Kevin Patrick, CNET Radio, San Francisco

"...an obliging and magnificently written mystery which is as entertaining as it is ultimately inspiring." —*The Midwest Book Review*

"...Allen's book will inspire many who believe in the power of faith — and enjoy a good story."   —*The Eagle* (Wichita, Kansas)

"...an eye-opener. *The Heart of Matthew Jade* is a compelling novel that will stay with you long after you put it down."
        —*The Charlotte Austin Review* (reviewed by Nancy Mehl)

"...this novel's strength is in the behind the scenes glimpses of faith behind bars."   —*The Bookdragon Review*
        (reviewed by Melanie C. Duncan)

"...destined to become a classic. Its mixture of love and hate, religion and fallacy grabs readers from the very beginning and never lets them go."
        —*The Lantern* (Butler County Community College)

"This compelling story chronicles the faith journey of a simple accountant from his sanitized office building into the maw of Hell as chaplain in a county jail."
        —Laurel Schunk, author of *Black and Secret Midnight*

A Clear North Light by Laurel Schunk

"Schunk solidly launches a new 'Lithuanian' trilogy, following one family's triumphs and tragedies through the generations."
        —*Library Journal*

"Schunk, author of the well-regarded coming-of-age story *Black and Secret Midnight* (1998), drops back to 1938 with *A Clear North Light*, the first installment of her Lithuanian Trilogy."   —*Booklist*

"...notable as much for its excellent character development as for its story line...Good reading..."—*nwsbrfs* (Wichita Press Women, Inc.)

"...dramatically illuminates the effect of deadly global politics on the private lives of all-too-human individuals caught up in events not of their making."
        —Gretchen Sprague, author of *Maquette for Murder*

"...pulls one into an historical drama with excitement and moral persuasiveness as Petras fights and searches for faith, meaning, and love..."   —James D. Yoder, author of *Lucy of the Trail of Tears*

Irregardless of Murder by Ellen Edwards Kennedy

"...good writing and solid plotting don't need a famous imprint...a satisfying cozy..."   —*Chicago Tribune*

"...a signature mystery..."   —*The Midwest Book Review*

"A delightful cozy mystery peopled with eccentric characters with the prospect of more in the future."
     —*The Bookdragon Review* (reviewed by Melanie C. Duncan)

"...a wonderful puzzle, complete with all its pieces; clever, entertaining and hard to put down."   —BookBrowser.com

"A warm and cozy evening's read."   —*I Love a Mystery*

"...an absolutely delightful mystery."
     —MyShelf.com (reviewed by Nancy Mehl)

"...one of the greatest mystery books of the year!"
     —*Book Review Café* (bookreviewcafe.com)

"...a treat and a triumph..."
     —*The Drood Review of Mystery*

"A delightful read. The characters are wonderful."
     —Anne George, author of The Southern Sisters Series

"It's got everything a great cozy story needs — a charming and sympathetic heroine, a colorful supporting cast...a little romance, and, of course, a murder that challenges the reader..."
     —Sarah Shaber, award-winning author of
     Simon Said and *Snipe Hunt*